Sing a New Song
Liberating Black Hymnody

Jon Michael Spencer

FORTRESS PRESS   *Minneapolis*

To Michele

The mingling of fighting experience with conjugal life deepens the relations between husband and wife and cements their union.

—Frantz Fanon

SING A NEW SONG
Liberating Black Hymnody

Unless otherwise noted, Scripture quotations are from the Revised Standard Version Bible copyright © 1989 by the Division of Christian Education of the National Council of the Churches of Christ in the United States of America. Used with permission.

Cover art: Detail from "Joyous Voices" by Morris Johnson, St. Petersburg, Florida, 1993. Watercolor and hand-printed paper collage.
Cover design: Peggy Lauritsen Design Group
Author photo: Valerie Ann Johnson

Library of Congress Cataloging-in-Publication Data

Spencer, Jon Michael.
    Sing a new song : liberating Black hymnody / Jon Michael Spencer.
      p.   cm.
    Includes bibliographical references (p.   ) and index.
    ISBN 0-8006-2722-9 :
    1. Afro-American churches—Hymns—History and criticism. 2. Afro-American public worship. 3. Hymns, English—United States—History and criticism. I. Title.
    BV313.S645   1995
    264'.2'08996073—dc20   94-34515
                                                 CIP

The paper used in this publication meets the minimum requirements of American National Standard for Information Sciences—Permanence of Paper for Printed Library Materials, ANSI Z329.48–1984. ∞™

Manufactured in the U.S.A.   AF 1-2722

99   98   97   96   95   1   2   3   4   5   6   7   8   9   10

CONTENTS

iii

P R E F A C E

Yes. No. . . . Two of the tiniest words in any language. But yes or no, one had to choose between them. To say "Yes" or "No" to unfairness, to injustice, to wrong-doing, to oppression, to treacherous betrayal, to the culture of fear, to the aesthetic of submissive acquiescence, one was choosing a particular world and a particular future.
　　—Ngũgĩ Wa Thiong'O, *Detained: A Writer's Prison Diary* (1981)

The theme of the 1992 annual conference of the Hymn Society of the United States and Canada was "You Are Ethnic," and that was supposed to be the title of my keynote address for that conference. However, I could not, in honesty, say to everyone in the audience, "You are ethnic." I could only attempt to persuade the participants that as authentic Christian hymnologists, who should have a salvational goal in mind when practicing their discipline, they ought to say yes to being ethnic. Some in the audience did not need convincing, but in order to convince the rest of the listeners that they ought to be ethnic, I needed to coin the term *ethnohymnology* and argue for them to adopt this discipline as their approach to the broader field of hymnology.

By the term *hymnology* I mean the study of *hymnody*, which is any congregationally sung music, music often (but not always) found in hymnals. By the term *black hymnody* I really mean black church hymnody, which includes any music sung congregationally in black churches and often (but not always) found in black denominational hymnals—such as spirituals, standard and gospel hymns, and gospel songs, all written by black or nonblack hymnists (hymn writers).

Ethnohymnology, I explained in my keynote address, is hymnology that stands over against the mainline hymnology of continental and diasporan Europe. It is a discipline that discourses about hymnody and that has as its overriding concern the plight of those groups in society most ethnic and therefore most alienated from extant hymnological tradition. These alienated groups include women, nonwhites, and the poor. In the Eurocentric ideology that has dominated Western history and modern hymnology, these are the heathens of society—women, nonwhites, and the poor. These groups are the invisible and dispossessed within the ideological domain of European patriarchy, white supremacy, and capitalistic landlordship. These three practices are the by-products of Eurocentrism—the placing of bourgeois Europe at the center of the cultural, economic, and political universe. Thus, for hymnologists to be able to say "We are ethnic" requires them first to say yes to being ethnic. In terms of hymnology, this constrains them to "sing a new song" that reminds them of their newly acquired conviction to be in solidarity with these ethnic groups—women, nonwhites, and the poor.

For those who are white, I am not speaking first and foremost about relinquishing rather slippery membership in the so-called white race. This is a membership granted not solely on having a more or less white skin but substantially on a certain frame of mind—namely, willingness to suppress a specific cultural ethnicity in favor of assimilation into what novelist Toni Morrison calls the "unraced" (those who view themselves as universal and, illusionally, as the world's majority). I am not speaking of relinquishing membership in this minority white collective of the one-third world in favor of celebrating one's particular cultural ethnicity, nor speaking of becoming raced in lieu of being unraced. Rather, I am speaking of relinquishing privileged immersion in patriarchy, supremacy, and landlordship in favor of becoming *a*white. In terms of the hymnological discipline, I am speaking of becoming an ethnohymnologist—one who discourses about hymnody that has as its overriding concern the plight of those groups in society most ethnic and therefore most alienated from extant hymnological tradition. One needs now to take sides: yes or no.

Of all the books on hymnology that I have written and that I foresee writing, this one, *Sing a New Song*, is the culmination of my having learned to take sides, of my having learned to choose between yes and no, of my having become an ethnohymnologist. My journey up to this point, to summarize, follows that of the formation of the "native intellectual" that Frantz Fanon outlines in *The Wretched of the Earth*. This journey begins with the native intellectual giving proof that he has assimilated into the dominating European culture, only subsequently, in the second phase, to feel a sense of inner disturbance and a need to remember who he is. "Finally, in the third phase, which is called the fighting phase, the native, after having tried to lose himself in the people and with the people, will on the contrary shake the people. Instead of according the people's lethargy an honored place in his esteem, he turns himself into an awakener of the people; hence comes a fighting literature, a revolutionary literature, and a national literature."[1] *Sing a New Song* is a product of this third phase—my having learned to take sides and choose between yes and no. No book in the field of hymnology, no book on the hymnody of the black church, has heretofore constituted what Fanon calls a "revolutionary literature." This is a first work in ethnohymnology.

1. Frantz Fanon, *The Wretched of the Earth*, trans. Constance Farrington (New York: Grove Press, 1966), 222–23.

    Much information and inspiration came from a number of people I wish to acknowledge: Wilfred Sebothoma and Simon Maimela, respectively, professors of New Testament and systematic theology at the University of South Africa (UNISA) in Pretoria; Richmon Ngwanya and Kobus Bohnen, professors of New Testament at the University of Fort Hare in South Africa; Tebogo Modise and Solomon January, South African seminarians; Leonorah Khanyile, of Soweto, in South Africa; J. Nathan Corbitt, professor of communications at Eastern College in Pennsylvania; Adande Washington, a friend and fellow student; and J. Michael West, senior editor at Fortress Press.

PART ONE

PETITION

1

The Requisite of Revision

Again, what is this theory of benevolent guardianship for women, for the masses, for Negroes—for "lesser breeds without the law"? It is simply the old cry of privilege, the old assumption that there are those in the world who know better what is best for others than those others know themselves, and who can be trusted to do this best.

To tap this mighty reservoir of experience, knowledge, beauty, love, and deed we must appeal not to the few, not to some souls, but to all. The narrower the appeal, the poorer the culture; the wider the appeal, the more magnificent are the possibilities. Infinite is human nature. We make it finite by choking back the masses . . . , by attempting to speak for others, to interpret and act for them, and we end by acting for ourselves and using the world as our private property.

—W. E. B. Du Bois, *Darkwater* (1920)

A civilization that chooses to close its eyes to its most crucial problems is a stricken civilization.

—Aimé Césaire, *Discourse on Colonialism* (1955)

In my book *Black Hymnody: A Hymnological History of the African-American Church* (1992), I give a historical reading of the black church through a study of the hymns that comprise the hymnbooks of ten denominations. These include black denominations of the Methodist, Baptist, Holiness, and Pentecostal persuasions, as well as the Catholic, Episcopal, and United Methodist churches, whose black minority memberships produced hymnbooks that reflect their African-American heritage. Because the hymns that are sung in the black church are an essential aspect of our religious worldview, my study of these denominational hymnbooks provided me with information regarding the status of our theological and doctrinal beliefs and social perspectives over the last two centuries. I close that book with a postscript that makes explicit some of the underlying implications in my hymnological history. I conclude that the black church and its hymnody are caught in a liberative lag as regards the self-identity and self-determination of African Americans who are Christians. That postscript to *Black Hymnody* is essentially the tacit prescript of the present book, in which I identify three primary aspects of this liberative lethargy. My claim is that black hymnody is by and large captive of Eurocentric biblical analysis, interpretation, and doctrinal guardianship that support the subordinationist traditions of sexism, racism, and classism.

Some of the hymns sung in the black church are also held captive to European-originated musical notation, particularly when that which is notated—especially the rhythm and the melody—becomes the expressive limit that black worshipers are timid about transcending through the African gift of improvisation. In this present book, however, I am concerned principally about hymnic texts that are Eurocentric—exacerbated by European worldview and ideology—to the degree that these texts incur the problems of sexism, racism, and classism. It is not that a "new song" that addresses these problems will alone revolutionize the people or that the old hymnody is the cause of these dilemmas; it is that the revolution that must be fashioned by and among the people at least must be supported by "new song."

Our hymnody is nowhere close to being able to offer support to needed change in the world. It has not even sufficiently distanced itself from the hymns written by people who held slaves or condoned slavery. Neither has our hymnody distanced itself from, for instance, such social Darwinist missionary hymns as Reginald Heber's "From Greenland's Icy Mountains." Heber's hymn has this telling couplet in stanza 2:

> Can men, whose souls are lighted with wisdom from
>   on high,
> Can they to men benighted the lamp of light deny?

This is the very phenomenon that led Ngũgĩ Wa Thiong'O, the Kenyan novelist and cultural critic, to complain about the hymns brought to Kenya by missionaries, hymns that create among Kenyans a mood of passivity and acceptance, hymns that include such phrases as "I'm a sinner" and "Wash me redeemer and I shall be whiter than snow."[1] Yet, as put by Canaan Banana, the first president of independent Zimbabwe, despite its long presence on the African continent, the church would not in the face of colonialism and neo-colonialism proceed beyond "a mere murmur and a hymnal squeak."[2] Because evangelicals will not proceed beyond a murmur and a squeak, today, say the black writers of the document *Evangelical Witness in South Africa* (1986), the crude attitudes of missionaries during colonial times still prevail in evangelical circles. These evangelicals still view blacks as the "mission field" and whites as the bearers of civilization, when it is the whites of South Africa (and America) who need the redemptive message.[3]

This is illustrated in the small tract "What Is the Answer?" put out by the Gospel Publishing House in Roodepoort, South Africa, which I picked up in Johannesburg in 1992. Accompanying this question on the cover page is a photograph

1. Ngũgĩ Wa Thiong'O, *Barrel of a Pen: Resistance to Repression in Neo-Colonial Kenya* (Trenton, N.J.: Africa World Press, 1983), 57.
2. Canaan Banana, *The Gospel according to the Ghetto*, rev. ed. (Gweru, Zimbabwe: Mambo Press, 1990), 169.
3. *Evangelical Witness in South Africa (Evangelicals Critique Their Own Theology and Practice)* (Dobsonville, South Africa: Concerned Evangelicals, 1986), 22, 33.

consisting of Nelson Mandela (top left), Mikhail Gorbachev
(top right), George Bush (bottom left), and John Major (bottom right). Inside the cover is a list of societal ills, among
which is the statement, "Racism divides our country." Ensuing
is the statement that the answer to these problems cannot be
found in politicians (no doubt those on the cover) but only
in Christ. It should strike our attention that Mandela was out
of place in the group of national leaders, while it was the
oppressive white, colonial South African government that
escaped the criticism. Mandela was imprisoned by the South
African government for twenty-seven years and yet, in a
Christlike spirit, has, without bitterness, called for racial harmony, a new South Africa based on a truly egalitarian and
ethical democracy. Why was Mandela on the cover of this tract
and not P. W. Botha or F. W. DeKlerk?

Indeed, our hymnody has not sufficiently distanced itself
from the hymns we learned from white slaveholders and col-
onizers, hymns that embody the kind of subtle racism found
in the above-mentioned tract. References to the need for
things "dark" to be washed "white" or made "light" are un-
countable. For instance, John H. Stockton's hymn, "Come,
Every Soul by Sin Oppressed," has this couplet:

> For Jesus shed His precious blood rich blessings to
>   bestow;
> Plunge now into the crimson flood that washes white
>   as snow.

The popular hymnic language of the church is certainly
as problematic in regard to sexism, not so much hymns that
explicitly degrade women but ones that exclude or subordinate them through the preponderance of male images and
pronouns relating to God and masculine nouns and pronouns
that refer to women. Among such hymns, really too numerous
to list, are Frederick W. Faber's "Faith of Our Fathers" and
Charles Wesley's "Come, Father, Son, and Holy Ghost," plus
the hymns of the patriarchal social gospel movement, such
as William Merrill's "Rise Up, O Men of God!"

That the patriarchy of a particular denomination also reveals itself in the hymns selected for hymnal compilations is illustrated in the two hymnbooks compiled by the Holiness denomination named The House of God, Which Is the Church of the Living God, The Pillar and Ground of Truth, Without Controversy, Inc., founded in 1903 by (Mother) Mary L. Tate.[4] The hymnbook compiled around 1944 by Mother (Bishop) Tate's successor, (Bishop) Mary F. L. Keith, titled *Spiritual Songs and Hymns*, omitted the old graybeard of patriarchal Protestantism, "Faith of Our Fathers," and instead contained six hymns about "mother": "Will My Mother Know Me There?" "If I Could Hear My Mother Pray Again," "You Know Your Mother Always Cares," "I Hear My Mother Call My Name," "Please Shake My Mother's Hand," and "Meeting Mother in the Skies." These six hymns were conspicuously excluded from the hymnal of the same title compiled under the bishopry of the first male "chief overseer," James W. Jenkins. While most gospel songs, prior to 1970, exhort that human relationships are carnal and not to be trusted, "mother" in these six pieces is viewed positively rather than negatively. In fact, in "Please Shake My Mother's Hand" all relatives but mother are depicted as sinners:

> My brother turned his back on Jesus,
> Sister sinful as can be;
> My father did not seem to want me,
> Please shake my mother's hand for me.

Another hymn, "You Know Your Mother Always Cares," hints at the possibility of viewing God, as revealed in Jesus, in traditional feminine characteristics:

> Your mother is your friend and she'll be to the end
> And if her hope and dreams will just come true.
> No bitterness or strife will even touch your life,
> You know your mother always cares for you.

4. See Jon Michael Spencer, *Black Hymnody: A Hymnological History of the African-American Church* (Knoxville, Tenn.: University of Tennessee Press, 1992), 119–29.

But when the denomination came under the leadership of a man, these hymns that affirm womanhood, motherhood, and the religious maturity of women were lost to the patriarchal "traditional."

At a hymn festival that I narrated at Christian Theological Seminary in Indianapolis, I went to an extreme in pointing out the problems of gender and hymnody. I mentioned that my reaction to the hymnic cadence "Amen," particularly at the end of hymns dominated by masculine images and pronouns, is that "Amen" *sounds* more like "*Awe men!*" (the ultimate glorification, even deification, of *men*). In other words, I am suggesting that this cadence works subconsciously on listeners to the detriment of women. Thus, I requested the hymn festival choir director to end the first of my three original hymns to be sung that night, "Our God Who Reigns Lord before Us," with a plagal cadence sung to the words "A-women" (Awe *women!*). He had the choir do it, and the point was made. But in all seriousness, what language shall we use? How could "amen," to illustrate the problems we face in revising our hymnody, be revised to suit a new hymnody? Since "amen" means essentially "so be it" or "yes" in Hebrew, then why not end with "yes" over the plagal cadence? Or, we could borrow from the denominational anthem of the Church of God in Christ and conclude our two-chord plagal cadence with the two-syllable phrase, "Yes, Lord!" The word "Lord" may be problematic gender-wise (masculine) but not, to my thinking, as problematic as "men" or even "king."

The point I am making is that the notion that Christ can make a woman "male" and suitable for entrance into God's "*king*dom" is not simply an extraneous idea found in the apocryphal *Gospel according to Thomas* (99:18-26); Christian hymnody implies the same, just as it implies that blacks, albeit allegedly "cursed," can be washed "white."

In challenging Afro-Christian hymnists to be sensitive to contemporary currents of social change spearheaded by visionary black intellectuals, I am responding in part to the challenge of some African-American biblical scholars to examine one of the black church's principal "near-canonical sources" that reinforces the subordinationist boundaries.[5] At least one of these biblical scholars feels that the various scholarly approaches to the African-American religious tradition— history, sociology, theology, and so forth—have neglected to examine the role the Bible has played in that tradition.[6] Therefore, when these scholars come to the consensus that they must lead the way in the adoption and dissemination of a liberationist rather than a precritical literalist interpretation of Scripture,[7] I take them to be challenging also the ethnohymnologist. "I assume that a primary responsibility of the African-American biblical scholar," says William Myers, "is to aid the African-American believing community in understanding, surviving, and altering its present socio-political situation through accurate and appropriate interpretation and application of Holy Scripture."[8] My goal as an ethnohymnologist, then, is to clarify the relationship between the biblical text and the wider source of canon that is our hymnody. This is important because, as hymnologist Benjamin Crawford said back in 1938, the development and the future of religious ideals rest on the hymns people sing. "For the average churchman the hymn book is more a book of religion than his Bible. More religious interest is brought him by song than by the scriptures. In fact much of scriptural truth is conveyed to him through hymns."[9] If this measurement of the role of hymnody in the religious life of laity is accurate, then a revised hymnody is a prerequisite in order to inform and uplift the Afro-Christian masses. If raising the level of thought among the masses is the goal (which it is), as opposed to cultivating the exceptional individual and leader, then it is hymnody—the

5. William H. Myers, "The Hermeneutical Dilemma of the African American Biblical Student," in *Stony the Road We Trod: African American Biblical Interpretation*, ed. Cain Hope Felder (Minneapolis: Fortress Press, 1991), 51, 53, 54.
6. Vincent L. Wimbush, "The Bible and African Americans: An Outline of an Interpretative History," in Felder, *Stony the Road We Trod*, 81–82.
7. Clarice J. Martin, "The *Haustafeln* (Household Codes) in African American Biblical Interpretation: 'Free Slaves' and 'Subordinate Women,' " in Felder, *Stony the Road We Trod*, 228.
8. Myers, "The Hermeneutical Dilemma," 44.
9. Benjamin F. Crawford, *Religious Trends in a Century of Hymns* (Carnegie, Pa.: Carnegie Church Press, 1938), 24.

popular source of the theology of the masses—that needs serious attention.

My reading of the research of black church scholars has informed me of a significant part of the problem: The black church is captive of the theological and doctrinal hegemony of Eurocentric biblical Christianity that emphasizes an overly dogmatic devotion to the Bible. This keeps our theological way of thinking bound, to a substantial degree, to the Greco-Roman metaphysical worldview as regards divinity.[10] Since Christianity was influenced by the values of Roman patriarchal and class societies that were prevalent at the time and place of its spread, it also forces modern marginalized readers—the victims of sexism, racism, and classism—to side against the marginalized groups in the Bible.[11] Thus there is something suspect about the Afro-Christian church being party to maintaining Christian orthodoxy when in fact that orthodoxy looks patronizingly upon traditions that are at best supplements and never alternatives to Eurocentric cultural preferences. This is especially the case when the Eurocentric preferences require (as is usually the case) the suppression of worldviews and values derived from being a woman, a person of color, or poor.

Quite aware of this dilemma, African-American biblical scholar Clarice Martin inquires as to why black men and male ministers reject the subordinationist ethos of master-over-slave while essentially accepting the kindred ethos of male-over-female.[12] As put by the womanist minister Willie Barrow, at the 1992 conference on the Black Church in America held at Morehouse and Spelman colleges, the black church is practicing "ecclesiastical apartheid" and "taxation without representation." Women are expected to function in the church as they have been traditionally held to functioning in the home—as spousal homemakers (missions, outreach ministries, and caring for the male pastor's needs). As put by Frene

10. Robert E. Hood, *Must God Remain Greek? Afro Cultures and God-Talk* (Minneapolis: Fortress Press, 1990), 110–11.
11. Renita J. Weems, "Reading *Her Way* through the Struggle: African American Women and the Bible," in Felder, *Stony the Road We Trod*, 72–73.
12. Martin, "The *Haustafeln*," 225.

Ginwala, a South African womanist, "We can no more accept even at a social level, a cultural practice that relegates the status of women, than we would accept a claim by Afrikaners that respect for their culture requires the separation or segregation of races."[13]

W. E. B. Du Bois recognized this as early as 1920, long before most men came anywhere close to articulating a language of gender liberation. He said that just as contempt for blacks rests on no scientific foundation and is but a "vicious habit of mind," so too contempt for women. "It could as easily be overthrown as our belief in war, as our international hatreds, as our old conception of the status of women, as our fear of educating the masses, and as our belief in the necessity of poverty."[14] Of the "old conception of the status of women," Du Bois says elsewhere, in his essay "The Damnation of Women":

> All womanhood is hampered today because the world on which it is emerging is a world that tries to worship both virgins and mothers and in the end despises motherhood and despoils virgins.
>
> The future woman must have a life work and economic independence. She must have knowledge. She must have the right of motherhood at her own discretion. The present mincing horror at free womanhood must pass if we are ever to be rid of the bestiality of free manhood; not by guarding the weak in weakness do we gain strength, but by making weakness free and strong.[15]

Of the black woman, Du Bois said in 1920: "What is today the message of the black women to America and to the world? The uplift of women is, next to the problem of the color line and peace movement, our greatest modern cause. When, now, two of these movements—women and color—

13. Cited in Desiree Hansson, "Working against Violence against Women," in *Putting Women on the Agenda*, ed. Susan Bazilli (Johannesburg, South Africa: Ravan Press, 1991), 182.
14. W. E. B. Du Bois, *Darkwater: Voices from within the Veil* (New York: Schocken Books, 1920), 73.
15. Ibid., 165.

combine in one, the combination has deep meaning."[16] In another man of color, Frantz Fanon, is to be found an additional model for the formation of the womanist black male. Fanon says that in underdeveloped countries (and Africa, continental and diasporan, *is* underdeveloped) every effort must be made to mobilize men and women, mobilize them free of the tradition of male superiority—an equality not in the rhetoric of a national constitution but in everyday life, from places of labor and education up to the high halls of government.[17] Women of color have at the very least, in participating in liberation struggles, earned, by their sheer strength, the right to cease being a complement for men.[18]

The same inquiry that Clarice Martin poses to men of color, regarding the repression of women in the light of their own quest for racial freedom, is worth presenting to feminists who allow the continuation of internal divisions based on race and class. In fact, in contrast to feminists who contend that racism will persist until the achievement of gender emancipation, Dorothy Blake Fardan, a white woman, suggests just the opposite:

> White women need to understand that their underside condition is due to the white man's aggressions against nonwhite peoples the world over, and that the keys which will unlock the door of freedom, justice and equality, lie not in the storerooms and pantries of America, but in the vast and ancient wealth of African and Native American spirituality and human wisdom that preceded any of the structures in which white people find themselves.[19]

White women also need to understand, says Fardan, that they are partners in the white man's aggressions against nonwhites:

16. Ibid., 181.
17. Frantz Fanon, *The Wretched of the Earth*, trans. Constance Farrington (New York: Grove Press, 1966), 202.
18. Frantz Fanon, *Studies in a Dying Colonialism*, trans. Haakon Chevalier (London: Earthscan Publications, 1989), 109.
19. Dorothy Blake Fardan, *Message to the White Man and Woman in America: Yakub and the Origins of White Supremacy* (Hampton, Va.: United Brothers and Sisters Communications Systems, 1991), 128.

> While white women have not constructed the white
> world, they have been "kept" by it, being allowed domicile
> and access to its material acquisitions and assets. Being
> the bearer of keys and the protector of the white man's
> profits and accumulated wealth, she has, in collaboration
> and complicity, perpetuated the kingdom of white su-
> premacy and the empire of material grand theft.[20]

It is the "orthodoxy" of this kind of hierarchical "body
politic"—a European head over an African foot, a male head
over a female foot, an elitist head over an impoverished foot—
that has resulted in the sickness in the Christian "body." The
problem with letting the Afro-Christian church continue this
pattern is that it has been party to this sickness, a sickness
that has split us up and cut us off from the root of our African
history, identity, and potentiality. What Afro-Christians (all
Christians of African descent) ought to be endorsing is not
uniformity and conformity but an ever-emerging church that
is permitted to mature into an institution of liberty (a community of redemptively free people), equality (a community
of individuals with equal rights and opportunities), and family
(a community of siblings free from patriarchy, race prejudice,
and elitist class divisiveness).

During our enslavement in the diaspora lands, there was
no mistake that the Christianity given us by our captors was
polluted and unchristian, and we produced revolutionaries
such as Nat Turner and Denmark Vesey. The white southern
(Christian) reaction to Reconstruction also left no doubt in
the minds of Afro-Christians that we were still under a colonial
system, and we produced revolutionaries such as Henry
McNeal Turner, Reverdy Ransom, Mary McLeod Bethune,
and Fannie Lou Hamer. At present, having been thrown the
bone of civil rights advances, our thrust toward liberation,
justice, and equality has been undercut. We have been dis-
armed by a few concessions, a few "victories," which have
falsely satisfied our longing to be treated on a par with all
other human beings. This continues to be worrisome to our

20. Ibid., 102.

public philosophers and leaders of radical change. It was worrisome to James Baldwin and Malcolm X, and it continues to be to C. Eric Lincoln, Cornel West, and bell hooks, to name only a few.

This very concern for the lack of Christian action in behalf of the "poor and needy" is what led Langston Hughes, even before the days of Malcom X, Lincoln, West, and Hooks, to write his infamous poem of 1931, "Goodbye Christ." He wrote the dramatic monologue, he said, "with the intention in mind of shocking into being in religious people a consciousness of the admitted shortcomings of the church in regard to the condition of the poor and oppressed of the world, particularly the Negro people." After touring the American southland and viewing the racial atrocities that held his people in social and economic degradation, he wrote the poem. "In the poem I contrasted what seemed to me the declared and forthright position of those who, on the religious side in America (in apparent actions toward my people) had said to Christ and the Christian principles, 'Goodbye, beat it on away from here now, you're done for.' I gave to such religionists what seemed to me to be their own words merged with the words of the orthodox Marxist who declared he had no further use nor need for religion."[21]

Intellectuals such as Hughes (and the others mentioned) understand that they must give their full attention to explaining carefully to the Afro-Christian public the intellectual warfare that continues to rage, so as to prevent them from being further burdened and bound by the intellectual maneuvering of the self-serving guardians of established traditions. As Fanon says of our people in *The Wretched of the Earth*, in the context of discussing the psychological impediments to the work of revolutionary decolonization by the colonized:

> They are so used to the settler's scorn and to his declared
> intention to maintain his oppression at whatever cost that

21. Langston Hughes, "Hughes Tells Why He Wrote Poem Entitled 'Goodbye Christ,'" *California Eagle*, 9 January 1941.

the slightest suggestion of any generous gesture or of
any good will is hailed with astonishment and delight,
and the native bursts into a hymn of praise. It must be
clearly explained to the rebel that he must on no account
be blindfolded by the enemy's concessions. These concessions . . . have no bearing on the essential question;
and from the native's point of view, we may lay down
that a concession has nothing to do with the essentials if
it does not affect the real nature of the colonial regime.[22]

The point is, the hymns of the Afro-Christian church are
largely colonized hymns, and the concession of finally allowing a few of these colonized "black hymns" into the hymnals
of predominantly white denominations does not affect the
real nature of the problem. Let us call the problem "Christendom" and define it more fully.

Søren Kierkegaard, in his *Attack upon "Christendom"*
(1855), defines "Christendom" as religion that stands dia-
metrically opposite New Testament Christianity: playing *at*
faith and worship, liturgical "pomp and circumstance" rather
than theological substance.[23] In Christian hymnody, Christendom is manifested in imagery where Christ is portrayed
as a royal *white* potentate surrounded by *white* angels that
worship *him* upon a mighty *throne*:

> All hail the power of Jesus' name!
> Let angels prostrate fall;
> Bring forth the royal diadem,
> And crown him Lord of all.

Where Christ is portrayed as male rather than as female (or
feminine), as white rather than as nonwhite (or oppressed),
as master rather than as servant (or impoverished), what
results is the hymnic tradition of gender, race, and class hierarchy rooted in Greco-Roman societal conventions and
philosophical sanctionings.

---

22. Fanon, *Wretched*, 142.
23. Søren Kierkegaard, *Attack upon "Christendom*," trans. Walter Lowrie (Princeton, N.J.: Princeton University Press, 1968), 121, 191, 212.

The intent of this critical assessment is not to denigrate the Afro-Christian church, which, probably worldwide, has been the most important institution owned and operated by Afro-peoples. Neither is the intent of the challenge I put forth to denigrate Afro-Christian hymnists, whose songs have helped sustain us over the last century. Indeed, the gospel hymns of Charles Albert Tindley (Methodist), Charles Price Jones (Holiness), and Lucie Campbell (Baptist) are frequently known by Afro-Christians throughout the world. The problem is, however, that these gospel hymns are so anticultural— all things and institutions of the world being portrayed so negatively—that even the value and the beauty of Afro-cultures are left unaffirmed. C. P. Jones's "I Am Happy with Jesus Alone" illustrates the point:

> Should father and mother forsake me alone,
> My bed upon the earth be a stone,
> I'll cling to my Savior, He loves me I know,
> I'm happy with Jesus alone.

In our traditional gospel hymns, Jesus Christ is everything and the world is worth nothing.

In search of a solution that would correspond with the immensity of the problem, I took Fanon up on his advice that black intellectuals ought to turn to Aimé Césaire for inspiration.[24] Indeed, I have also turned to Fanon himself for reasons that I will let his biographer, Irene Gendzier, explain:

> Fanon's initial appeal in American black circles was not based on his considerations of national culture, nor on his discussion of negritude. Yet he has been cited as the intellectual guide in the awakening that has characterized the black community and that has involved a reconsideration of the question of black culture. Fanon's role in this can be attributed to his powerful exposé of the psychology of colonization and the process of total psychic alienation common to the colonized and the oppressed, whom he increasingly identified with one another. Out

24. Frantz Fanon, *Black Skin, White Masks*, trans. Charles Lam Markmann (New York: Grove Press, 1967), 187.

of this has come the endorsement for self-affirmation, for rejection of masks and the false identity they imply.[25] I also took Haki Madhubuti, the African-American poet and cultural critic, up on his suggestion that studying the work of Cheikh Anta Diop and kindred African and African diaspora Africanists is a requisite initial step to recapturing the minds of Afro-peoples.[26] As this book will evidence, I did turn to Diop and Césaire, as well as to John Henrik Clarke, Nawal El Saadawi, and others, for the information and inspiration to forge ahead with research and a resultant practical proposal. I also heard the call of Canaan Banana in his book of poetry and essays, *The Gospel of the Ghetto* (1980), in which he states prefatorily: "It is my hope that these thoughts can form the basis of the kind of study that will stimulate the reader to creative action."[27]

I believe the Africanists posit a viable possibility in petitioning Afro-peoples to allow an African anteriority (a retrospective look to African cultures) to function as the basis of reconceived and renewed Afro-cultures. This is what Afrocentrism is to me: not an ideology but the placing of Africa, the habitat and culture from which continental and diasporan Africans have come, at the center of our self-understanding so that we are no longer alienated from ourselves; and the placing of Africa and Afro-peoples back into the truer historical perspective, a historical balance that has been denied us by the Eurocentric ideology. Thus it is partly upon the shoulders of the aforementioned scholars that I stand in calling for a renaissance in the Afro-Christian church that can begin with a revised black hymnody. From the church, the renaissance can overflow into the community. "Without the full participation of the church," says Molefi Asante, "we cannot have a genuine re-creation. In fact, our history shows

25. Irene L. Gendzier, *Frantz Fanon: A Critical Study* (New York: Grove Press, 1973), 263.
26. Haki R. Madhubuti, *Enemies: The Clash of Races* (Chicago: Third World Press, 1978), 49.
27. Banana, *The Gospel*, xiv-v.

that the church, sooner or later, establishes itself as transmitter of the new visions within our community."[28]

If I depend alone on the shoulders of those whom I have mentioned in order to propose ideas that are themselves balanced, I will, according to Anthony Appiah, surely fall. Diop, and the other "Egyptianists," says Appiah, require us to view Africa's modern identity as a cultural unity, which will only divert us from the problems of the present and the possibilities of the future.[29] Thus Appiah warns us not to rely too heavily on the traditional concept of race as found in the works of scholars ranging from Du Bois to Diop:

> But these objections to a biologically rooted conception of race may still seem all too theoretical: if Africans can get together around the idea of the Black Person, if they can create through this notion of productive alliances with African-Americans and people of African descent in Europe and the Caribbean, surely these theoretical objections should pale in the light of the practical value of these alliances. But there is every reason to doubt they can. Within Africa . . . racialization has produced arbitrary boundaries and exacerbated tensions. . . .
>
> In short, I think it is clear enough that a biologically rooted conception of race is both dangerous in practice and misleading in theory: African unity, African identity, need securer foundations than race.[30]

Appiah concludes his point about the possibility of a Pan-Africanism without racism as a source of African identity, saying:

> To accept that Africa can be . . . a usable identity is not to forget that all of us belong to multifarious communities with their local customs; it is not to dream of a single African state and to forget the complex different trajectories of the continent's so many languages and cultures.

28. Molefi Kete Asante, *Afrocentricity*, rev. ed. (Trenton, N.J.: Africa World Press, 1988), 71.

29. Kwame Anthony Appiah, *In My Father's House: Africa in the Philosophy of Culture* (New York: Oxford University Press, 1992), 176.

30. Ibid., 175–76.

> "African solidarity" can surely be a vital and enabling
> rallying cry; but in this world of genders, ethnicities, and
> classes, of families, religions, and nations, it is as well to
> remember that there are times when Africa is not the
> banner we need.[31]

Accepting this word of caution, I think we can proceed enthusiastically, but carefully, in petitioning for an African anteriority to function as the basis of a reconceived and renewed Afro-Christian church.

On the other hand, although we need to proceed with some caution as we posit new ideas for new song, the reality is that we must proceed with a measure of haste. The Afro-Christian church has been for too long held captive to the theological, doctrinal, and social hegemony of the Eurocentric ideology that works to stifle the impetus of Afro-peoples toward self-identity and self-determination, inwardly as well as in the larger social milieus. It is in this respect that religion works as an opiate in our societal bloodstream: We are divesting ourselves of personal power by investing the God presented to us by the guardians of orthodoxy with all power. We are doing this to the degree that we are left marginalized and, worse, submissive to or indifferent toward the subordinationist practices of that guarded tradition. Religion itself is not necessarily responsible for this opiate effect. Religion easily can be, but need not be, limited to functioning as a mere stage in the process of human maturation; and it does not have to quell human aspiration and achievement. Afro-Christian self-identity and self-determination should be achievable in and through religious and theological growth. This is our challenge in the field of ethnohymnology and hymn writing.

By what means, then, can we alleviate the problems reflected in black hymnody and more rapidly progress, through the vehicle of our religion, toward gender, race, and class liberation? It must be understood, first of all, that the problem is not simply reflected in our hymnody; to a considerable

31. Ibid., 180.

degree the problem *is* our hymnody. Replacing it with a song that recovers the best of our African heritages, while also remembering past struggles that Afro-peoples have overcome and future hurdles that we must overcome, could possibly help launch us toward the alleviation of gender, race, and class hierarchies, for it is in the midst of liberation struggles that we have traditionally transcended these forms of captivity that impede our self-identity and self-determination. Such a new corpus of hymnody perhaps could build upon the base of the songs Afro-peoples created as they struggled for freedom from slavery and colonialism, from the freedom songs of America's civil rights marchers to those of Kenya's Mau Mau liberation fighters. This hymnic corpus could include modern expressions of faith that recoup the best of an African anteriority, all in order to institutionalize gender, race, and class egalitarianism. We can also contemplate the meaning of W. E. B. Du Bois's *Prayers for Dark People* and create a "new song" that is not timid about facing head-on, with even "radical" language, the dilemmas of our day. We can contemplate Du Bois's poem of 1899:

> I am the smoke king
> I am black
> I am darkening with song;
> I am hearkening to wrong;
> I will be black as blackness can . . .
> I am carving God in night,
> I am painting hell in white,
> I am smoke king
> I am black.[32]

I can hear Fanon in this: "I am black: I am the incarnation of a complete fusion with the world, an intuitive understanding of the earth, an abandonment of my ego in the heart of the cosmos. . . . If I am black, it is not the result of a curse, but it is because, having offered my skin, I have been able to

32. W. E. B. Du Bois, "The Song of the Smoke," in *Selected Poems* (Accra, Ghana: Ghana University Press, 1964), 12.

absorb all the cosmic *effluvia*. I am truly a ray of sunlight under the earth."[33]

This acceptance of one's blackness, this esteeming of what heretofore had been denigrated, is the antithesis of what Fanon sarcastically critiques in a book titled *Je suis martinquaise* (1948) by the (black) Martiniquan, Mayotte Capecia. Fanon says the American film *Green Pastures*, in which God and the angels are black, was a brutal shock to Capecia, who wrote: "How is it possible to imagine God with Negro characteristics: This is not my vision of paradise." Fanon's sarcasm lights up: "Indeed no, the good and merciful God cannot be black: He is a white man with bright pink cheeks. From black to white is the course of mutation. One is white as one is rich, as one is beautiful, as one is intelligent."[34]

Behind Du Bois's poem is not only an African anteriority that would help us bypass the attitude of Capecia but more specifically an Egyptian anteriority, the same that is predicated by Diop and that, for both Diop and Du Bois, resulted in a petition for gender equality. More recently, the Egyptian womanist Nawal El Saadawi has turned to ancient Egypt of the first four dynasties for a paradigm of gender equality. At this time, prior to landownership and resultant class divisions, women held high status in society as well as in the realms of religion and government:

> The earliest and perhaps greatest of all ancient civilizations has been a fertile field for historical research. Scholars and Egyptologists repeatedly registered the fact that, in the preliminary stages of Egyptian society, women were frequently drawn and engraved on the walls, and their size corresponded to that of men, indicating equality in status and prestige. But, later on, the female size started to decrease which meant that women were losing position in relation to men. This change was found to correspond with the appearance of private property extending from the VIIth to the Xth Dynasty (2420–2140 B.C.).[35]

33. Fanon, *Black Skin*, 45.
34. Ibid., 51–52.
35. Nawal El Saadawi, *The Hidden Face of Eve: Women in the Arab World* (London: Zed Press, 1980), 108.

Preventing the possibility of such an African anteriority is a silent consensus among us (and those outsiders who observe us): Not only do whites, says Andrew Hacker, seem to feel that we stand in need of their tutelage, as if we lack the capacity to comprehend our own interests;[36] we in fact give the impression that we cannot comprehend or practice Christianity without European interpretation, without European hymns to sing, without the white-colored Jesus sanctioning the validity of our religion. Fanon makes this very comment with regard to the strategy of European colonialism:

> When we consider the efforts made to carry out the cultural estrangement so characteristic of the colonial epoch, we realize that nothing has been left to chance and that the total result looked for by colonial domination was indeed to convince the natives that colonialism came to lighten their darkness. The effect consciously sought by colonialism was to drive into the natives' heads the idea that if the settlers were to leave, they would at once fall back into barbarism, degradation, and bestiality.[37]

I understand Appiah's point that it is too late to escape the way in which Europe and people of European origin have shaped our identities as people of African descent.[38] But I agree with Madhubuti, who says, "We in our search for meaning generally go the way of European-American 'Correctness,' not realizing that what is 'normal' for others may be deadly for us."[39] African-American historian Asa Hilliard, in his foreword to the 1976 reprint of George G. M. James's *Stolen Legacy* (1954), concurs, saying, "Mental bondage is invisible violence."[40] Ngũgĩ Wa Thiong'O adds that "intellectual slavery masquerading as sophistication is the worst form of slavery."[41]

36. Andrew Hacker, *Two Nations: Black and White, Separate, Hostile, Unequal* (New York: Charles Scribner's Sons, 1992), 43.
37. Fanon, *Wretched*, 210–11.
38. Appiah, *In My Father's House*, 72.
39. Madhubuti, *Enemies*, 117.
40. Cited in John A. Williams, "The Stolen Legacy," in *African Presence in Early Europe*, ed. Ivan Van Sertima (New Brunswick, N.J.: Transaction Publishers, 1985), 84.
41. Ngũgĩ Wa Thiong'O, *Detained: A Writer's Prison Diary* (Nairobi, Kenya: Heinemann Kenya, 1981), 143.

To this Fanon adjoins a psychological analysis that explains the need of those who have been not only culturally but mentally colonized to turn back toward their unknown cultural roots. "This tearing away, painful and difficult though it may be, is however necessary. If it is not accomplished there will be serious psycho-affective injuries and the result will be individuals without an anchor, without a horizon, colorless, stateless, rootless—a race of angels."[42] Fanon concludes, "European achievements, European techniques, and the European style ought no longer to tempt us and to throw us off our balance."[43] Indeed, European hymns ought no longer throw us off our balance by "washing us white as snow." Rather, still pursuing the psychology of Fanon, we should become conscious of this unconscious "hallucinatory whitening":

> In other words, the black man should no longer be confronted by the dilemma, *turn white or disappear*; but he should be able to take cognizance of a possibility of existence. In still other words, if society makes difficulties for him because of his color, if in his dreams I establish the expression of an unconscious desire to change color, my objective will not be that of dissuading him from it by advising him to "keep his place"; on the contrary, my objective, once his motivations have been brought into consciousness, will be to put him in a position to *choose* action (or passivity) with respect to the real source of conflict—that is, toward the social structures.[44]

To preclude our becoming "a race of angels," I am calling for a reformation, a renaissance, comprised of a renewed look at the history, cultures, and cosmologies of Africa in order to create a hymnody that, somewhat like the poetic and narrative literature of the Hebrew Bible,[45] esteems Africa. One example

42. Fanon, *Wretched*, 218.
43. Ibid., 312.
44. Fanon, *Black Skin*, 100.
45. See Randall C. Bailey, "Beyond Identification: The Use of Africans in Old Testament Poetry and Narratives," in Felder, *Stony the Road We Trod*, 183.

is the hymn "Nkosi Sikelel' iAfrika" ("God Bless Africa"), written in 1897 by the Xhosa teacher of Johannesburg's Nance-
field location, Enoch Sontonga, and popularized by Reuben
T. Caluza, the Zulu composer. It is a hymn that became the
official anthem of the African National Congress (ANC) in
1925 and has been adopted as the national anthem of several
southern African countries, including Zimbabwe and now
South Africa.[46] The first verse is:

> Lord, bless Africa
> May her horn rise high up;
> Hear Thou our prayers
> And bless us.

Subsequent verses, written by the Xhosa poet S. E. Mqayi,
petition for the blessing of the chiefs, the public men, the
youth, the wives and young women, the ministers of the
churches, and the agriculture and livestock so as to abolish
all famine and disease. The last two verses are especially
important:

> Bless our efforts
> Of union and self-uplift
> Of education and mutual understanding
> And bless them.

> Lord, bless Africa;
> Blot out all its wickedness
> And its transgressions and sins,
> And bless it.

Appiah is convincing in his argument that there is no
united Africa or homogeneous African worldview,[47] but I do
not find that this hymn, which petitions for a united Africa,
is anywhere problematic. Neither do I find it problematic that
we should look back to Africa for the inspiration to move
forward. In fact, I agree with African-American historian

---

46. David B. Coplan, *In Township Tonight! South Africa's Black City Music and
Theatre* (Johannesburg, South Africa: Ravan Press, 1985), 46.
47. Appiah, *In My Father's House*, 26, 82.

John Henrik Clarke, who says, "If we have to change tomorrow we are going to have to look back in order to look
forward. We will have to look back with some courage, warm
our hands on the revolutionary fires of those who came before
us and understand that we have within ourselves, nationally
and internationally, the ability to regain what we lost and to
build a new humanity for ourselves, first and foremost, and
for the whole world ultimately."[48] According to Nawal El
Saadawi, this looking back in order to look forward is exactly
what is occurring among the people of North and Sub-
Saharan Africa:

> Peoples everywhere are not only breaking the bonds of
> political and economic dependence, but also the cultural
> chains that imprison the mind. They are probing into
> their past, rediscovering their origins, their roots, their
> history; they are searching for a cultural identity, learning
> anew about their own civilization, moulding a personality
> genuine enough and strong enough and resolute enough
> to resist the onslaught of Western interests and to take
> back what was plundered over the centuries: natural re-
> sources, labour producing value, goods and profits, and
> the creations of intellect and culture . . . and to restore
> the roots that take their sustenance in the past and their
> nourishment in cultural heritage. For without these roots
> the life of a people dries up, becomes weak and futile
> like a tree cut off from the depths of the soil, and loses
> both its physical and moral force.[49]

The general point I am making actually corresponds with
what Appiah identifies as the difference between the contemporary African writer and the contemporary European writer:
the European's search for self and the African's search for a
culture.[50] "So that though the European may feel that the
problem of who he or she is can be a private problem, the

48. John Henrik Clarke, "African Resistance and Colonial Dominance: The
Africans in the Americas," in *New Dimensions in African History: The London Lectures
of Dr. Yosef ben-Jochannan and Dr. John Henrik Clarke*, ed. John Henrik Clarke (Trenton,
N.J.: Africa World Press, 1991), 33–34.
    49. Saadawi, *The Hidden Face of Eve*, v.
    50. Appiah, *In My Father's House*, 74.

African asks always not 'who am I?' but 'who are we?' and 'my' problem is not mine alone but 'ours.' "[51]

When I shared these very ideas in a lecture at a theological seminary, a biblical scholar retorted negatively regarding my suggestion for reconciling the historical imbalance in white and black Christian outlooks—namely, my suggestion that Afro-peoples place Africa back into truer biblical perspective. The worst part of her retort is that she fell back on the most common excuse for opposing Afrocentrism—that to put Africa and Afro-peoples at the center of inquiry is to be exclusionary of all other peoples whose hues are not black. Political scientist Andrew Hacker (who is white) can answer this query for that professor. He agrees that all nonwhite people have suffered discrimination at the hands of white Americans, but he says these "intermediate groups" have been allowed by whites, who grant and impose racial memberships, to keep a visible lacuna between themselves and black people. "Put most simply, none of the presumptions of inferiority associated with Africa and slavery are imposed on these other ethnicities."[52]

Beyond this, I have been clear from the beginning. I am working for Afro-peoples whom I know best in the light of our common enslavement and colonial exploitation by whites. I resonate with what Aimé Césaire said in 1967 in the context of European colonialism in Africa:

> We lived in an atmosphere of rejection, and we developed an inferiority complex. I have always thought that the black man was searching for his identity. And it has seemed to me that if what we want is to establish this identity, then we must have a concrete consciousness of what we are—that is, of the first fact of our lives: that we are black; that we are black and have a history, a history that contains certain cultural elements of great value; and that Negroes were not, as you put it, born yesterday, because there have been beautiful and important black civilizations. At the time we began to write

51. Ibid., 76.
52. Hacker, *Two Nations*, 15, 16.

people could write a history of world civilization without
devoting a single chapter to Africa, as if Africa had made
no contributions to the world. Therefore, we affirmed
that we were Negroes and that we were proud of it, and
that we thought that Africa was not some sort of blank
page in the history of humanity; in sum, we asserted that
our Negro heritage was worthy of respect, and that this
heritage was not relegated to the past, that its values were
values that could still make an important contribution to
the world.[53]

The fact is, unless it is recognized that there is a dilemma
with the historical record of the Euro-Christians, in regard
to the way they have treated black people and with respect
to certain self-serving theological presuppositions prolifer-
ated in the white church, then all of my solutions will be
found to be problematic, flawed, unnecessary, and exclusionary. This book will be found to be a work of black nationalism
rather than a work of black liberation.

There is another criticism I have heard that I should
address. Given my suggestion that Afro-Christians engage in
an African anteriority for the purpose of engendering a
hymnic renaissance, the critical person might also question
how I can, without contradiction, draw on the thought of
Eurocentric scholars, particularly since I am critical of their
historical record. Indeed, I am critical of their record, as are
most people who are ethnic. This is part of what it means to
be what I defined an ethnohymnologist to be in my preface.
Furthermore, this book-length petition to "sing a new song"
is not, I repeat, a work of black nationalism; it is an attempt
to attain black liberation. Therefore I am free to choose selectively from any thought that theorizes about liberation, not
to mention that I take pleasure in showing that some of the
words of the opposition in fact corroborate my arguments for
liberation. Chancellor Williams makes my point when he says
that even the most racist writers usually prove the opposite

---

53. Aimé Césaire, "An Interview," in *Discourse on Colonialism*, trans. Joan Pinkham
(New York: Monthly Review Press, 1972), 76.

of what they intend to assert. "Indeed, it is doubtful whether anyone, even a devil, could write a book completely devoid of truth."[54] Diop also makes a useful point when he says that Egypt is the root and basis of Western cultures, so that most of the ideas that appear foreign to African peoples are but the modified, reversed, or misconstrued thought of Africa.[55] "Consequently, no thought, no ideology is, in essence, foreign to Africa, which was their birthplace," says Diop. "It is therefore with total liberty that Africans can draw from the common intellectual heritage of humanity, letting themselves be guided only by the notions of utility and efficiency."[56] Or, if one does not accept the Egyptianist portrait of Africa, which Appiah calls "a fancied past of shared glories,"[57] then perhaps Appiah's own point will be satisfactory. The point suffices for my argument:

> We may acknowledge that the truth is the property of no culture, that we should take the truths we need wherever we find them. But for truths to become the basis of . . . natural life, they must be believed, and whether or not whatever new truths we take from the West *will* be believed depends in large measure on how we are able to manage the relations between our conceptual heritage and the ideas that rush at us from worlds elsewhere.[58]

There are no doubt some radical Afrocentrists who will not want to believe in any "truth" if it comes from "a devil," those Afrocentrists who maintain what Appiah calls an unnecessary "nativism." In spite of these suspicions, which will always persist among all Afrocentrists to a degree, I agree with Diop for his reasons and Appiah for his that "nativism"— which rejects all "foreign" thought—is unnecessarily self-limiting in the quest for liberation. In regard to our choice

54. Cited in Runoko Rashidi, "Blacks in Early Britain," in Sertima, *African Presence in Early Europe*, 252.
55. Cheikh Anta Diop, *Civilization or Barbarism: An Authentic Anthropology*, ed. Harold J. Salemson and Marjolijn de Jager, trans. Yaa-Lengi Meema Ngemi (New York: Lawrence Hill Books, 1991), 3.
56. Ibid., 4.
57. Appiah, *In My Father's House*, 176.
58. Ibid., 5.

of what "foreign" hymns to sing, I only insist on selectivity, critical review, and frequent revision. I have been suggesting that these review processes, as regards our hymnody, could be based on the legitimizing and systematizing of measurements derived from an African anteriority. If we choose to maintain some aspect of orthodoxy in our hymnody, it should be as a result of our having reviewed it in the light of our own history and cultures and our quest for liberation. The precedent is in the customary dependence of Eurocentric hymnologists and hymnists on a Greco-Roman philosophical anteriority.

I understand fully that my petition is a progressive step that at present seems even to be an impossibility. I know that I face the disposition of such persons as the black clergyman who responded to my ideas at the conference on the black church hosted at Morehouse and Spelman colleges (which I mentioned in the Preface). After my presentation, the clergyman handed me a note that read, "In the hymn 'From Greenland's Icy Mountains' does the word 'benighted' refer to black people or [just] people lost in the darkness of sin? [Regarding] 'white as snow' check Isaiah 1:18. Is this only for white people? Does it mean that black people cannot be washed 'white as snow' because they are black? Or, does it mean that anyone can be washed white as snow from sin?"

I had a similar experience as I lectured on this topic at the Baptist International Theological Seminary (BITS) in Debe Nek, in the former homeland of Ciskei in South Africa. I spent four days (two hours a day) teaching thirty-two African students about the need for a "new song" that reconciles the problems of gender, race, and class. During the end of their second-period class on the last day, their visiting professor, Nathan Corbitt, had them compose original hymns. After doing so in groups over a brief ten-minute span, they sang them. All of the five or six hymns praised Jesus or celebrated the heavenly salvation Jesus promised. None of them, after all that I had taught about the need for a new song, even came close to reflecting some of what I petitioned for during the week. New song is hard to come by.

Indeed, I understand fully that my petition is a progressive step. Hesitance for progressivism has been repeatedly manifested in our cultures. For instance, although "Lift Every Voice and Sing" is now accepted by most African Americans as the Black National Anthem, there was a time when the idea of having a black national anthem was unacceptable to many African Americans pushing upward to middle-class status in the milieu of early-twentieth-century modern urbanity. It is worth quoting in full a commentary of 1939 published in the black-owned *Chicago Defender*:

> The attempt to force upon the American people a so-called "Negro National Anthem" is both ludicrous and dangerous. If we admit beyond a shadow of a doubt that American blacks, in the very nature of specific provisions of the United States Constitution, are citizens of this country, then it follows logically that our national anthem is that which is generally accepted and sung by all of the citizens of this country.
>
> The 13th Amendment to the Constitution abolished slavery. The 14th Amendment states "All persons born or naturalized in the United States, and subject to the jurisdiction thereof, are citizens of the United States." Unless we wish to circumvent the meaning of this amendment by putting ourselves outside the pale of the application implied therein, we should not muddle up the stream of our freedom and citizenship rights by the creation of a farcical separate national anthem.
>
> When the late James Weldon Johnson wrote the words to his "Lift Every Voice and Sing," he was prompted by a motive which has been prostituted by injudicious minds. As principal of a high school in Florida, Johnson sought to compose for his student body, a poem that would inspire them to higher heights. The special circumstances that gave birth to it remove any question as to the purpose and intent of the author.
>
> Are we not polluting the stream of democracy: are we not contributing to segregation and discrimination when we undertake the promotion of a separate national anthem?

One fortunate aspect of the "Negro National Anthem"—although the music was written by Johnson's brother—is that it is beyond the vocal range of the average person. In fact, nobody knows the tune and words thereof except those few persons who try to force the anthem upon the people. The efforts at singing this anthem are met on every occasion with pathetic failure. So many discordant notes are registered that even the casual observer not knowing the historical circumstances of the hymn would be inclined to think, on hearing it sung, that a large part of the audience had imbibed spiritus frumenti too freely. For there is more harmony in a quartette of drunkards singing "Sweet Adeline" in a bar room than can be found wherever the "Negro National Anthem" is sung:

> Sing a song full of the faith that the dark
>   past has taught us,
> Sing a song full of the hope that the present
>   has brought us;
> Facing the rising sun of our new day begun,
> Let us march on till victory is won.

Beautiful as these words may be, they cannot be made to become the sentiment of a national hymn. "The Star Spangled Banner" is our national anthem. For heaven sake, let us learn to sing it. It is difficult enough.[59]

Even the writer from Dallas, Texas, who disagreed with the commentator's remark about the merits of the poetry and music of "Lift Every Voice and Sing," agreed that it should not be adopted as a racial anthem:

> Editor *Chicago Defender*: I find it in my heart to agree with you in last week's editorial criticism of the practice of labeling James Weldon's and J. Rosamond Johnson's composition, "The Negro National Anthem." I've always contended that it is nothing of the sort, either by official or unofficial sanction. Why not designate it, if classifying label is required, a "hymn" which is probably more expressive of its content and theme.

59. "Why an Anthem?" *Chicago Defender*, 25 February 1939, 16.

Some of us, though, may disagree with you as to the worthwhile nature of the words and music that make up the composition. Musicians and critics, better judges, perhaps, than either of us as to the literary and lyrical excellence, have commended the piece as a worthy example of the song writers' art. Personally, while I can't for the life of me sing it, the gentle admonitions and the deep spiritual implications that run through the melody seem vastly superior to the inflammatory blood and thunder of the national anthems of most of the nations of the world, including our own.

Dr. Edward A. Steiner, illustrious professor of sociology of Grinnell College, Iowa, says "Lift Every Voice and Sing" ranks high among the recent musical and poetical expressions of national and racial aspirations.[60]

So, I understand fully that my petition for us to "sing a new song" is a progressive step, one that can be easily misunderstood and logically discredited. This is because the Afro-Christian populace is too deeply entrenched in tradition, too attached to the old "songs of Zion," to accept suddenly more compelling expressions of self-identity and self-determination rooted in an African anteriority. This is because our hymns have functioned at a "tertiary level of canonicity" that makes them difficult to change.[61] If the solution I posit seems extreme, it is because I am convinced that the solution must correspond with the extent of the dilemma.

A far less extreme, as a beginning, is to do what the moral abolitionists, social gospelers, and civil rights freedom fighters did in the United States to help give momentum to their movements: We can choose selectively from extant hymnody and revise it so it resonates with the specific ethos and needs of the times. Creating new hymns or omitting or revising old hymns that contain sexist, racist, and classist language and imagery—for the purpose of restoring balance to our self-identity and self-determination—will require some

60. "The National Anthem," *Chicago Defender*, 11 March 1939, 16.
61. James A. Sanders, *Canon and Community* (Philadelphia: Fortress Press, 1984), 14–15. Cited in Myers, "The Hermeneutical Dilemma," 53.

progressive steps. It will require the prerequisite of some hermeneutical freedom (which I discuss in chapter 2), freedom that seeks to liberate our minds from perceiving the biblical canon and its cognate canon of hymnody as completed entities whose meanings are static for all time.

As regards the dilemma surrounding gender and hymnody, hymnologist Helen Pearson suggests that her disciplinary colleagues engage in "hymnic exegesis" in order to ask certain critical questions about the text, just as biblical scholars engage in scriptural exegeses.[62] In order to carry out such hymnic exegesis to the necessary degree, so that we get at the very mythological substance (rather than the form) of these dilemmas, I contend that hymnologists must also engage in biblical exegesis. Since scriptural myths and writings have been misused in the past to perpetuate the problems surrounding gender and race, I contend that gender and racial discrimination are still symptoms of a mythological/ideological flaw. I think this mythological/ideological flaw is what is repeatedly hinted at when scholars speak of the deeper or subconscious causes of discrimination. For instance, Frene Ginwala, a South African lawyer who was director of research for the office of the president of the African National Congress (ANC), says: "Discrimination is more a symptom than a cause. . . . To attack it, then, we have not only to legislate and act against it itself but also to work for shifts in the deeper causes which underlie it."[63] Andrew Hacker uses similar language in trying to pinpoint the source of racism. He says, "It transcends prejudice, discrimination, and even bigotry because it arises from assumptions of which whites are essentially unaware."[64]

The two "myths"—"deeper causes" of which people are "essentially unaware"—that have thus found their way into our hymnody are that women are depraved and inferior because of the disobedience of Eve in the Garden of Eden and

62. Helen Bruch Pearson, "The Battered Bartered Bride," *The Hymn* 34 (October 1983): 216.
63. Frene Ginwala, "Women and the Elephant: The Need to Redress Gender Oppression," in Bazilli, *Putting Women on the Agenda*, 62.
64. Hacker, *Two Nations*, 19–20.

that blacks are cursed and natural slaves because of the transgression of Ham. The narratives of the blaming of Eve (Gen.
3:1-6) and the so-called curse of Ham (Gen. 9:18-27) are the
two segments of Scripture that must be exegeted, their misinterpretations uncovered and corrected, by Afro-Christian
biblical scholars as preludes to a revised black hymnody and
a gender-blind and class-neutral society.

Perhaps we can think of only a few people who might
seriously agree that the Genesis story of the fall implies that
females are inferior and even fewer who would say that the
curse of Ham implies black inferiority, except possibly the
Afrikaners of South Africa, the "Rhodesians" who still refuse
to recognize the independence of Zimbabwe, and the
Mormons in the United States. Regarding the Afrikaners'
theology, Dutch Reformed Church minister J. A. Loubser
contends in his book *The Apartheid Bible* (1987) that the curse
of Ham theory was once used to justify slavery but eventually
became obsolete during the early part of the twentieth century.[65] However, elsewhere, in his discussion of various myths
that circulate among many white South Africans about blacks,
Loubser implies that even the curse of Ham myth may lie
latent in the subconscience of racists: "Even among regular
church members there are still individuals who almost seriously assure one that 'Blacks cannot go to heaven' and that
'it does not pay to do missionary work, because they fall back
into sin the moment they are converted.' These are only some
examples of the many myths in circulation."[66] For those who
actually have escaped being mythologically minded, the mythological exterior of racism, once stripped away, leaves a de-
mythologized interior—the social, political, and economic
remnant of the myth. Of course, it is even questionable
whether the notion that whites are "blessed" is in fact a de-
mythologization of its antithesis at all. Regarding the demy-
thologized remnant of the curse of Ham myth, Hacker asks
whether it must be admitted that the residues of slavery and

65. J. A. Loubser, *The Apartheid Bible: A Critical Review of Racial Theology in South
Africa* (Cape Town, South Africa: Maskew Miller Longman, 1987), 7–8.
66. Ibid., 133.

the ideology that provides its rationale continue to exist. He answers yes and says further:

> What other Americans know and remember is that blacks alone were brought as chattels to be bought and sold like livestock. As has been noted, textbooks now point out that surviving slavery took a skill and stamina that no other race has been called upon to sustain. Yet this is not what others choose to recall. Rather, there remains an unarticulated suspicion: might there be something about the black race that suited them for slavery? This is not to say anyone argues that human bondage was justified. Still, the facts that slavery existed for so long and was so taken for granted cannot be erased from American minds. This is not the least reason why other Americans—again, without openly saying so—find it not improper that blacks still serve as maids and janitors, occupations seen as involving physical skills rather than mental aptitudes.[67]

Others, such as Fanon, allude to the existence of a mythological root beneath the modern dilemma of white racism. He says, "For the Negro there is a myth to be faced. A solidly established myth. The Negro is unaware of it as long as his existence is limited to his own environment; but the first encounter with a white man oppresses him with the whole weight of his blackness."[68] My "petition," then, is for us to get at the mythological root beneath racism and sexism by critically reapproaching two biblical myths that have ideological residue in our folk, classic, and popular cultures.

Given this, it may seem that classism should not be included alongside these two problems in Christian hymnody, since no biblical myth has been misused to apologize for classist division and elitist exploitation. In fact, Jesus' defense of the poor hints at the exceptionalism of the poor and the inferiority of the wealthy and the elite. No one can miss the symbolism of Jesus' birth in a stable, his riding into Jerusalem

67. Hacker, *Two Nations*, 14.
68. Fanon, *Black Skin*, 150.

on a donkey, and his depiction of wealth as an impediment to salvation. Neither is there any mistaking the fact that Jesus reversed the hierarchical order of society so that the "poor and needy" were the blessed. Even the apostle Paul is implored by the apostles of the Jerusalem church to remember the poor in his mission to the Greeks; "which very thing I was eager to do," responds Paul (Gal. 2:10). In spite of these passages (frequently cited by systematic theologians to support their liberation theology), history repeatedly manifests religious individuals and groups that believe (or act as though they believe) poverty is a curse and the best thing that can be done for the impoverished is to facilitate their genocide. Like its partial progenitor, Islam, early Christianity was a call to social equality, a call for the liberation of the oppressed; but also like Islam, there arose in Christianity a perpetual struggle between those who stood for social justice and equality and those who stood for class privilege. Even in the post-independence countries of Africa, in which Christianity has a strong presence, elitism has substituted for racism. "But the tragic effects on the poor," says Canaan Banana, "are the same if not worse."[69]

Although there is not a biblical myth to which elitists can turn for the defense of their class biases, the master-slave dialectic in Paul's letter to Philemon (Philemon 8-21) can help us understand the dynamics of classism in modern times. This is because Paul's letter perfectly illustrates the tension between the rhetoric of equality and the reality of social hierarchy. What the apostle Paul intended for Philemon (the slave-holder) regarding Onesimus (the runaway slave), and what the wealthy or elitists of today are to do regarding such modern forms of slavery as classism, seem to reduce to what the apostle meant by these words:

> Perhaps this is why [Onesimus] was parted from you for a while, that you might have him back for ever, no longer as a slave but more than a slave, as a beloved brother. (Philemon 15-16)

69. Banana, *The Gospel*, 70.

As I will detail in chapter 5, what we have here are the problems of hierarchy and religious propaganda that typify the way the bourgeoisie deal with the proletariat, the way the rich deal with the poor. The elite or well-to-do speak of fraternity and equality between the social classes, but it is largely this defective, insincere kind of equality. It is akin to the former South African government speaking of "law and order" when what was meant was that the dispossessed masses must submit in an orderly way to their oppressors. As put by the writers of *Evangelical Witness in South Africa*, this is the "Law of Satan and the Order of Hell."[70]

This search for some biblical understanding regarding classism is especially timely since Eurocentric scholars have begun to present biblical evidence that early Christianity was not just a religion of and for the poor. These scholarly findings certainly contribute to our understanding of the early church, but these scholars excavate biblical tidbits essentially, it seems, to underwrite their wealth while ignoring the pragmatic problems surrounding gender, race, and class, problems that can be dealt with on biblical exegetical terms—contextual exegesis.

The need for Afro-Christian scholars to engage in biblical exegesis, and for our hymnists to give their findings serious consideration, is based on the fact that the Scriptures have been used by the guardians of orthodoxy to perpetuate sexism, racism, and classism. Although the Bible and its interpretation have been, as African-American biblical scholar Charles Copher says, a source of blessings to millions of people, it also has been a source of some of the most solemn curses humankind has ever known.[71] I believe that part of the reason why Christian hymnody perpetuates these "curses" and why we have been hesitant to make the appropriate hymnic revisions is that we still practice the doctrinal way of reading the Scriptures. That is, we read the Scriptures literally

70. *Evangelical Witness in South Africa*, 19.
71. Charles B. Copher, "Three Thousand Years of Biblical Interpretation with Reference to Black Peoples," in *African American Religious Studies: An Interdisciplinary Anthology*, ed. Gayraud S. Wilmore (Durham, N.C.: Duke University Press, 1989), 105.

and maintain outmoded interpretations of them that have been perpetuated through the Eurocentric subordinationist reading tradition.

Afro-Christian hymnists need to give serious attention to Afro-Christian biblical scholarship that applies the historical-critical method of exegesis. In brief, I agree with African-American biblical scholar Thomas Hoyt that the historical-critical method serves as a defense against the problems of biblicism (dogmatic literalist interpretation) and fundamentalism.[72] The historical-critical method, practiced by the brightest Afro-Christian biblical scholars, will help our hymnists recognize Scripture as embodying a history of writing, editing, canonization, translation, and commercial publishing, all of which have contributed to the perpetuation of gender, race, and class hierarchy (oppression). Ultimately, this method, by helping our hymnists understand original contexts, meanings, and intents, will allow them to help rid our hymnody of sexist, racist, and classist language, even though hierarchism pervades the Scriptures. If we can move beyond the point of simply reading the Bible to the point of critically studying it, I believe we can begin to progress uninhibitedly toward a postpatriarchal, postracist, postclassist hymnody.

72. Thomas J. Hoyt, Jr., "Interpreting Biblical Scholarship for the Black Church Tradition," in Felder, *Stony the Road We Trod*, 24.

2

The Prerequisite
of Exegetical Freedom

The same fetters that bind the captive bind the captor,
and the American people are captives of their own myths,
woven so cleverly and so imperceptibly into the fabric of
our national experience.
— C. Eric Lincoln, *Race, Religion, and the Continuing
American Dilemma* (1984)

The process of decoding a power system and its culture
is a necessary first step to achieve behavioral mastery
over that system/culture. The attainment of such mastery
is an essential step in the process of total liberation for
the victims who wish to end that oppression and regain
their self-respect and mental health. Without this process
of decoding, the oppressed fail to fully understand what
they are dealing with.
— Frances Cress Welsing, *The Isis Papers* (1991)

An uninformed literalist reading of the Bible is still prevalent among the masses of the Afro-Christian church. As an

39

ethnohymnologist, I feel some responsibility for contributing
to the resolution of this quandary, as do some of the African-
American biblical scholars cited in the previous chapter. I feel
this sense of urgency because an uninformed literalist reading
of the Bible is a sleeping pill to black people and is killing us
by degree, a death that is preceded only by its turning us
"white as snow." This approach to biblical interpretation probably began during our enslavement and colonization. As we
became increasingly literate after slavery and colonialism, it
probably developed as a rudimentary literalist reading of the
Bible learned during the formative years of our individual
churchgoing lives. Even today this literalist interpretation is
perpetuated by Sunday school graduates who often move on
to amateur Bible study classes only to become the next generation of Sunday school teachers, still critically (exegetically)
uninformed.

In order to break out of this traumatic cycle—which I
think is partly based on a false perception of the Bible as
comprised of a homogeneous history, doctrine, and
theology—we must critically examine the myths that, inform-
ing our hymnody, undergird our religious worldviews. Most
literalists do not realize, for instance, that there are two versions of the creation in Genesis (Gen. 1:1–2:4a and 2:4b-24).
Both creation stories cannot be literally true. In fact, since
there are two versions, both included in the one Bible and in
the very same biblical book, what this ought to suggest to us
is that neither is literally true. My first exegetical prelude will,
I hope, help us to see that the creation myth is not intended
to lock us into some fixed historical event (especially when
the writing of that myth may have been ideologically motivated) but to give us some cosmological rootedness in the
world. I hope, too, it will accomplish this while also capturing
submerged truths about our existential experience—such as
the monocentric and monogenetic birth of modern humankind, Homo sapiens sapiens. In his usual way, Malcolm X
states the point bluntly:

> It was alright when you were a little baby to believe that
> God made a little god out of sand or mud and breathed

on it and that was the first man. When you were a child
it was alright to believe like that, but here in 1962 with
all this information floating around in everybody's
ears. . . . Why, you should open up your mind and your
head and realize that you have been led by a lie. And
today it is time to listen to the undiluted truth. And
when you know the truth, as Jesus said, truth
will make you free. . . . When you know the truth,
you're free.[1]

Malcolm X chose the extreme of abandoning Christianity, as did, among many other well-known leaders, the late
Ugandan poet Okot p'Bitek.[2] But there are many Afro-
Christians who, if they do not fully abandon the church,
become borderline Christians. They often do so because in-
stitutionalized Christianity seems to them to be too mythologically otherworldly, especially in regard to the misuse of
certain Christian writing to perpetuate gender, race, and class
subjugation. This is essentially the point raised by the group
of black South African evangelicals who wrote *Evangelical
Witness in South Africa* (1986), which recognizes the inadequacy
of their own theology insofar as it is influenced by that of
American and European missionaries:

> Called as we are to minister good news, we find ourselves
> in the midst of bloodshed and death, of increasing bit-
> terness and polarisation, and of rising anger in the town-
> ships. Our proclamation therefore, has been swallowed
> up by the cries of the poor and oppressed that it is now
> even impossible to hold conventional evangelistic cam-
> paigns in this war situation. These voices have become
> so loud that it has become impossible to hear the
> church preach.
>
> Besides the crisis in the country, Black Christians
> (especially those who are evangelicals) in the townships
> are facing *a crisis of faith*. This crisis of faith is caused by
> the contradictions they have to live with on a daily basis

1. Malcolm X, "The Black Man's History" (recorded speech, 1962).
2. Okot p'Bitek, *Song of Lawino and Song of Ocol* (Nairobi, Kenya: Heinemann
Kenya, 1984), 3–4.

as they try to live their faith in this crisis situation. This
crisis of faith is caused by the dilemma of being oppressed
and exploited by people who claim to be Christians, especially those who claim to be "born-again."[3]

The Swiss theologian Hans Küng also recognizes that the
unassailable facts of history stand weightily on the side of
people who cannot or refuse to hear the church preach: "Obviously there is the other possibility, and those who have chosen it often enough were not the bad Christians. This is to
break with the Church because of its decline, for the sake of
higher values, perhaps even for the sake of being a genuine
Christian. There are Christians—and, at least as borderline
cases, Christian groups—outside the Church as institution.
Such a decision is to be respected, it can even be understood. . . . And any committed and informed Christian could
certainly list as many reasons for leaving as those who have
in fact gone."[4]

I am by no means suggesting that Afro-Christians follow
those who have abandoned Christianity or that we become
borderline Christians, but I am suggesting that we seek religious truth, a process that must begin by our reforming the
way in which we approach the interpretation of the Bible.
The importance of the human search for religious truth is
even recognized theoretically by the Roman Catholic Church,
the Christian institution most deeply entrenched in problems
of gender, race, and class not simply because of its Roman
roots but because of its Eurocentric guardianship of the Christian tradition, as I will describe momentarily. The Second
Vatican's *Dignitatis humanae*, "Declaration on Religious Liberty" (Dec. 7, 1965), reads in part: "It is in accordance with
their dignity that all men, because they are persons, that is,
beings endowed with reason and free will and therefore bearing personal responsibility, are both impelled by their nature
and bound by a moral obligation to seek the truth, especially

3. *Evangelical Witness in South Africa (Evangelicals Critique Their Own Theology and Practice* (Dobsonville, South Africa: Concerned Evangelicals, 1986), 2, 4, 5.
4. Hans Küng, *On Being a Christian* (Garden City, N.Y.: Image Books, 1984), 523.

religious truth. They are also bound to adhere to the truth once they come to know it and direct their whole lives in accordance with the demands of truth."[5] Of course, Catholic women, who are oppressed in their church, are also bound by a moral obligation to seek religious truth (as are non-Catholic women, people of color, and the poor). Many people among these oppressed groups are beginning to respond to this obligation to find truth by exercising, for themselves, what African-American biblical scholar Vincent Wimbush calls biblical "hermeneutical control":

> Without an increased measure of *hermeneutical control* over the Bible, it will prove impossible for Afro-Christian churches to articulate self-understanding, maintain integrity as separate Christian communities, and determine their mission in the world.
>
> Needed are both a defense from alien, imperialistic hermeneutical constructs (and with them symbols, concepts, rituals, social orientation) and the capacity to assume control over, to evaluate critically, and advance their own traditions. Basically *pre-critical* in their hermeneutic, African American churches find themselves unable to fend off alien and competing claims from other traditions, especially those which court with the same doctrinal language and polity. . . . Critical facility for the historical study of both the self, viz., the Afro-Christian tradition, is required for self-defense and self-criticism, as well as the capacity for the construction of a more affirming, indigenous hermeneutic built on the tradition.[6]

Wimbush's conclusion is brief and memorizable: "Perhaps what liberation initially requires is exegetical room."[7]

This is all that I am suggesting as regards specifically our hymnody, which depends so significantly on how we understand the biblical writings. For women who wish to be

5. *Vatican Council II: The Conciliar and Post Conciliar Documents*, vol. 1, ed. Austin Flannery, rev. ed. (Northport, N.Y.: Costello, 1988), 801.

6. Vincent L. Wimbush, "Biblical Historical Study as Liberation: Toward an Afro-Christian Hermeneutic," in *African American Religious Studies: An Interdisciplinary Anthology*, ed. Gayraud S. Wilmore (Durham, N.C.: Duke University Press, 1989), 144–45.

7. Ibid., 152.

liberated from male dominance in the church and in society, for inferiorized blacks who wish to attain psychological parity in the face of historical and personal effacement by nonblacks, and for the subjects of class subjugation and elitist exploitation who wish to engender true democracy, what is initially required in this quest is "exegetical room." Otherwise, as African Egyptologist Yosef ben-Jochannan says with tacit reference to literalist hermeneutics, we might as well accept our enslavement and genocide:

> If the Black communities throughout the United States and elsewhere can intelligently accept the type of genocide committed by the Hebrews against the Amalakites, Hittites, Jebusites, and countless other nations of people, and the enslavement of others still, on the sole basis that their conduct was "the command of God"—Jehovah; then they must equally accept that their own enslavement and attempted liquidation by the descendants of the same element of the Bible people was the "command" of the same "God"—Jehovah. Herein lies the fundamental challenge to the Black Christian, Jew, and Moslem.[8]

The same holds true specifically for African-American men: If we can accept and use the Bible to apologize for our subjugation of women, then we must accept our own enslavement, for female subjugation and slaveholding were co-codes in the Greco-Roman societal system that found their way into the biblical writings.

I believe our problematic biblical hermeneutics, which prevents us from having "exegetical space" in our hymnody, is partly based on our false perception of the Bible as a homogeneous entity. For instance, we tend to view the culture captured in the writings of the Old and New Testaments as being singularly Jewish, when in fact what we have is acculturation—the symbiotic exchange of Egyptian, Palestinian (Canaanite), Greek, and Roman cultures (to name the principal ones). Our perception of the Bible as a homogeneous

8. Yosef A. ben-Jochannan, *Africa: Mother of Western Civilization* (Baltimore: Black Classic Press, 1988), 570.

entity is probably also due to our unknowing enmeshing of the biblical narratives. We not only read the Old Testament through the prism of the New (rather than the requisite reverse), we also read certain books in the New Testament through the prism of other New Testament books. All of the epistles (even those that are not Pauline) tend to be read through the prism of Paul's authentic and most prominent epistles, those to the Romans and the Corinthians. Likewise, the Gospel of John tends to be read through the prism of the Synoptic Gospels (Matthew, Mark, and Luke), and often the reverse occurs. For example, John reduces the teachings of Jesus to the command to love, but we tend to read into this notion of love Jesus' teachings in the Synoptics regarding the love of neighbor and enemy. Indeed, we read into John's view of love the parable of the Good Samaritan, assuming that there is theological homogeneity among the four Gospels when there is not. In addition, the biblical narratives rarely (if ever) explain the psychological motivations behind certain behaviors among the biblical characters, so we constantly (and unconsciously) read into these events motivations derived from Eurocentric biases concerning, for instance, gender, race, and class. We are unable to fend off these alien claims when they appear in the hymns we sing, particularly when they speak the doctrinal language we have been taught and with which we are familiar.

Inevitably the amalgamation of the Gospels into a false homogeneity fashions not so much what is a "fifth gospel" (a piecing together of bits from the four) but what is essentially perceived as *the* gospel. The ultimate symbol of this enmeshing in black church music is "gospel music"; a more accurate designation would be "music of the gospels." *The* gospel, fabricated by the doctrinal way of reading Scripture, is apparently *the* story of *the* ministry of Jesus based on an unknowing coalescence of the four Gospels. This story is given further fictitious character by our reading thereupon biased motivations, derived ultimately from the Eurocentric guardianship over biblical interpretation, that cause *the* story's characters to behave as they do. *The* gospel, then, is not the "gospel truth," for even though there is some continuity amid the discontinuity in the Gospels, everything in them cannot be simultaneously true. Yet it is *the* gospel—which, canonically speaking, simply does not exist—that is typically the basis of our hymnody.

To understand this, let us look further into the relationship between the Old and the New Testament and then into the relationship between the Gospels, all of which impact the interpretations embodied in our hymnody. The Old Testament is frequently apologetically quoted in the New by Jews who were out to convert other Jews to their belief in the messiahship of Jesus. It was necessary for these Christ-believing Jews to show that Jesus' death was not defeat (crucifixion) but victory (resurrection) and that all the events that transpired were carried out "according to the scriptures." Therefore it is quite legitimate for us to wonder whether we are reading theological apology and rhetorical argument by believers who want others to believe as they or whether we are reading (as we formerly believed) objective religious history—sacred, untouchable documentation. Extrascriptural sources, such as the writings of first-century C.E. Jewish historian Flavius Josephus, can help us realize that biblical history is substantially more subjective than our modern notions about objective history. The Gospels may be "historical" according to the standards of ancient "sacred biography," but sacred biography hardly approaches historical objectivity according to modern standards. The same thing is true in regard to the Old Testament. For the most part, the Old Testament writings are not historical documents; they comprise a theological (interpretive) history of Israel, a history—we might conclude after reading the next two chapters—that was fraught with political and ideological concerns.

A case in point is that Josephus's account of John the Baptist's death is distinctly different from that in the Gospels, not to mention that Josephus historicizes Jesus as but a human prophet. Josephus's history is biased too, no doubt; but considering the fact that the Old Testament seems to comprehend

who God is better than the New seems to understand who
Jesus is, and that Jesus himself may not have agreed with
what his disciples were preaching about him after his crucifixion, one wonders who is (in our modern sense) the most
historically objective: Josephus or Luke. That Luke could have
been subjective (religiously motivated) in his Gospel account
of the ministry of Jesus is evidenced by the fact that he is
apparently religiously subjective in his account of the spread
of the early church in his authored Book of Acts. In Acts,
Luke gives us the impression that Christianity dispersed
smoothly across the Greco-Roman world, from Jerusalem to
Rome. From our current historical purview of perceived
Christian dominance in the world (no matter how inaccurate
this perception may be), the smooth dispensation of Christianity seems feasible and even, from a fundamentalist purview, accurate. However, Paul's epistles, which have priority
over Acts in terms of historical facticity (given his involvement
in the actual evangelizing), show otherwise. The early church
was never unified but was plagued by conflicts and diversities,
much like the church today—much like the Afro-Christian
church today.

Thus we need to come to grips with the realization that
the Gospels are biased historical accounts because of their
attempt to cultivate sympathy for and allegiance to the man
the Gospel writers profess to be the Christ. To understand
the Gospels otherwise is to perpetuate the notion that there
is *a* gospel, frozen in perpetuity, from which is derivable an
unalterable doctrine and "orthodox" hymnody. Such a hymnody is bound to be plagued by problems of gender, race,
and class hierarchy since its content and meaning are consequently bound to the time and place in which the Scriptures
first had meaning—societies, as we will see, in which female
subordination and slavery were accepted customs.

Let us now, as a means of my asserting this process of
reasoning, consider the "theory of Markan priority"—the theory that Mark was the first to write a Gospel, which was used
independently by Matthew and Luke along with their additional common source known as Q (*Quelle* = source). This

theory forces us to reconsider our customary belief that the Gospels were independently composed in the order in which they appear in the Bible—Matthew, Mark, Luke, and John. That Matthew and Luke, according to careful parallel readings of their Gospels against that of Mark,[9] improve Mark's Gospel grammatically, theologically, and historically presupposes that there is something imperfect or inaccurate in that which fundamentalist biblical interpreters hold to be literally true or even divinely infallible. That Matthew and Luke have a higher Christology—omitting parts in Mark's Gospel that portray Jesus as somewhat of a common man—forces us to consider the strong possibility that the spiritual biography of the Gospels involves an inherently subjective element. Added to this is the fact that the Gospels do not claim to be (and most likely are not) written by Jesus' disciples or even by persons who were eyewitnesses of his prophetic career. Rather, they were written by persons who were probably witnesses of the original teachings about Jesus. This means there is no way of really knowing how much of the Gospels is historical fact and how much is theological interpretation based on the writers' personal (even biased) understanding of the tradition that developed after Jesus' life. Gospel music, to make the point as regards my petition for a revision of our hymnody, tends to reflect the antithesis of an informed biblical hermeneutic. This means it tends to be held captive (and it holds us captive) to an essential otherworldliness.

Finally, let us consider the basic differences between the first three Gospels and the fourth. This can force us to confront the dilemma of biblical literalism. Our traditional Sunday school learning actually has most of us believing that the Gospels are literally identical (or at least complementary) rather than contradictory in their myriad details regarding the ministry and identity of Jesus. Yet a close examination of Christian belief—such as in gospel music—reveals that Christians are divisible into two groups: those who essentially subscribe to Johannine theology (the fourth Gospel) and those

---

9. See Burton H. Throckmorton, Jr., ed., *Gospel Parallels: A Synopsis of the First Three Gospels* (Nashville: Thomas Nelson, 1979).

who essentially subscribe to the Synoptics' theology (Matthew, Mark, and Luke). I would say that black Methodists and Baptists, as evidenced by their doctrine and composed hymnody, tend to be synoptic Christians and that black Holiness and Pentecostals, as evidenced by their doctrine and composed hymnody, tend to be Johannine. In John's Gospel, Jesus does not specifically teach people; there is no Sermon on the Mount, as in the Synoptics. Rather, Jesus engages in protracted debates regarding his identity. Holiness and Pentecostals, as Johannine Christians, tend to consider the identity of Jesus to be more important than the question of what they, according to his teachings, are to do ethically in the "world" (the social and political realm). This is clearly evident in the theology of the traditional gospel favorites they sing. Second, while synoptic Christians interpret the meaning of "neighbor" through Luke's parable of the Good Samaritan, the Johannines, again as their traditional gospel favorites show, interpret "neighbor" far more exclusively. John's portrayal of the church as sectarian is correlative to his definition of love as being something practiced only between members of the church. This is homologous with modern Johannine Christians' view of love as something to be shared only between those of their particular denomination.

Not only is there a dichotomy between synoptic and Johannine Christians and further sectarianism among separatist Johannine communities (the Holiness versus the Pentecostals), but within the synoptic group are Christians who prefer to be Lukan versus Matthean. Matthew evidently spiritualizes the common source he and Luke use for the Beatitudes. For instance, while Matthew understands the status of being "poor" in a spiritual sense ("poor in spirit"), Luke understands it in the socioeconomic sense. While Matthew's Gospel says, "Blessed are those who hunger and thirst for righteousness," Luke's says, "Blessed are you that hunger *now*." Although being "poor in spirit" implies a spirit antithetical to elitism and an ideology of gender and racial supremacy, Luke tends to deal directly with aspects concerning the socially and economically oppressed. This is further evidenced in the fact that his Gospel is the only one that includes the parable of the Good Samaritan, which is Jesus' radical improvement of the customary meaning of "neighbor." In this respect, the theology and the hymnody of the early-nineteenth-century antislavery abolitionists, the early-twentieth-century social gospelers, and the mid-twentieth-century civil rights freedom fighters tend to be Lukan. Womanists (black) and feminists (white) also tend to prefer Luke's version of the Jesus tradition because of Luke's recognition of the prominent roles that women played as followers of Jesus and in the establishment and administration of the early church. For this reason, liberation theologians tend to prefer Luke to Matthew and the other Gospels and to prefer (according to their writings) the black spirituals and the blues to gospel music. I am not suggesting that a revised black hymnody ignore the Gospels other than Luke, only that there is a body of critical understanding that supports thematizing the Lukan perspective in a "new song."

All of these considerations simply go to illustrate that there is no historical, doctrinal, or theological homogeneity in the New Testament or the Old. There is no such thing as *the* gospel, no one correct account of Jesus' ministry, no comprehensive answer to the question of who Jesus is, and no divinely sanctionable gospel music. This means that the Scriptures are not the infallible word of God in the literal sense, personally dictated by God to the biblical writers, and neither is the near-canonical source that is our hymnody divinely infallible. To be able to procure hermeneutical control by forging out exegetical room is to be able to fashion enough space to sing a new song.

To appropriate seriously this perspective, through the examples I have provided, should cause a reassessment of all that Sunday school and Bible study have ever taught us. Unfortunately this potentially rude awakening will cause some of us to cling even more adamantly to our traditional beliefs and our old favorite hymns and to label as mere "worldly knowledge" the exegetical space that can actually begin to liberate us. Conversely, to arrive at the conclusion that Scripture is merely the fallible work of human beings who reflect only their cultural biases and political preferences will lead some of us to question the integrity of the biblical authors themselves. In any case, I think it is necessary to exercise the kind of hermeneutical control over the Bible that is, for example, evidenced in a drawing of 1952 by black political cartoonist Jay Jackson. The drawing pictured a black man who appeared to be Paul Robeson helping Jesus carry the cross (the cross was labeled "Persecution"). The caption of the drawing read, "He, Too, Helped Bear the Cross."[10] This exercising of hermeneutical control is also evidenced in *The Gospel according to the Ghetto* (1980) by Canaan Banana, the first president of independent Zimbabwe, a man who saw his nation's war of independence as God's call, "Let my people go":[11]

> Since I have been personally involved in the struggle for our freedom, many passages from the Bible have assumed new and compelling meanings. When Jesus says, "I have come that they may have life and have it in all its fullness," to me the implications of this are clear: it means man must be free to live life in all its fullness. When man is denied any part of his life, he must reclaim it.[12]

Banana's reading of the Bible through the lens of liberation rather than that of the legitimation of social stratification is captured in the poetry that comprises most of his book. His version of the Lord's Prayer begins, "Our Father which art in the Ghetto, / Degraded is your name." God's name is degraded, he continues, because the divine will is "mocked" as "pie in the sky."[13] His version of the Apostles' Creed, titled "The People's Creed," is a confession about Jesus Christ, "Who was ridiculed, disfigured, and executed, / Who

---

10. "He, Too, Helped Bear the Cross," *California Eagle*, 10 April 1952, 5.
11. Canaan Banana, *The Gospel according to the Ghetto*, rev. ed. (Gweru, Zimbabwe: Mambo Press, 1990), 142.
12. Ibid., 52.
13. Ibid., 1.

on the third day rose and fought back."[14] Du Bois, in his "Credo," exercises similar hermeneutical control. In addition to believing in God "who made of one blood all nations that on earth do dwell," he believes in the demonic: "I believe in the Devil and his angels, who wantonly work to narrow the opportunity of struggling human beings, especially if they be black; who spit in the faces of the fallen, strike them that cannot strike again, believe the worst and work to prove it, hating the image which their Maker stamped on a brother's soul."[15]

Continuing with examples that illustrate Banana's exercise of hermeneutical control, the Ninth Commandment in his rendition of the Ten Commandments, which he calls "The Ten Gates of Emancipation," is "Thou shalt neither classify nor humiliate your neighbor, for racism perverts the Soul."[16] The Sermon on the Mount becomes "The Sermon at the Market Place," and blessed are those who "hunger and thirst after freedom," those who are "the advocates of the underdog." It is they, he concludes, who shall be saved.[17] Banana's treatment of the famous Pauline passage on love in 1 Corinthians says that though he may espouse the sacrality of human life, if he just sits on his hands and does nothing about the oppression of his people, he is a hypocrite. He continues, "Though I approve of the goals of human liberation and profess love for freedom, if I do not act on this love, it is worthless."[18] Finally, as one last example of Banana's good use of hermeneutical control, Banana interprets another familiar Pauline passage. He says, "When we were slaves, we spoke as slaves, we understood as slaves, we thought as slaves but as we became free, we cast off all the chains of servitude." Faith, love, and hope must abide, he concludes, but without freedom and dignity they remain "hollow shadows."[19] Summarizing the essential thrust behind this kind of exercise of

14. Ibid., 2.
15. W. E. B. Du Bois, *Darkwater: Voices from within the Veil* (New York: Schocken Books, 1920), 3.
16. Banana, *The Gospel*, 7.
17. Ibid., 12.
18. Ibid., 15.
19. Ibid., 16.

hermeneutical control, Banana says: "It will never be necessary any longer to resort to the Bible as the magic book in which all the answers are found and all positions legitimized, but as the Holy book in which the struggle of mankind along history is symbolized. Life is not a textbook of theories but a battlefield of practical realities."[20]

African-American biblical scholar Cain Hope Felder also exercises hermeneutical control in his scholarship. For instance, Felder notes that the social and political realities of gentile Rome (and Hellenism in general) diminish the New Testament writers' visions of universalism and inclusivism. "The immediate significance of this New Testament tendency to focus on Rome instead of Jerusalem is that the darker races outside the Roman orbit are for the most part overlooked by the New Testament writers."[21] Such an observation should prompt us to be careful not to force any remnants of Greek ethnocentrism in the biblical text onto our hymnody.

Felder's observation also leads us directly to the question of whom the New Testament canon belongs to. The answer is important because it has some bearing on the question of whose biblical interpretation can be legitimately central in our hymn writing. Christianized Jews and their progeny certainly can lay claim to the New Testament, insofar as Christianity originated as one of several sects of Judaism. This is evidenced in the debate within the early church as to whether Gentiles had first to become Jews (circumcised) in order to become Christians (Gal. 2:2-11). Because of Paul's protecting the freedom of gentile Christians from impingement by Jewish law, and because the New Testament books were written in and for the churches of the gentile Mediterranean world, it is evident that the European descendants of the Greco-Roman world can also lay claim to Christianity—and by all means they do! Since Christianity was being expressed in the West through Roman culture, Christian officials came to see that culture as the ideal one to be propagated along with the

20. Ibid., 112.
21. Cain Hope Felder, *Troubling Biblical Waters: Race, Class, and Family* (Maryknoll, N.Y.: Orbis Books, 1989), 46.

Christian message. This led Christians of European origin,
who claim Roman culture as their cultural progenitor, also
to claim Christianity as *their* religion. In fact, during the nineteenth century, European scholars, who resented the substantial credit given to the Semites, increasingly sought
to establish Hellenic and thus (they said) Aryan primacy in
Christianity.[22]

While the preponderance of hymnody of European origin and emphasis demonstrates the European claim to Christianity in nearly every stanza, the fact that women can also
lay claim to Christianity is sorely lacking in our hymnody.
Only in recent decades has the tradition of androcentrism
been revised systematically by womanist and feminist biblical
scholars (including some men). Prior to womanists and feminists forging out this new mind-set, it was generally understood by men (and by women ruled by the male ideology)
that women played no part in the establishment of the early
church. The parts they did play were overshadowed by the
androcentric interests of the writers and editors of the Hebrew
Bible and the New Testament. Their biases are written into
the canons and laws of Judaism and have fashioned the very
character of Christianity. This fact has been obscured by modern Eurocentric scholars for the same reason the biblical writers, seemingly intentionally, avoided documenting the cults
they attempted to displace by their male deity (Jehovah). In
taking hermeneutical control over the Bible, womanists and
feminists refuse to be lulled into contentment, for instance,
by the early church's elevation of the mother of Jesus (essentially due to the church's competition with the cult of Isis) to
the status almost equaling that of the Egyptian goddess.[23] All
of the hymns that laud "mother Mary," particularly in the
Catholic tradition, have been of no consequence in the face

22. Martin Bernal, "Black Athena: The African and Levantine Roots of Greece,"
in *African Presence in Early Europe*, ed. Ivan Van Sertima (New Brunswick, N.J.:
Transaction Publishers, 1985), 69.
23. Danita Redd, "Black Madonnas of Europe: Diffusion of the African Isis,"
in *Black Women in Antiquity*, ed. Ivan Van Sertima, rev. ed. (New Brunswick, N.J.:
Rutgers University Press, 1987), 170–71. Also see James Bonwick, *Egyptian Belief
and Modern Thought* (London: African Publication Society, 1983), 147–48.

of female subordination—most Christian women being prohibited from pursuing their dreams and potentials within the
denomination they have chosen as their Christian affiliation,
including their right to be ordained as ministers, priests, and
bishops.

Because of the persistence of womanist and feminist
scholars, the predominantly male church leadership has begun to come into broader inclusiveness, and male biblical
scholars and hymnologists have begun to do so in their scriptural interpretations. In a section of *Anatomy of the New Testament* titled "The Role of Women," for example, authors
Robert Spivey and D. Moody Smith (without implicating men
for a history of female suppression) say, "When the genuine
Pauline letters and the gospels, particularly [Luke] and John,
are considered, the reader is struck with the role played by
women among the disciples of Jesus and in the first
churches."[24]

For the same reason (probably social and market forces
but, it is hoped, for the sake of historical truth), Eurocentric
scholars must be inclusive enough to discuss, and hymnists
to thematize, the roles that Africa and Africans played in the
biblical narratives. Afro-Christians deserve to know, partly for
the crucial sake of their self-identity and self-determination,
that we are not latecomers to participation in salvation history.
This needs to be seen as partial rectification of the ideological
suppression of this knowledge, a suppression that has been
used historically in the systemic process of black inferioriza-
tion, "Bantu education." As I explained in chapter 1 with
reference to hymnologist Benjamin Crawford, the future of
our religious ideals rests significantly on our hymnody because the average worshipers glean more of their religious
interest from the hymns they sing than from the Scriptures
alone.[25] Until historical truth is recovered regarding the African impact on the Bible and until our hymnody is revised

24. Robert A. Spivey and D. Moody Smith, *Anatomy of the New Testament: A Guide
to Its Structure and Meaning*, 4th ed. (New York: Macmillan Publishing Co., 1989), 443.
25. Benjamin F. Crawford, *Religious Trends in a Century of Hymns* (Carnegie, Pa.:
Carnegie Church Press, 1938), 24.

accordingly, we will remain unable to establish in our minds that we too can claim authentic ownership of Christianity and citizenship in God's kingdom and that we need not view ourselves as the Christian products of slaveholders and colonialists.

That the African presence in the Bible is overlooked, when in the Old and New Testament narratives it is so obvious that Africa had meaning to the Israelites and the New Testament community, is evidently a matter of an ideology of Eurocentric biblical guardianship. With regard to such an ideology, African-American biblical scholar William Myers explains that subordination and the suppression of the rights of others are not maintained by controlling only political, economic, and social systems but also the signal "charter documents" (such as the Bible and the U.S. Constitution) and especially the interpretation of these documents.[26] African-American church historian Robert E. Hood says this "theological hegemony" and "doctrinal guardianship" over what is legitimate, authentic, and true for Christian thought is maintained by theologians, bishops, councils, liturgists, and hymnists who reflect their own Eurocentric cultural preferences to the exclusion of other interpretations.[27] "The Graeco-Roman packaging of Christian theology, dogmatics, language, and traditions particularly raises acute issues of cultural and religious hegemony, called by less charitable people 'cultural imperialism.' Western Christians continue to exercise exclusive guardianship over the shape of Christian theology and over the debate about the meaning of Jesus Christ for a multicultural church and world."[28] What is worse, says Hood, is that these "guardians of orthodoxy" act as though any other perspectives on Christianity are at best supplements and never alternatives or replacements to their own perspectives which

26. William H. Myers, "The Hermeneutical Dilemma of the African American Biblical Student," in *Stony the Road We Trod*, ed. Cain Hope Felder (Minneapolis: Fortress Press, 1991), 45.
27. Robert E. Hood, *Must God Remain Greek? Afro Cultures and God-Talk* (Minneapolis: Fortress Press, 1990), 109, 246, 248.
28. Ibid., 7.

they deem "universal."[29] The problem is, as African Egyptologist Yosef ben-Jochannan explains, that white scholars, ministers, and missionaries still equate Christianity with European civilization, Caucasianism, and even capitalism. "For this very reason," he says, "it is necessary [for them] to ignore the reference to the Africans of Ethiopia in the book of Acts. . . . It is also necessary [for them] to convert the Africans—Tertullian, St. Cyprian and St. Augustine, 'Fathers of the Christian Church,' into 'Caucasian Europeans,' thereby perpetuating the myth that 'Christianity had its origins in Rome as an organized institution.' "[30]

This de-Africanization of Scripture, so evident in Christian hymnody, is paralleled by and illustrated in Eurocentric cartography. In the familiar Mercator map, first developed in 1569 for European navigators by the German cartographic scholar Gerhard Kremer, and in many of the modern derivatives of this map, the equator is placed below the middle of the map. This gives unequal prominence to the northern hemisphere, where whites have quantitatively dominated; it makes Africa, in the southern hemisphere, appear to be much smaller than what was once the Soviet Union and about the same size as Europe. To the contrary, Africa (11.6 million square miles) is about 3 million square miles larger than what was the Soviet Union (8.7 million square miles) and is about 8 million square miles larger than Europe (3.8 million square miles).[31]

The maps that Eurocentrists have made of the "Bible lands" also demonstrate that the European colonization of geography, through cartography, is part and parcel of their colonization of historical information. Where maps of the so-called ancient Near East venture beyond the Syria-Palestine region or areas east of there, they generally omit the African nations of, for instance, Cush, Put, and Cyrene and include only Egypt, the ideological assumption being that Egypt was

29. Ibid., 107.
30. Ben-Jochannan, *Africa*, 645–46.
31. Ward L. Kaiser, *A New View of the World: A Handbook to the World Map: Peters Projection* (New York: Friendship Press, 1987), 6, 8, 12, 13.

part of the West rather than of Africa.[32] Manning Marable,
who understands well this political act of claimed ownership,
comments that white Christianity continues to fail to liberate
the deceived conscience of white America. He says, "The
principal victims of this failure have been African American
people. White Christianity's God is still a white God."[33]

What is worse is that the minds of Afro-Christians have
been violently colonized by the image of this "white God"
through a white-colored Jesus. Ngũgĩ Wa Thiong'O says:

> But these values are reinforced by Christianity, partic-
> ularly the version brought by missionaries. To the Euro-
> pean colonizer the African has no religion, he knows not
> God. He is superstitious, and worships idols and several
> Gods. There is only one God, though he has a Son,
> begotten by the Holy Spirit. This God is white: his angels
> are white; and when the saved finally go to heaven, they
> will wear white robes of purity. But the devil is black; his
> angels are black; sin itself is black; and when the sinful
> finally go to Hell, they'll be burnt to black charcoal. Is it
> surprising that the African converts sing in pleading ter-
> ror: Wash me Redeemer and I shall be whiter than snow?
> Is it any wonder that African converts wear white robes
> of virgin purity during their white wedding? And is it
> any wonder that African women often buy red, blond,
> or brunette wigs to hide their black hair? And is it any
> wonder that African women and men will apply *Ambi*
> and other skinwhitening creams to lighten their dark
> skins?[34]

Ngũgĩ's question—"Is it any wonder?"—is as applicable to
the African continent, because of colonialism, as it is in the
African diaspora, because of slavery. This symbol of oppression, exported by what Ngũgĩ calls the "Jesus-is-thy-Savior

32. Randall C. Bailey, "Beyond Identification: The Use of Africans in Old
Testament Poetry and Narratives," in Felder, *Stony the Road We Trod*, 166, 168.

33. Manning Marable, "Religion and Black Protest in African American History,"
in Wilmore, *African American Religious Studies*, 336.

34. Ngũgĩ Wa Thiong'O, *Barrel of a Pen: Resistance to Repression in Neo-Colonial
Kenya* (Trenton, N.J.: Africa World Press, 1983), 94.

missionaries," helps maintain the mind-set of neo-colonialism—the "new colonial Jerusalem" in Africa.[35] Because all is now well in "imperialist heaven" because there is "peace on neo-colonial earth," says Ngũgĩ, the settlers construct churches to thank a white God for delivering their white race from the toils of Adam; and they invite their African laborers to share in their expression of thanksgiving.[36] The prayer on the lips of these neo-colonialist rulers, says Ngũgĩ, begins:

> Our father in Europe and America
> Hallowed be thy name
> Thy kingdom come
> Thy will be done
> In our wealthy Africa.[37]

"Need we ever again," asks Ngũgĩ, "kneel before foreign gods and languages and other people's icons of culture?"[38]

African-American psychologist Na'im Akbar identifies the image of the white-colored Jesus, which he says has become an unconscious controlling factor in our psychology, as inferiorizing and dehumanizing to black people. This impelled him to be instrumental in getting a resolution passed to this effect at the 1980 meeting of the National Association of Black Psychologists.[39] Indeed, the white-colored Jesus in the Afro-Christian church is the most visible sign of the cultural and psychological trauma brought about by slavery and colonialism.

I have been using the term "white-*colored* Jesus" intentionally, with sardonic irony in mind—sardonic with the intent of gleaning a grin in order to keep from sobbing. I chose this description after reading a black newspaper article of 1949, "White People Are 'Colored' Negroes Are 'Colorless,' " in

35. Ngũgĩ Wa Thiong'O, *Detained: A Writer's Prison Diary* (Nairobi, Kenya: Heinemann Kenya, 1981), 44, 61.
36. Ibid., 60.
37. Ibid., 62.
38. Ibid., 189.
39. Na'im Akbar, *Chains and Images of Psychological Slavery* (Jersey City, N.J.: New Mind Productions, 1984), 50, 59.

which the author, John Minkins, uses his college-level study in introductory physics to poke fun at white racism. He explains that there are only seven primary colors—violet, indigo, blue, green, yellow, orange, and red—the colors that show up when the white light of the sun is reflected through a prism. When reflected back through a prism, these colors again form white, which is not a color in itself but a combination of the seven primary colors. Thus, to be white, he deduces, is to be "colored." On the other hand, he continues, the complete absence of light or color from natural or artificial sources is blackness. Thus, the nearer people are to being black, the less "colored" they are.[40] Despite the oversimplification of Minkins's logic, or despite his attempt to poke fun at white racism, it was his article that led me to call the portrayal of Jesus as white, which Akbar identifies as inferiorizing to us, the "white-colored Jesus." The point is, for Jesus to be portrayed as white, particularly in the black church, is ludicrous.

Akbar makes the same point about the anthropomorphism that portrays God as male as he does about the anthropomorphism that portrays Jesus as white-colored. He says, "There are considerable problems in making the deity 'man' as opposed to 'woman.' If God is just a man, then that means that there are 50% of human possibilities that God is not. This means that you have cut off God's possibilities and limited your concept. You have introduced an unnatural psychology into those who are women, who would see themselves less favored because God is of a different gender."[41] In both instances—God as white-colored and God as male—language, which is the greatest of the symbols of worship, contributes to the dropping of what Ngũgĩ calls the "cultural bomb":

> The effect of a cultural bomb is to annihilate a people's belief in their names, in their languages, in their environment, in their heritage of struggle, in their unity, in

40. John C. Minkins, "White People Are 'Colored' Negroes Are 'Colorless,' " *California Eagle*, 15 [or 5] September 1949, 1, 3.
41. Akbar, *Chains and Images*, 41.

their capacities and ultimately in themselves. It makes
them see their past as one wasteland of nonachievement
and it makes them want to distance themselves from that
wasteland. It makes them want to identify with that which
is furthest removed from themselves.[42]

Having so colonized geography, historical information,
and the African mind, and having maintained a strict guardianship over biblical interpretation, Eurocentric ecclesiolo-
gists, liturgists, and hymnologists conclude, as did the French
Cardinal Roger Etchegaray, that problems such as racism are
mysteries. The Vatican's document "Racism in the Church,
Toward a More Fraternal Society," written in 1989 by Cardinal
Etchegaray, begins by saying racism is "a wound in humanity's
side that mysteriously remains open." The same thing could
be said about sexism, with even more carefully construed and
evasive language. However, racism and sexism, as Marable
and Akbar have said, are not wounds in humanity's side; they
are sicknesses in humanity's mind, sicknesses derived from
the same root disease. Neither is there anything "mysterious"
about the perpetuation of racism (or sexism and classism) by
the Eurocentric powers that maintain historical and doctrinal
guardianship. To say that our continued bleeding from the
open wound of racism is "mysterious" is but a conservative
escapism that protects individual Christians from the burden
of having to account for their unchristian decisions. Were the
truth to be told about the essential African contribution to
Christianity, some of the traditional beliefs that delude the
mind and allow racism to persist would be undermined.
Racism increasingly would be religiously, apologetically,
indefensible.

In the New Testament, for instance, mention is made of
Simeon, called "Niger" ("Niger" being a Latinism for "black"),
who was one of the leaders at the Antioch church (Acts 13:1).
We also read about the Nubian official baptized by Philip as
he traveled the road from Jerusalem to Gaza (Acts 8:26-40).

42. Ngũgĩ Wa Thiong'O, *Decolonising the Mind: The Politics of Language in African
Literature* (Nairobi, Kenya: Heinemann Kenya, 1986), 3.

How can modern biblical scholars and hymnologists fail to
celebrate the fact that this Ethiopian eunuch, who, tradition
holds, became an apostle to his and other countries, was quite
possibly the first Gentile to receive Christian baptism when
such early church scholars as Irenaeus, Eusebius, and Jerome
recognized this?[43] Clearly, Eurocentric scholars who avoid this
kind of information are the kindred ideologues of those
paleoanthropologists who, against Charles Darwin's advice,
spent nearly two generations searching in Europe and Asia
for evidence of human beginnings when that evidence had
been, as Darwin suspected, in Africa all along.[44] These Eurocentric biblicists are also the kindred of those paleoanthropologists who searched for evidence of human beginnings in Africa but, as Ngũgĩ points out, hated Africans
themselves: "To the Leakeys, it often seems that the archaeological ancestors of Africans were more lovable and noble
than the current ones—an apparent case of regressive evolution. Colonel Leakey, and even Lewis Leakey, hated Africans
and proposed ways of killing off nationalism, while praising
skulls of dead Africans as precursors of humanity."[45] Certainly
if pushed on the matter, the Eurocentric biblical scholars I
am speaking of would (to continue the parallel with Eurocentric anthropology) simply posit the alternative of their
kindred American anthropologist of the mid-twentieth century, Carlton Coon. "If Africa is the birthplace of the human
race it is only the undifferentiated kindergarten," wrote Coon.
"Europe and Asia are the true schools of mankind."[46]

Thus, there are three ways Coonian Europeans revise
history to fit a preconceived colonial mold and thus perpetuate their claims to supremacy and to the guardianship of
tradition. They separate Africans from their achievements by
identifying Africans (Egyptians, Moors) as any race but black;
they denigrate black accomplishments where it cannot be dis-
proved that the culture is African; or they ignore African

43. See Frank M. Snowden, Jr., *Blacks in Antiquity: Ethiopians in the Greco-Roman
Experience* (Cambridge: Harvard University Press, Belknap Press, 1970), 206, 335.
44. Charles S. Finch, "Race and Evolution in Prehistory," in Sertima, *African
Presence in Early Europe*, 289.
45. Ngũgĩ, *Detained*, 31.
46. Cited in Finch, "Race and Evolution," 296.

civilization altogether. As Napoleon once said, which is quite applicable here, "History is a set of lies agreed upon."[47] The lie in this case, which has been agreed upon far too long, is specifically that which was stated by Joseph Arthur Gobineau in his *Essay on the Inequality of the Human Races*: "The only history is white."[48]

Afro-Christians must become informed enough to counter Eurocentric de-Africanization of the biblical text and Christian tradition. For instance, as a means of countering Europeanist "Egyptomania" we must become informed enough to understand that the theological dependency of Christianity on Egyptian theology is undeniable. German historian of religions Karl Luckert, in a work that sets out to distinguish between Egyptian and Hebrew contributions to Christianity, says much that should be taken into serious consideration:

> The Hellenic tradition of philosophy has greatly affected the formation of the early Christian church. This happened especially by way of Neoplatonism, which, as we now know, has been Greek philosophy's homecoming to neo-Egyptian ontology. Whereas the history of Greek philosophy does now read like the homecoming of Greek minds to Egypt, Christianity by and large represents a similar return to Egypt by way of mythology, theology, and ritual. Hellenic philosophy, Christianity, Gnosticism—and some of the mystery cults that flourished during the time we call Hellenistic—were ancient Egypt's parting gifts to Mediterranean and Western civilization.[49]

Out of the Egyptian religious and philosophical cosmology, three thousand years before Jesus lived, came the ideas that, in part by way of Judaism and the Old Testament, were appropriated by Christianity: monotheism, messianic

47. Cited in Wayne B. Chandler, "The Moor: Light of Europe's Dark Ages," in Sertima, *African Presence in Early Europe*, 171.

48. Cited in Aimé Césaire, *Discourse on Colonialism*, trans. Joan Pinkham (New York: Monthly Review Press, 1972), 54.

49. Karl W. Luckert, *Egyptian Light and Hebrew Fire: Theological and Philosophical Roots of Christendom in Evolutionary Perspective* (Albany: State University of New York Press, 1991), 180.

expectation, trinitarianism, incarnation, virginal conception, redemption, passion, resurrection, reincarnation, sabbath, prayer, baptism, circumcision, eucharist, transubstantiation, judgment, millennialism, damnation, and salvation.[50] In fact, according to Luckert, Christianity was more theologically dependent on ancient Egypt than on the Hebrew tradition. "Only, let it be told already now, that over against the background of Egyptian theology it can no longer be said that the Christian religion was 'merely,' or even 'primarily,' an offspring of Semitic religion in general or of Judaism in particular."[51] Let us take as an example the idea of resurrection, which Luckert calls an instance of "Christianized Egyptian soteriology":

> When speculating about the source of Pharisaic belief in resurrection, scholars usually point to Iranian Mazdaism. Indeed, Persian influence on the history of Judaism is a fact of history, so too is Persia's contact with Egypt. Mircea Eliade was correct when he renamed the Iranian belief in the "resurrection of the dead" as "recreation of bodies." Elsewhere he has summarized how, according to Mazdaism, after the final judgment a human soul "will recover a resuscitated and glorious body."
>
> While influences from Mazdaism on Pharisaic Judaism and on early Christian belief need not be ruled out completely, the specific resurrection gospel that got Christendom started was definitely something more. First, the apparitions of Christ's resurrection body were temporary; they represented not a re-created and permanent state, precipitated on him by divine Judgment. His apparitions ceased when he returned to his Father. Second, in the Christian context, the savior's resurrection and ascension were notions very much dependent on his

        50. See Bonwick, *Egyptian Belief*; Ben-Jochannan, *Africa*, 179–82, 348–74; and Cheikh Anta Diop, *Civilization or Barbarism: An Authentic Anthropology*, ed. Harold J. Salemson and Marjolijn de Jager, trans. Yaa-Lengi Meema Ngemi (New York: Lawrence Hill Books, 1991), 311–12, 324, 331. For a summary, see Maulana Karenga, *Introduction to Black Studies* (Los Angeles: University of Sankore Press, 1982), 169–74.
        51. Luckert, *Egyptian Light*, 106.

earlier descent. The Father's begetting and the Son's returning constitute a single gospel event, a single round
trip journey. From ancient Egypt we can derive the model
for this entire round trip, whereas from latter-day Iran
we can derive only the return journey. The probability
of an ideological link with Egyptian soteriology therefore
is considerably stronger.[52]

The Egyptians were possibly also the progenitors of
ethics and *logos* (Johannine) theology, wherein the Sun God,
Ra, who creates through the word, conceives being that then
comes into existence.[53] Thus the prologue to the Gospel of
John can be seen as a clear summary of ancient Egyptian
theology: "In the beginning was the Word, and the Word was
with God, and the Word was God. He was in the beginning
with God; all things were made through him, and without
him was not anything made that was made. In him was life,
and the life was the light of men. The light shines in the
darkness, and the darkness has not overcome it" (John 1:
1-5). Akin to this, it is the god Amon, in the cosmogony of
Thebes, who first says the familiar line of the Johannine Gospel, "I am the God who became by himself, and who was not
created."[54] Even the word "Christ" is of Egyptian origin.[55]

Some biblical scholars also assert that certain passages
in the Old Testament are near-duplicates of Egyptian moral
texts. Eight of the Ten Commandments are clearly derived,
with no real modification, from the *Book of Coming Forth by
Day* (the *Book of the Dead*),[56] which had its beginnings around
3000 B.C.E., at the time of the first Egyptian dynasties.[57] Some
scholars have also acknowledged the strong similarity between
Israelite and Egyptian wisdom literature[58] and, more specifically, have recognized the strong similarity in form and
content between Psalm 104 and the "Hymn to the Sun" by

52. Ibid., 287, 319.
53. Diop, *Civilization or Barbarism*, 311.
54. Ibid., 330.
55. Ibid., 312.
56. See Karenga, *Introduction to Black Studies*, 171–72.
57. Diop, *Civilization or Barbarism*, 329.
58. See Bailey, "Beyond Identification," 175.

Pharaoh Akhenaton.[59] A comparative examination of the
biblical Proverbs and the poetry and songs of Pharaoh
Amen-em-ope, in *The Teachings of Amen-Em-Ope*, will reveal
the source from which many of the proverbs were taken (occasionally word for word).[60] "It is startling at first to realize
that supposed Christian dogmas are not novelties," concludes
Egyptologist James Bonwick. "Once granting that men in the
days of the pyramids knew more of evangelic truth, and
received higher and clearer inspirational teaching, than
the Old Testament saints and prophets, the Bible, as the
source of religious light, may seem to lower its flag to the
stony pyramid."[61]

In this respect, according to these scholars, the religion
received by the Ethiopian eunuch at the hand of Philip had
come full circle: Ethiopia was the mother of Egypt, which was
the "cradle of civilization" and the progenitor of modern religion. Christianity was in part a derivative of the religion
passed on to the Semitic world by the Egyptians. On this
reading, the Hellenic world owed part of its cultural enlight-
enment to Egypt (as well as to Ethiopia and Sudan). Ben-
Jochannan also draws a circle beginning in and leading back
to Africa:

> The co-option of the "sacred scriptures" (writings) by
> various religious groups was common among the an-
> cients. This practise came down through the adaptation
> of the basic tenets from the indigenous Nile Valley Af-
> ricans' "Mystery System" into Judaism. Christendom ex-
> tended it when it made Judaism its foundation. From
> this historical background it re-entered the various in-
> digenous African traditional religions through coloni-
> alism and imperialism. In the Americas, including the
> Caribbean Islands, the indigenous African religions the
> enslaved Africans brought with them from the West,
> Central, North, South, and East Africa were over-
> shadowed. But, in this co-optation the African-Americans

59. Diop, *Civilization or Barbarism*, 82.
60. For a side-by-side comparison, see Yosef A. ben-Jochannan, *African Origins of the Major "Western Religions"* (Baltimore: Black Classic Press, 1991), 164–65.
61. Bonwick, *Egyptian Belief*, 403.

were able to retain much of their ancient heritage through Judaism and Christianity, otherwise called "Judaeo-Christianity."[62]

There is no reason for the Afro-Christian church and its hymnody, with such available African anteriority, to continue to exist on the periphery of a Eurocentric worldview. This is particularly the case since Pauline Christianity has been appropriated by Europeans and interpretively attenuated to their ethnocentric perspective. What Europeans subsequently gave Africans in the context of missionary expansion, says African philosopher John Mbiti, was a thoroughly hellenized God—patriarchy, individualism, exploitation, and "rhythmless hymns."[63] "The traditional solidarity in which the individual says, 'I am because we are, and since we are, therefore I am,' is constantly being smashed, undermined and in some respects destroyed. Emphasis is shifting from the 'we' of traditional corporate life to the 'I' of modern individualism."[64] Mbiti concludes that the "I" of modern individualism among Africans has even led to religious doubt and radical disbelief (atheism).[65] Have African and African-diasporan Christians no hymnody without the "rhythmless hymns" of Isaac Watts and Charles Wesley, who are the ultimate hymnological symbols of Eurocentric Protestant Christianity?

Since the ideas of Christianity reveal something of their Egyptian ancestry, and since the religion received by the Ethiopian eunuch at the hand of Philip had come full circle, Afro-Christians (as African kin to the Ethiopians) have good reason to exercise "exegetical room" by way of a return to Egyptian thought prior to its hellenization. This is especially true since Egyptian religion influenced Yoruba religion,[66] which influenced African-American religion. I am not suggesting a return to Alexandrian Christianity, but perhaps Egypt can shed

62. Ben-Jochannan, *African Origins,* 167.
63. John S. Mbiti, *African Religions and Philosophy* (New York: Doubleday & Co., Anchor Books, 1970), 285, 289, 305.
64. Ibid., 293.
65. Ibid., 288.
66. Diop, *Civilization or Barbarism,* 324.

light not only on Africa south of the Sahara but on the culture
of the African diaspora. Europeans had no difficulty sub-
merging themselves in the reservoir of knowledge—mathe-
matics, astronomy, physics, medicine—held by the Muslim
"renaissance men" of Egypt's Dar-el-Hikma, the House of
Wisdom, built in Cairo in 1005 c.e. It was from this well
that the twelfth-century renaissance sprang.[67] Thus Afro-
Christians have good reason to look back to Egypt or to other
parts of Africa for the best ideas in theology and ethics that
might be valuable and usable in a new hymnody, liturgy, and
theology.

That our African ancestors were a root of the religious
cosmology that produced Christianity and were participants
in the formation of the early church and in the dispensation
of Christianity is certainly historically significant. We too must
do historical-critical scholarship so that it can serve the Afro-
Christian church well in our quest to reveal truth and recover
liberation—and to revise our hymnody.

Biblical scholars also contribute to the notion that the
Bible is the possession of "European civilization" not only by
trying to begin civilized history with the Greeks and through
their selective purview on the biblical text but also by their
overwhelming production of Eurocentric exegesis and interpretation, which ignore Africa and Africans. Their enormous
scholarly output and agreement on certain basic Eurocentric
presuppositions, and their institutionalization of those presuppositions in academia, have had the tendency to imply the
correctness of their interpretations and to justify the tradition
that has limited the spiritual growth and cultural breadth of
Christian hymnody. The extensive scholarly output of these
Eurocentric exegetes consequently achieves a certain level of
canonicity that reinforces their implied claim to the guardianship of Christianity. This, in turn, reinforces their suppression of readings of the Scriptures they fear can begin to
usurp the preeminence of the "select few" by liberating
women, blacks, and the poor.

67. Beatrice Lumpkin and Siham Zitzler, "Cairo: Science Academy of the Middle
Ages," in Sertima, *African Presence in Early Europe*, 176, 182, 188.

The scholastic imperialism I am speaking of is epito-
mized when the guardians of Christianity, the officials of Western civilization, inquire as to why blacks turned to "their"
(white) religion at the hands of our white "masters." This
question is just as loaded with implications of supremacist
ideology as the rhetorical inquiry made by a journalist to
James Baldwin in the 1960s. The journalist asked what Negroes had ever contributed to civilization.[68] If these questions
were not being asked from a mind-set of institutional ownership (part and parcel of racist ideology), then a far more
appropriate query of Afro-Christians would be: Is there some
cosmological connection or collective consciousness between
modern peoples of African origin and the religion and worldview of the African civilization of Egypt that made the Christian ideas and narratives—we agree, derived largely from
Egyptian religion and philosophy—attractive to the enslaved
or the colonized even though the so-called "new" religion was
transmitted to them through their oppressors?

The fact of the matter is, Christianity is, in more ways
than one, an indigenous religion in Africa. The minister of
the Ethiopian queen, spoken of in Acts 8:26-28, can be re-
garded as the first Christian, in the sense that prior to the
conversion of the Gentiles this "new" religion was but a sect
of Judaism. Furthermore, in the light of my earlier statement
about the religion the Ethiopians received having come full
circle, we can understand Mbiti's statement that Christianity
is an indigenous African religion:

> Christianity in Africa is so old that it can rightly be de-
> scribed as an indigenous, traditional and African religion.
> Long before the start of Islam in the seventh century,
> Christianity was well established all over north Africa,
> Egypt, parts of the Sudan and Ethiopia. It was a dynamic
> form of Christianity, producing great scholars and the-
> ologians like Tertullian, Origen, Clement of Alexandria

68. Cited in John A. Williams, "The Stolen Legacy," in Sertima, *African Presence
in Early Europe*, 83.

and Augustine. African Christianity made a great contribution to Christendom through scholarship, participation in Church councils, defense of the Faith, movements like monasticism, theology, translation and
preservation of the Scriptures, martyrdom, the famous
Catechetical School of Alexandria, liturgy and even her-
esies and controversies.[69]

Ben-Jochannan makes the same point about Christianity being an indigenous Egyptian religion: "In Egypt (Sais) Christianity was basically indigenous—Egyptian in almost every
aspect. As Christianity moved across North Africa to Numidia
and Carthage (birthplaces of the African Christian 'Fathers
of the Church') the indigenous Africans there reformed and
adopted much of its Egyptian format to suit Numidian and
Carthagenian culture and religious customs."[70]

The problem, then, is that the Eurocentric guardians of
Christian tradition know better than to ask the historically
correct questions. By asking insignificant or incorrect questions, they are able to support their doctrinal guardianship
and perpetuate ignorance among the Christian masses in regard to the evil of sexism, racism, and classism. So, the Eurocentric scholar will ask us a question such as why we became
involved in the "Western religion" of Christianity when we
were held captive by whites, while the Africa-centered scholar
will ask a question such as Ben-Jochannan's: "How much
longer are we to remain outside of the religions we originated
in our 'Mysteries' in Egypt and other High-Cultures along
the Nile?"[71] Ben-Jochannan's answer to this question is basically a criticism of the Eurocentric guardianship of the Christian tradition: "But as long as *racism* remains the basis upon
which these religions are taught, rejection of the indigenous
African and Asian peoples' contribution to them shall continue to be camouflaged into the authorship of those who did
least to start them, but most to continue them as their own
exclusive domain."[72]

69. Mbiti, *African Religions*, 300.
70. Ben-Jochannan, *African Origins*, 115.
71. Ibid., xiii.
72. Ibid., x–xi.

Indeed, my own theological education in the white academy was a kind of "Bantu education." Here I am drawing my language from Sipho Sepamla's poem "Civilization Aha," in his anthology *The Soweto I Love* (1977). Explaining the way by which the Eurocentric guardianship of Christian tradition had come to affect him, Sepamla wrote:

> i must be honest/it wasn't only bantu education
> it was all part of what they say is western/civilization.[73]

This "Bantu education" is what Carter G. Woodson calls "miseducation" in his long-lived book of 1933, *The Mis-Education of the Negro*:

> For example, the philosophy and ethics resulting from our educational system have justified slavery, peonage, segregation, and lynching. The oppressor has the right to exploit, to handicap, and to kill the oppressed. Negroes daily educated in the tenets of such a religion of the strong have accepted the status of the weak as divinely ordained, and during the last three generations of their nominal freedom they have done practically nothing to change it.[74]

Woodson says further, "In schools of theology Negroes are taught the interpretation of the Bible worked out by those who have justified segregation and winked at the economic debasement of the Negro sometimes almost to the point of starvation."[75] Hymnologically speaking, the misleading queries and teaching of Western "Bantu education," posited by Eurocentric scholars from a self-proclaimed seat of judgment, prevents the masses from realizing the necessity of singing new song.

I illustrated this point earlier in this chapter when I explained that I selected the term "white-*colored* Jesus" after reading John Minkins's sardonic newspaper piece of

73. Sipho Sepamla, *The Soweto I Love* (London: Rex Collins; Cape Town, South Africa: David Philip, 1977), 27.
74. Carter G. Woodson, *The Mis-Education of the Negro* (1933; reprint, Washington, D.C.: Associated Publishers, 1969), xxxii.
75. Ibid., 4–5.

1949, "White People Are 'Colored' Negroes Are 'Colorless.' "
Minkins concludes that article, which pokes fun at white racism, with a serious, yet still sardonic, comment on the failure
of some people to ask the right questions, questions that would
lead to unwanted answers: "It merely emphasizes the 'white'
man's propensity for ignoring his own definitions and conclusions whenever it suits his purpose to do so, regardless of
the dictionary and of even elementary science."[76]

Allow me to illustrate Minkins's point and my claim about
white doctrinal guardianship by way of reference to the book
The Problem of Christianity (1918) by the American philosopher
Josiah Royce. Royce identifies the singular problem of Christianity as the sin of individualism—individual disloyalty to
community. He perceives Christianity not simply as a religion
based on love but as the most advanced religion of loyalty, a
virtue he says the apostle Paul learned amid the early church
communities that were the interpreters of Jesus' teaching on
God's kingdom.[77] The individual who becomes estranged
from the "beloved community" can be reconciled with God
by means of the community leading the lost back into the
fold within reach of the kingdom that is at hand.[78] Afro-
Christian theology basically agrees with this view of redemption and salvation being available through the church
community. However, while Royce works out the intricacies
of a philosophical response to the problem (singular) of Christianity, his discourse hovers above the pragmatic problems
(plural) surrounding gender, race, and class. He claims that
a consciousness of unity creates community among a pluralism of peoples because of the existence of a common history,
memory, foregone unity, and future hope;[79] but are unity and
cooperation possible in a community of personal and structural hierarchy rooted in a Eurocentric tradition? When Royce
says "European civilization" is transformed and guided by the

76. Minkins, "White People Are 'Colored' Negroes Are 'Colorless,' " 1, 3.
77. Josiah Royce, *The Problem of Christianity* (1913; reprint, Chicago: University
of Chicago Press, 1968), 42, 50, 69, 76.
78. Ibid., 50.
79. Ibid., 260.

ideas of Christianity,[80] it becomes starkly evident that his underlying assumption is that people of European origin are the guardians of Christianity. Given this, our response is now less understanding and more critical; it is the response of Ngũgĩ: "All is now well in imperialist heaven for there is peace on neo-colonial earth."[81]

Our response is critical and sardonic, like Minkins's above, because Royce's perspective is revealed to be naked Eurocentric exclusiveness when put up to the light of historical reality. But Roi Ottley's comment in *No Green Pastures* (1952), much like Mbiti's comment above, serves sufficiently for a sober probation:

> The fact is, so many Negroes have been prominent in the history of the Church that everyone in Italy accepts this racial development as the natural course of things. Even a cursory investigation reveals that four popes of Rome are believed to have been Negroes—Victor, Melchiades, Gelasius and Adrian. Melchiades led Christianity to its final triumph against the Roman Empire. There are eighteen Black Madonnas and nearly twenty Negroes have been elevated to sainthood; principally Benedict, Cyprian, Simon, De Porres, Maurice, Moses, and Augustine, who incidentally held that no true believer in God could assert a Negro was not the equal of a white man.[82]

Fully ignoring this information, which was available even during his day, Royce preempts a common history and memory with Afro-Christians by misnaming the salvational agent for individualism as being the "beloved community," when actually it is the exclusive community of "European civilization" of which he speaks. The hymns of this "beloved community," one will see upon examination, reinforce the European claim to guardianship over Christianity.

80. Ibid., 214.
81. Ngũgĩ, *Detained*, 14.
82. Cited in Edward Scobie, "The Black in Western Europe," in Sertima, *African Presence in Early Europe*, 196.

Because of the utter particularity and exclusivity of Royce's "beloved community," his ideas are but "metaphysical idealism"—the fruits of an academic theology comprised of an abstract system of universal ideals. His metaphysical idealism is akin to men, whites, and elitists respectively saying that the "mysteries" of sexism, racism, and classism are their own moral problems. The reality is that sexism, racism, and classism are the respective problems of women, people of color, and the poor, each of whom are at the killing end of these "ideological weapons of death" in the hands of men, whites, and wealthy elitists. Royce's metaphysical idealism is simply a kind of conservative escapism, for there is no theological engagement with the crucial pragmatic problems of gender, race, and class. As Manning Marable recognizes, "The passion of white Christianity transfers critical thought to an idealist or supernatural plane, removing individual Christians from making moral decisions within the secular world, allowing 'the sadistic extermination of the weak' to continue."[83]

The reason Royce's ideas hover above the pragmatic problems surrounding gender, race, and class is not due alone to his metaphysical idealism. It is principally that his idea of a "beloved community" is derived from his rootage in "European civilization," whose societal progenitor—the Greco-Roman worldview—is the historical source of the hierarchism that perpetuates these problems. Part of the problem with the Greco-Roman worldview is the dualistic division between the spiritual and the material, such that the gospel is seen as being concerned with only the spiritual and not also the social in human life. This was explained by the black writers of *Evangelical Witness in South Africa*, who view this dualism as foreign to African and Judeo-Christian traditions:

> The consequence of this dualistic form of life has been disastrous for evangelical faith. This dualism enables one to live a pietistic "spiritual" life and still continue to oppress, exploit, and dehumanize people. And those who

83. Marable, "Religion and Black Protest," 320.

are victims of this oppression, exploitation and dehu-
manization are prohibited from complaining or resist-
ing it because this would amount to worrying about
material things that have nothing to do with one's
spirituality. . . . In this way the oppressors of this world
are able to maintain their system by conveniently con-
fining the gospel to the spiritual realm alone.[84]

That the difficulty with Royce's idea is not simply at-
tributable to his metaphysical idealism but in fact is due to
Eurocentrism is evident in an examination of Reinhold
Niebuhr's so-called Christian realism, which theoretically
should be antithetical to metaphysical idealism. Even though
Niebuhr rejects utopian forms of moral rhetoric and his is no
mere academic theology, his Christian realism actually legit-
imated and promoted United States imperialism and European colonialism while denying visibility and autonomy to the
marginalized communities of the world.[85] As ethicist James
McClendon says, in agreement with theologian Herbert
Edwards, Niebuhr's "Christian realism" is in effect complacent
racism—a commitment to the racist status quo despite the
fact that he, more than any other theologian, denounced
"racial pride."[86] Niebuhr's book, *The Structure of Nations and
Empires*, contains the greatest celebration of Anglo-Saxon supremacy, says Edwards, since that of Josiah Strong.[87] The
Europeanist bias of Niebuhr's Christian realism is therefore
ideologically identical to that in Royce's metaphysical idealism
because of the implied claim of both scholars to European
guardianship over Christianity.

Our current dilemma is that this Eurocentrism does not
cease with the scholars of Royce's and Niebuhr's generation
or with the hymns their contemporaries sang. As African-
American philosopher Cornel West understands, the distinc-
tive feature of even contemporary Christian thought is its

84. *Evangelical Witness in South Africa*, 9, 10.
85. Cornel West, "Christian Realism as Religious Insights and Europeanist Ideology," in *Prophetic Fragments* (Grand Rapids: Wm. B. Eerdmans Publishing Co.;
Trenton, N.J.: Africa World Press, 1988), 148, 151.
86. James W. McClendon, Jr., *Biography as Theology: How Life Stories Can Remake
Today's Theology* (Philadelphia: Trinity Press International, 1990), 11–12.
87. Cited in McClendon, *Biography*, 11.

mediocrity, owing to a lack of courage by white theologians to probe the pragmatic problems facing our existence.[88] Some white scholars know quite a lot about these matters we have been discussing; but, despite a possible inclination to disclose their knowledge, they fear saying too much lest they incur the ire of their Eurocentric colleagues.

Thus the value of Afro-Christians being liberated from the doctrinal way of reading the Bible is that we can begin to ask the historically correct and morally right questions, to reinterpret the gospel we preach and the doctrine we teach, and to revise the hymns we sing. We can respond to the need for a revised hymnody free from the constrictions of the Scriptures themselves and the European guardianship over their interpretation. We can do this knowing that faith, in the early church, preceded Scripture and therefore that the Bible is neither the beginning nor the end of Christianity, religion, or God. In other words, religion itself does not have to be responsible for the suppression of our human aspirations and the prevention of our liberation. Neither does religion have to function as a mere stage through which we must pass if we are ever to gain human maturity. Human maturity should be achievable in and through religious adulthood. For Afro-Christians, religious adulthood might in fact be achievable only through an African anteriority.

My trilogy of biblical exegeses that follow in Part Two—intended to serve as critical preludes to just such a religious adulthood—is for the purpose of proving the necessity of a revised black hymnody. My first exegetical prelude (chapter 3) addresses the problem of sexism. I discuss the "blaming of Eve" by searching out the original meaning of Genesis 3:1-6, a segment of the larger narrative (Gen. 2:4b–3:24) whose setting is the Garden of Eden. The episode of temptation and disobedience involving the characters of Eve, Adam, and the serpent has been used by the early church fathers of the Greco-Roman world and their sons of "European civilization" to develop and perpetuate the dogmatic

88. West, *Prophetic Fragments*, 195.

tradition of patriarchy—the ideology of male supremacy— and a hymnody that has been the curse of women ever since. Did Eve really beguile an innocent Adam and thus deservingly receive a punishment that has been and will continue to be transmitted to every woman of every generation in the form of gender subordination? Were the early dogmaticians correct in naming this event the "fall"—the origination of original sin—and in placing its responsibility on Eve (and every woman)? In a word, who was really to blame for the problem of female subjugation: Eve (and every woman) or the early church fathers and their sons (every man)?

In general, androcentric readings of this myth in Catholicism, Protestantism, and secular popular culture have adversely affected religious doctrines, ethical theories, civil laws, social customs, and personal characterizations. This tradition, perpetuated in church liturgies through the sexist language and images of hymnody, has caused deception and fostered human oppression rather than liberation. To discover the real Eve of the biblical myth, as we will try to do in the first exegetical prelude (chapter 3), will be to begin to see the damage the Eurocentric guardians of biblical orthodoxy have wreaked on certain constituencies of the so-called beloved community.

My presupposition is that women's emancipation is not just a private, domestic issue but is the concern of all apartheid societies, societies deeply entrenched in the multiple oppressions of gender, race, and class. This, then, is a quest for the full emancipation of women and the true equality between the sexes, not for the so-called equal rights held by a minority of women belonging to the elite classes, women who are sometimes ultraconservative and as inconsiderate as males in their disposition toward other women. When full emancipation is achieved, when a gender-neutral society is reached, it will be recognizable not by the election of a woman prime minister or president but by statistics that show that gender violence— sexual harassment and assault, domestic violence, and rape— ceases to be the problem that it currently is throughout the

world. We will see that fallenness has less to do with Eve than
it does with a subordinationist Eurocentric tradition that has
perpetuated these social problems.

The disclosure of a history of biased biblical misinterpretation will show us not only why traditional masculine
language in hymnody is offensive to women who understand
its ideological implications and social effects but also why
traditional racist language is offensive to people of color who
understand its implications and social effects. Just as the so-
called temptation of Eve has been misused by the Southern
Baptists as recently as 1984 to deny women the right to min-
isterial ordination, so has the so-called curse of Ham been
misused by the Mormons as recently as the 1970s to deny
African Americans entrance into the Mormon priesthood.
The second exegetical prelude, on race and hymnody (chapter
4), is also connected to chapter 3 by the fact that white supremacist pseudoscholars have read the Eden narrative of
temptation and disobedience through the modern prism of
modern racialism. The best known of the pseudoscholars is
Charles Carroll. In his book *The Tempter of Eve* (1902), Carroll
details his theory that the Eden serpent was a pre-Adamic
"negress" who was Eden's gardener.

The questions I raise and answer in examining the so-
called curse of Ham in the story of Noah and his sons (Gen.
9:18-27) are akin to the questions addressed regarding Eve
and every woman in chapter 3. In a word, was Noah's cursing
of Ham's son Canaan meant to predict and prescribe and
therefore to justify the enslavement, segregation, and abom-
ination of people of African origin throughout ancient and
modern times? In spite of answers in the negative, even by
modern Eurocentric scholars, I contend that the curse Noah
uttered has been lacerated into the flesh of black people up
to this very day: "Cursed be Canaan; a slave of slaves shall
he be to his brothers" (v. 25). This curse—whether it was
intended to predict and prescribe or not—is also the beginning of a long hymnic tradition that commences with explicit
references to the black "curse" and ends with things black

or dark representing transgression, debauchery, danger, and death. As I will explain in this exegetical prelude, the narrative of Noah and his sons was meant originally to explain and justify how the Canaanites (Canaan), whose land Palestine had been, came to be subjugated by the Israelites or Semites (Shem). But the misconstrual of the story was procured, protracted, and perniciously perpetuated by the officials of "European civilization," and it crystallized in the Christian justification of Europe's colonialism in Africa and its Atlantic slave trade. The result, as Leo Frobenius put it in *The History of African Civilizations*: "The idea of the barbaric Negro is a European invention."[89] "Let us have the courage to say outright," adds Fanon. "It is the racist who creates his inferior."[90]

Antebellum preachers, quasi-scholars, and other theological apologists for slavery, backed by the pseudoscientific theories of social Darwinists, were especially prolific in using the so-called curse of Ham to justify their merchandising of African flesh. These alleged "sons of Japheth" (American whites) were also backed by a rather social-Darwinistic corpus of nineteenth-century hymnody. In fact, because their hymnody portrayed all things "white," "fair," and "light" to be pure, divine, and equated with life, and all things "black" and "dark" as evil, "sin-sick," "poor and needy," and equated with death, it was not even necessary for them to create a proslavery hymnody to counter the growing corpus of American antislavery hymnody.

That the above symbolic language—the dialectic between black and white—is to be taken seriously in terms of its probable (almost certain) contribution to the residue of the curse of Ham myth is put well by Fanon. While white is viewed as symbolizing justice, truth, and virginity, he says, the use of black to symbolize evil translates into actual societal perceptions of black people. "I knew an Antillean who said of another Antillean, 'His body is black, his language is black,

89. Cited in Césaire, *Discourse*, 32.
90. Frantz Fanon, *Black Skin, White Masks*, trans. Charles Lam Markmann (New York: Grove Press, 1967), 93.

his soul must be black too.' This logic is put into daily practice by the white man. The black man is the symbol of Evil and Ugliness."[91] Du Bois said the same, that the assumption of whites is that darker peoples are dark not only in body but in mind, that they are "of dark, uncertain, and imperfect descent."[92] Fanon expounds:

> *In Europe, the black man is the symbol of evil....* The torturer is the black man, Satan is black, one talks of shadows, when one is dirty one is black—whether one is thinking of physical dirtiness or moral dirtiness. It would be astonishing, if the trouble were taken to bring them all together, to see the vast number of expressions that make the black man the equivalent of sin. In Europe, whether concretely or symbolically, the black man stands for the bad side of the character. As long as one cannot understand this fact, one is doomed to talk in circles about the "black problem." Blackness, darkness, shadow, shades, night, the labyrinths of the earth, abysmal depths, black someone's reputation; and, on the other side, the bright look of innocence, the white dove of peace, magical, heavenly light. A magnificent blond child—how much peace there is in that phrase, how much joy, and above all how much hope! There is no comparison with a magnificent black child: literally, such a thing is unwonted. Just the same, I shall not go back into the stories of black angels. In Europe, that is to say, in every civilized and civilizing country, the Negro is the symbol of sin. The archetype of the lowest values is represented by the Negro.[93]

South African poet Stanley Motjuwadi calls this being "brain-whitewashed" in his poem titled "White Lies."[94]

The European slave trade was eventually squelched, but the problem of racism has yet to receive an adequate response in the hymnody of either the white church or the Afro-Christian church. In fact, similar to the Mormons' misuse of

91. Ibid., 180.
92. Du Bois, *Darkwater*, 41–42.
93. Fanon, *Black Skin*, 189.
94. Robert Royston, ed., *To Whom It May Concern: An Anthology of South African Poetry* (Johannesburg, South Africa: Ad. Donker, 1973), 12.

the so-called curse of Ham, an annotated Bible (first published in 1961 and reprinted as recently as 1981) refers to the story of Noah and his sons as the "great racial prophecy." Titled *Dake's Annotated Reference Bible*, this volume evidences that a substantial number of white Christians, especially fundamentalists, still view the myth as the divine ethnological charter for race relations and racism. We must also take into consideration the query raised by the writers of *Evangelical Witness in South Africa*, who ask: "Are the black people the only sinners on earth, to warrant such a flood of white missionaries and evangelists from America?"[95]

That there remains this constituency of racist Christians means that history's chapter on slavery (its myriad forms) is not yet closed. In my third exegetical prelude (chapter 5), I reopen a reading of that inauspicious segment of Eurohistory, and justifiably so since less perceptible forms of slavery undoubtedly persist today: economic exploitation, unjust criminal imprisonment, and police brutality, all of which point to a prevailing "underclass" status. We will see in chapter 5, then, that the meaning of the apostle Paul's most personal (albeit ambiguous) address on the problem of slavery—his letter to Philemon—has significant bearing on the contemporary issue of class division, divisiveness, and exploitation, particularly as it is perpetuated in our hymnody.

The story surrounding Paul's letter to Philemon, which we will carefully examine in the third and final prelude, has Paul imprisoned in Rome or Ephesus. From his prison cell he has written to Philemon, a member of the church at Colossae, regarding Philemon's slave Onesimus, who had run away. Onesimus had located Paul and become a Christian under his teaching, and now Paul was sending Onesimus back to Philemon with a letter regarding their master-slave relationship. But the letter is somewhat ambiguous, leaving its contemporary readers with perhaps the same interpretive problem it probably left with its original recipient. Was Paul seeking the unconditional manumission of Onesimus (now

95. *Evangelical Witness in South Africa*, 33.

that he was a Christian) or manumission based on the condition that Onesimus return to help Paul in his evangelism? Or was Paul simply trying to humanize the master-slave relationship by suggesting that Onesimus be received back by Philemon not *just* as a slave but *also* as a Christian brother? Freedom under the condition that a slave can be more useful free than bound is not true liberation: It makes one a "free slave," which is the equivalent of the status of today's "underclass." Neither is redemption true liberation when it is a substitute for, rather than prerequisite to, emancipation (the liberation of human beings by human beings). Yet Paul's dealing with the former master-slave relationship seems to reduce to his imploring Philemon to receive Onesimus back as "no longer a slave but more than a slave, as a beloved brother." But if "in Christ" there is neither slave nor free, then how can one be "more" than a slave unless the former master-slave relation, the institution of slavery, the existence of socioeconomic hierarchy, or a mentality of slavehood is still a permitted and existent reality?

The point of the chapter is not to counter Lloyd Lewis's claim that black biblical scholars, wielding an optimistic hermeneutic, have an opportunity to claim Paul's letter to Philemon as "good news" regarding human liberation;[96] it is to counter the view of numerous Eurocentric scholars that Paul is suggesting that Onesimus could be both Philemon's slave and his Christian brother. These interpreters are suggesting that rather than Onesimus being treated as a mere tool, Paul may have wanted the slave to be treated with some dignity and respect. That Paul may have wanted Philemon to receive Onesimus back as no longer *just* a slave but *also* a Christian brother is an interpretation that numerous Eurocentric scholars favor; it is also typical of the hierarchism that results in and perpetuates classism.

One final way of looking at this is that slavery and the slave trade become transformed into antislavery and colonialism.[97] Du Bois says this regarding Britain's sudden turn from

96. Lloyd A. Lewis, "An African American Appraisal of the Philemon-Paul-Onesimus Triangle," in Felder, *Stony the Road We Trod*, 246.

97. W. E. B. Du Bois, *The World and Africa: An Inquiry into the Part Which Africa Has Played in World History*, enlarged ed. (New York: International Publ., 1965), 74.

establishing slavery in America to suppressing the expansion of the Arab slave trade in East and Central Africa for the purpose of building their colonial empire there. This is the same strategy that is descriptive of what has occurred in America: Slavery and the slave trade suddenly have become antislavery tagged with a domestic colonialism based on the maintenance of a permanent black underclass.

My response to Eurocentric exegesis, which in longhand is this very book, can be most concisely stated in Fanon's words: "It is our right to say that we are not satisfied. It is our duty to show the author how we differ from him."[98]

Sexism, racism, and classism—these three comprise a subordinationist tradition in the Afro-Christian church that finds expression in our hymnody. They are "curses," ideological weapons of death, the poverty of Christianity among Afro-peoples. Let us now carefully examine each of these subordinationist traditions so that we will understand why it is crucial that we pursue a postpatriarchal, postracialist, postclassist hymnody by achieving hermeneutical control over the Bible.

---

98. Fanon, *Black Skin*, 13.

PART TWO

EXEGESES

3

Gender and Hymnody

Women in Europe and America may not be exposed to
surgical removal of the clitoris. Nevertheless, they are
victims of cultural and psychological clitoridectomy. . . .
   No doubt, the physical ablation of the clitoris appears a much more savage and cruel procedure than its
psychological removal. Nevertheless, the consequences
can be exactly the same. . . . Psychological surgery might
even be more malicious and harmful because it tends to
produce the illusion of being complete. . . . It can create
the illusion of being free, whereas in actual fact freedom
has been lost.
   — Nawal El Saadawi, *The Hidden Face of Eve* (1980)

Discrimination against women (sexism) is probably the
oldest form of human bigotry in the Christian church and its
hymnody. The most ancient theological support for this bigotry of gender hierarchy and gender oppression is found in
the "primeval history" of the Book of Genesis: the story of
the so-called temptation of Eve in the Eden narrative (Gen.
3:1-6). Other customary sources that are used to support the

87

suppression of women—the household codes in Colossians
3:18–4:1; Ephesians 5:21–6:9; and 1 Peter 2:18–3:7—will
be dealt with indirectly in chapter 5. In that chapter, through
a discussion of the master-slave dialectic, we will come to some
resolution regarding the tension of social hierarchy and
Christianity.

The Fall Interpreted in
Ancient and Modern Times

It is not difficult to discover the roots of the misinterpretation of the Eden story by Christian scholars, ministers,
hymnologists, and hymnists. The misinterpretations that have
infiltrated practically every aspect of contemporary folk, classic, and popular culture were largely begun in the rabbinic
lore of late Judaism, the deutero-Pauline writings, the apocryphal and pseudepigraphical books, and in the writings of
Tertullian and Augustine. Rather than following the lead of
some of the early gnostic Christians who interpreted Eve
allegorically as the feminine power that engendered spiritual awakening,[1] the orthodox fathers viewed her as (in
Tertullian's words) "the devil's gateway." While the Song of
Songs or the edification of the mother of Jesus may have
served as a partial recompense for the misconstrual of the
Eden tale of paradise lost, the requisite recompense on our
part is to try finally to understand the true nature and intention of this narrative. If we do not carry through in this
respect, then any reproach to patriarchalism and androcentrism on our part will amount to little more than the alleviation
of sexist language in hymnody. I contend that without this
exegetical prelude no revisionary impact will have been made
on the deeper mythological notions used to justify the outer
forms of female subjugation. Thus, I want to trace the development and dispensation of the misinterpreted Eden narrative that has shaped our history and hymnody.

One of the earliest instances of an androcentric reading
of the text in question is a brief commentary on the Eden act

1. Elaine Pagels, *Adam, Eve, and the Serpent* (New York: Random House,
1988), 45.

of disobedience in the Book of Sirach (or the Wisdom of Ben Sira), found in the Bible used by the Roman Catholic Church:

> From a woman did sin originate
> And because of her we all must die. (Sir. 25:24)[2]

Subsequent to this, the pseudepigraphical work *The Books of Adam and Eve* gave an elaborate reading of the paradise narrative through Ben Sira's eyes.[3] Near the opening of the drama, which picks up immediately following the primal couple's expulsion from paradise, Eve sorrowfully utters these words to Adam: "Wilt thou slay me? that I may die, and perchance God the Lord will bring thee into paradise, for on my account hast thou been driven thence" (3:2). Farther along in the story, Eve beckons her children and her grandchildren to listen to her recount the way she *alone* was deceived, thus causing sin to be passed on to all the generations (15:1):

> And I cried out in that hour, "Adam, Adam, where art thou? Rise up, come to me and I will show thee a great secret." But when your father came, I spake to him words of transgression. For, when he came, I opened my mouth and the devil was speaking, and I began to exhort him and said, "Come hither, my lord Adam, hearken to me and eat of the fruit of the tree of which God told us not to eat of it, and thou shalt be as a God." And your father answered and said, "I fear lest God be wroth with me." And I said to him, "Fear not, for as soon as thou hast eaten thou shalt know good and evil." And speedily I persuaded him, and he ate and straightway his eyes were opened and he too knew his nakedness. And to me he saith, "O wicked woman! what have I done to thee that thou hast deprived me of the glory of God?" (21:1-6)

Such narratives as these, which possibly were present as early as the time of Jesus, entered into Christian doctrine and tradition largely through the pseudepigraphical Pauline writings that scholars call deutero-Pauline. From there, in particular, this doctrine impacted Christian hymnody. In the

2. R. H. Charles, ed., *The Apocrypha and Pseudepigrapha of the Old Testament* (Oxford: Clarendon Press, 1913), 1:402.
    3. Ibid., 2:134–54.

deutero-Pauline letter First Timothy is found the only biblical passage in which Eve is explicitly and scathingly blamed for the Eden transgression:

> Let a woman learn in silence with all submissiveness. I permit no woman to teach or to have authority over men; she is to keep silent. For Adam was formed first, then Eve; and Adam was not deceived, but the woman was deceived and became a transgressor. Yet woman will be saved through bearing children, if she continues in faith and love and holiness, with modesty. (1 Tim. 2:11-15)

The negative view, the hatred, of Eve was given elaboration in the writings of the medieval church fathers who were following the lead of Augustine, whose theology affected not only centuries but millennia. In his book *The City of God*, Augustine portrays the primordial woman as weaker than the man, and the serpent (Satan) as cunning in his decision to use the so-called weaker vessel to beguile "mankind." Regarding the serpent, Augustine says:

> He assumed that a man is less gullible and can be more easily tricked into following a bad example than into making a mistake himself. . . . So, too, we must believe that Adam transgressed the law of God, not because he was deceived into believing that the lie was true, but because in obedience to a social compulsion he yielded to Eve, as husband to wife, as the only man in the world to the only woman. It was not without reason that the Apostle wrote: "Adam was not deceived but the woman was deceived." He means, no doubt, that Eve accepted the serpent's word as true, whereas Adam refused to be separated from his partner even in a union of sin—not, of course, that he was, on that account, any less guilty, since he sinned knowingly and deliberately.[4]

Although Augustine played a prominent part in the process of transforming Eve into the Christian twin of the Greek Pandora, he was neither the only one to do so nor the first.

4. Augustine, *City of God*, trans. Gerald G. Walsh et al. (New York: Image Books, 1958), bk. 14, chap. 11.

Tertullian was familiar with the Pandora myth and managed to superimpose Pandora's gullibility on the character of Eve. His descriptive images of "opening" and "unsealing" are noticeably recollective of Pandora's raising the lid of a box (originally a jar) containing the earth's evils. Speaking to every woman, Tertullian said:

> Do you not know that each of you is an Eve? God's sentence on your gender lives even in our times, and so it is necessary that the guilt must also continue. You are the one who opened the devil's door; you unsealed the forbidden tree; you first betrayed the divine law; you are the one who enticed him whom the devil was too weak to attack. How easily you destroyed man, the image of God! Because of the death which you brought upon us, even the Son of God had to die.[5]

All of the foregoing prejudices toward Eve certainly had bearing on John Milton, the seventeenth-century Puritan whose *Paradise Lost* is probably the most influential piece of biblically derived misogyny that English literature has ever produced. Even though it is a secular epic poem, its popularity was such that it probably impacted the church's hymnody. Following the lead of Jerome's translation of the Hebrew Bible, namely, the omission of the pivotal prepositional phrase "with her" (that Adam was *with* Eve), Milton's epic poem built upon the notion that Eve was alone when the serpent beguiled her in the garden. Hence it seems that Adam's excuse—that the disobedient act was the woman's fault (Gen. 3:12)—was the basis of Milton's account of the fall rather than the narrative itself being the basis of Milton's account. As Phillip Cary says, anyone who wishes to blame the Eden transgression solely on the woman must remove the man from the scene of the crime; thus a substantial history of misogyny rests on the intentional omission of the phrase "with her."[6]

5. Cited in William E. Phipps, "Eve and Pandora Contrasted," *Theology Today* 45, no. 1 (April 1988): 42.
6. Phillip Cary, "Seeing through Adam's Excuse," *Daughters of Sarah* 14, no. 4 (July-August 1988): 8.

Merlin Stone would take issue with putting so much weight on Jerome's omitting the phrase "with her." She contends that the entire Adam and Eve story (along with a substantial part of both the Old and the New Testament) is a veiled political maneuver by the male leadership of the Hebrew tribes, especially the Levite priests, to destroy the ancient goddess religion that threatened their system of patriarchy.[7] Stone says, "It was the ideological inventions of the advocates of the later male deities, imposed upon that ancient worship with the intention of destroying it and its customs, that are still, through their subsequent absorption into education, law, literature, economics, philosophy, psychology, media and general social attitudes, imposed upon even the most nonreligious people of today."[8] Thus Stone's assessment of Western society's self-perception is that Adam and Eve define the images of male and female.[9]

What Augustine and Milton and Christian hymnists have perpetuated through their continued authority and popularity has, it seems, irrevocably tainted modern views of the female gender. As recently as 1984, for instance, the Southern Baptist Convention passed a resolution that, following the passage in First Timothy, maintains that women are to be excluded from pastoral leadership because man was the first in creation and woman the first in the fall.[10] Bill Leonard, a Southern Baptist liberal, sternly criticizes the conservatives in his denomination for such explicit use of the Bible to support their sexism: "If Southern Baptists want to condemn the ordination of women, that is one thing. They are free to do so, given our form of democratic polity. . . . But blaming Eve—that is really unfair."[11] The tendency to perpetuate "curses," concludes Leonard, is probably the most fatal of flaws in the fundamentalism of the current Southern Baptist kind.[12]

7. Merlin Stone, *When God Was a Woman* (New York: Harcourt Brace Jovanovich, 1976), 61.
8. Ibid., xxv.
9. Ibid., 7.
10. Cited in Bill Leonard, "Forgiving Eve," *The Christian Century* 101, no. 34 (7 November 1984): 1039.
11. Leonard, "Forgiving Eve," 1039.
12. Ibid.

Samuel Terrien goes further in his criticism of fundamentalism, arguing that the attempt to transform the Eden myth into a historical event is an effort to deny that *all* human beings are akin to Eve and Adam in their subjection to the limitations of sin and death.[13]

Like the Southern Baptist Convention, the Afro-Christian church and its hymnody are caught in a fundamentalistic liberative lag that maintains fixed boundaries of hierarchical biblical interpretation. To draw one case in point, the first hymnal of the Progressive National Baptist Convention, a "progressive" African-American denomination formed in 1962, was a 1976 "special edition" of the thirty-six-year-old Southern Baptist hymnal, *The Broadman Hymnal* (1940)— an outmoded hand-me-down that the Progressive Baptists did not even replace until 1982. If the doctrine of a fundamentalist white denomination is suspect in regard to women (and blacks), then ought not its hymnody be suspect too? In order to begin to forge the exegetical room that can give us hermeneutical control over the Bible, and to avoid becoming entrapped by uncharitable interpretations, let us examine closely the biblical narrative that has been a "text of terror" for women of modern history. Let us begin the serious exegesis that must be practiced by those scholars who would be ethnohymnologists.

Genesis 3:1-6

Now the serpent was more subtle than any other wild creature that the Lord God had made. He said to the woman, "Did God say, 'You shall not eat of any tree of the garden'?" And the woman said to the serpent, "We may eat of the fruit of the trees of the garden; but God said, 'You shall not eat of the fruit of the tree which is in the midst of the garden, neither shall you touch it, lest you die.' " But the serpent said to the woman, "You will not die. For God knows that when you eat of it your eyes will be opened, and you will be like God, knowing

13. Samuel Terrien, *Till the Heart Sings: A Biblical Theology of Manhood and Womanhood* (Philadelphia: Fortress Press, 1985), 27.

good and evil." So when the woman saw that the tree
was good for food, and that it was a delight to the eyes,
and that the tree was to be desired to make one wise, she
took of its fruit and ate; and she also gave some to her
husband, and he ate.

The foregoing episode of temptation and transgression,
perhaps the most familiar of events in the Book of Genesis,
was used by the early church fathers to infer a fully developed
moral system that has shaped the whole of Christianity, including its hymnody. As we give this scene a close reading,
the entire two-act drama of creation and paradise (Gen. 2:4b–
3:24) will necessarily come into play; but Genesis 3:1-6
alone is sufficient for our reconsideration of the so-called
temptation of Eve. The questions this passage raises are myriad in the light of its longtime use as an instrument of oppression: Did or did not Eve tempt and beguile Adam to eat
of the forbidden fruit? Was Adam present or absent at the
time of the temptation? Were the early theologians accurate
in naming this event the fall and in designating it the inception
of original sin, or were these misnomers imposed by a mis-
informed or biased tradition of Christian dogmatism? Have
these dogmatic doctrines been used wrongly to portray Eve
as the Hebrew counterpart to the Greek mythic Pandora? In
essence, I, as an ethnohymnologist, am seeking an answer to
the question of whether the story of the so-called temptation
and transgression implies that Eve really is a Pandora figure
or whether this interpretation of the paradise story is the
consequence of continued patriarchal prejudice in modern
church and society. Who is to blame, Eve (and every woman)
or the early church fathers and their sons—male scholars,
ministers, hymnologists, and hymnists?

These questions are neither outdated nor sufficiently
answered, especially not sufficiently answered for the ethnohymnologist and hymnist. They are important questions and
must be perpetually reconsidered because the answers given
characterize not only Eve (and Adam) but all women (and all
men) at every point in modern history. Indeed, Eve not only

represents every woman who lived in ancient Israel when the myth took final shape in about the tenth century B.C.E., she is the archetypal woman to all who embrace the Eden story as a part of their religious heritage. If we are ever to expose sexism as a pernicious ideology of a dominant patriarchy and rid our hymnody of such prejudice, we must discover the real Eve whose innocence is buried beneath thick historical layers of androcentric interpretation and Eurocentric guardianship over the Christian tradition. Once we see that this tenth-century B.C.E. Israelite text is erroneously read with twentieth-century C.E. post-Israelite eyes or that the text was contrived as pejorative toward women for ideological reasons, we will recognize not only the malignity of sexism but also the dire need for a hymnic renaissance. In other words, our retreading of this old exegetical ground is no waste of time or mind. My goal is to bring us to the point where we, as Afro-Christians generally unfamiliar with this exegetical ground, will understand and even appreciate the need for radical reform of our hymnody. Let us begin by discussing the kind of narrative we are reading, namely, its literary genre and form.

The Primeval Story of Genesis

The Eden narrative of Genesis 2–3 (2:4b–3:24) synthesizes at least two literary genres—creation myth and etiology (a historic tale explaining some present state of affairs). It comprises the formation of a human being, the fashioning of paradise, the placement of the human being therein, the creation of the animals, and the formation of woman from the rib or side of the first human being. This is a typical Israelite narrative that corresponds to like stories in the "primeval history" (Genesis 1–11) because of its thematizing of disobedience and punishment. Similar narratives in Genesis are the stories about Cain and Abel (4:1-6), the illegitimate interaction between the sons of God and daughters of men (6:1-4), the flood (chaps. 6–9), Noah and his sons (9:18-27), and the tower of Babel (11:1-9). As the first of the disobedience-punishment narratives in the primeval history, the creation-paradise story serves also as an overture to the patriarchal narratives (Genesis 12–50). Most of these narratives have been either thematized or alluded to in Christian hymnody.

There are two creation narratives in the first few chapters of Genesis—the creation story of Genesis 1:1–2:4a and the creation-paradise story of Genesis 2:4b–3:24. The latter (2:4b–3:24), which includes the disobedience-punishment narrative, is derived from a literary source different from the former (1:1–2:4a)—that is, a different source prior to their being brought together in the edited anthology we call the Bible. The creation-paradise story is a product of what biblical scholars call the Yahwist (J) source, which was finalized around the tenth century B.C.E. The first creation story is a product of the Priestly (P) source, which dates around five hundred years later (the fifth century B.C.E.). Because the era of the Yahwistic writer was a period of prideful nationalism and self-satisfaction for an Israel united under the powerful Davidic and Solomonic monarchies, the creation-paradise narrative, which portrays Eve and Adam as being tempted to turn away from faith and obedience, may have been intended to serve as a chastising response to the secularization and pride of these royal regimes.

Also characteristic of J source material, Genesis 2–3 is a conflation of different stories and various literary segments. From the larger perspective, the two acts of the extended Genesis 2–3 drama may evidence two literary segments that were once independent stories: a story about the creation of the world and man and woman (2:4b-25) and a story about paradise and the primal couple's expulsion therefrom (3:1-24). Ingeniously synthesized, these stories (possibly once independent) have become a single narrative event in two acts, one act about the creation of paradise and the other about the loss of paradise. Or, if we prefer, the whole can be divided into four parts or scenes: (1) 2:4b-17, the placement of a human being in the garden; (2) 2:18-25, the formation of the woman; (3) 3:1-7, disobedience and transgression; and

(4) 3:18-24, judgment and expulsion.[14] The latter two scenes, which comprise the second act of the drama (3:1-24), are further divisible into smaller units. The first scene of act 2 is divisible into two parts—the so-called temptation (3:1-5) and the act of disobedience (3:6-7). The second scene of act 2 is divisible into four parts—the exposure (3:8-10), trial (3:11-13), verdict and punishment (3:14-19), and conclusion (3:20-24).

A closer examination of the creation-paradise narrative reveals that within these four scenes set in two acts are other embellishments, such as motifs from other story traditions and editorial transitions (some of which account for the inconsistencies generally found in the narrative). The two acts of the drama, for instance, are fused together by a crucial transition, probably provided by the Yahwistic writer. Following the creation of the primal being (2:7) and *its* placement in the garden (2:15) and prior to the creation of the woman (2:22), the editor evidently added the segment that reads: "And the LORD God commanded the man, saying, 'You may freely eat of every tree of the garden; but of the tree of the knowledge of good and evil you shall not eat, for in the day that you eat of it you shall die' " (2:16-17). This transition makes the first act about creation an exposition that ascends to a climax in the second act's narratives of temptation and disobedience.

The scene of temptation is an added bonus in this drama of disobedience and punishment, for not all such narratives incorporate a temptation motif. While punishment is an essential part of the drama, it may very well be that the original punishment for the disobedience was simply expulsion from the garden (2:23-24) and that the extended punishment of 2:14-19 was an elaboration by the editor. Biblical scholar Claus Westermann says, "The trial and sentence then are elaborations of J in which he makes explicit his intention of referring the primeval event of crime and punishment to humankind

14. Walter Brueggemann, *Genesis: A Bible Commentary for Teaching and Preaching* (Atlanta: John Knox Press, 1982), 44–45.

in community. J, with surprising readiness, fits into his narrative traditional primeval motifs which are recognizable from their etiological character."[15] With the creation story (act 1) functioning as an exposition to the paradise story (act 2), it is evident that the drama as a whole has set out to thematize disobedience and punishment. What is distinct about this particular treatment of this favorite Yahwistic theme (disobedience and punishment) is that the creation-paradise story is the only biblical narrative where God deals with human beings face-to-face: God states a prohibition, discovers the disobedience, conducts the trial, pronounces the verdict, and carries out the punishment.[16]

The story of creation may have originally concluded with God creating the woman from the rib or side of the first human being (2:22) and the man exclaiming his great pleasure: "This at last is bone of my bones and flesh of my flesh; she shall be called Woman, because she was taken out of Man" (2:23). What follows in 2:24 is an etiological reflection possibly added to the narrative at a later time: "Therefore a man leaves his father and his mother and cleaves to his wife, and they become one flesh." Verse 25 then links this story of creation (act 1) with the narrative of disobedience and punishment (act 2): "And the man and his wife were both naked, and were not ashamed." This transitional verse is important because it describes the worldview of the woman and the man prior to their act of disobedience, thus preparing for the new consciousness caused by their eating from the tree of wisdom— their awareness of their nakedness (3:7a). In terms of the continuity and movement of the drama, the new consciousness is important only to the degree that it provides the evidence that leads God to question whether the primal couple had been disobedient (3:11) and finally to convict and punish them.

The creation of paradise (act 1) does more than function as an exposition of the loss of paradise (act 2). It links the

15. Claus Westermann, *Genesis 1–11: A Commentary*, trans. John J. Sullivan (Minneapolis: Augsburg Publishing House, 1984), 195.
16. Ibid., 193.

event of human disobedience to one of the most powerful of all myths—creation. Hence, in the brief transitional verse (2:25) that links acts 1 and 2 of this drama lies one of the channels by which the myth of the so-called temptation of Eve has gleaned some of its enormous influence over the human imagination. Merlin Stone, in agreement with other scholarly speculations, believes that the story of Adam and Eve was intentionally included in the creation myth to lend greater weight to the attack of the ancient goddess religion, with which the new patriarchal religion of the Hebrews was in competition.[17]

Let us now take an even closer, verse-by-verse examination of the temptation and transgression, so that no stone, no matter how small, is left unturned in my ethnohymnological argument for increased exegetical room, hermeneutical control, and a revised black hymnody.

A Verse-by-Verse Study of the Temptation and Transgression

Now the serpent was more subtle than any other wild creature that the LORD God had made. He said to the woman, "Did God say, 'You shall not eat of any tree of the garden'?" (Gen. 3:1)

There have been many attempts to explain what or who the serpent represents in this story, and Christian hymnody has probably reflected the entire spectrum of surmises. Answers to the question of who or what the serpent is range from Satan or evil to a phallic or sexual symbol implying the iniquity of sexuality. Augustine posited the former, that the serpent is the spokesperson of the fallen angel Lucifer.[18] Most biblical scholars outside the fundamentalist tradition reject this idea, and for good reason, as we will see.

Augustine's interpretation certainly is not as ludicrous as the notion that the serpent is an ape-like "negro" female (a "negress") who was the gardener of Eden even prior to the

17. Stone, *When God Was a Woman*, 197.
18. Augustine, *City of God*, bk. 14, chap. 11.

creation of Eve and Adam.[19] Charles Carroll, in his book *The Tempter of Eve* (1902), argued that the "negro" is the only "animal" with a mental capacity capable of devising a scheme that could deceive "man."[20] This sounds like an echo of the racist theory of the nineteenth-century French precursor of the Nazi theoreticians, Joseph Arthur Gobineau, which claimed that the black "female" races are the seducers and corrupters of the white "male" races.[21] Carroll's racist theory is reversed later in the twentieth century by the black Muslim leader Elijah Muhammad, who exercised hermeneutical control in a way that was just as oppressive to women as the interpretations of Eurocentric scholars. Muhammad's explanation, which still left women entrapped by the patriarchalism typical of mainline Islam, is that the serpent is the white man and he uses black Eve to tempt the black man, Adam.[22] We will see, through our careful reading of the text, that there is no evidence to support these subordinationist ideas and that we should therefore cease to sing (or we should radically revise) all hymns that suggest such interpretations.

At present, there is really no sure way of knowing what images may have arisen in the minds of the story's writers and original hearers. On the basis of the text alone, it seems that what the serpent represents is rather unimportant, that the animal merely serves as a prop in the drama: a means of temptation for the primal couple, by which the drama's plot gleans action and gains momentum. As Claus Westermann says, the reason an animal is used to play the role of tempter is simply that the story is about the primal couple, which prevents the inclusion of any other human characters.[23] Westermann also reckons that what the serpent represents is less important than the idea that the origin of evil remains a

19. Charles Carroll, *The Tempter of Eve* (St. Louis: Adamic Publishing Co., 1902), 367, 402.

20. Ibid., 392, 405.

21. See Martin Bernal, *Black Athena: The Afroasiatic Roots of Classical Civilization* (New Brunswick, N.J.: Rutgers University Press, 1987), 1:354–55.

22. Elijah Muhammad, *Message to the Blackman in America* (Chicago: Muhammad Mosque of Islam No. 2, 1965), 123, 126, 127.

23. Westermann, *Genesis 1–11*, 236.

mystery: "When J allows the man and the woman to be led astray by the clever snake, creature of God, he is saying that it is not possible to know the origin of evil. We are at a complete loss in face of the fact that God has created a being that can lead people to disobedience. The origin of evil remains a complete mystery. The most important thing that J has to say here is that there is no etiology for the origin of evil."[24] Carrying Westermann's point further, Hugh White comments on the effectiveness of the narrative's use of an animal character:

> By permitting an animal to speak, the narrator opens a new realm which is not under the prohibition, and thus makes possible the utterance of transgressive thoughts. Further, by permitting the transgressive thought to originate in the neutral arena of the animal world by means of a singular instance of speech by an animal, the source of evil is rendered totally ambiguous. . . . The writer thus avoids creating a traditional villain, and thereby throws the emphasis of the narrative upon the inner human conflict.[25]

Perhaps, then, the serpent is merely a nontraditional villain that, by virtue of its being an animal, is unable to upstage the more critical theme of inner human conflict initiated when the woman is asked: "Did God say, 'You shall not eat of any tree of the garden'?"

On the other hand, Merlin Stone, basing her theory on research that has substantial scholarly support, finds nothing mysterious or nontraditional about this so-called villain. The Israelites, who were being warned and chastised at every turn not to become involved in the goddess religion, understood the serpent to be the instrument or symbol of divine counsel for the prophetesses of that despised religion.[26] The reason Adam and Eve were not to eat of the tree of knowledge of

24. Ibid., 239.

25. Hugh C. White, "Direct and Third Person Discourse in the Narrative of the 'Fall,' " *Semeia* 18 (1980): 97.

26. Stone, *When God Was a Woman*, 220–21.

good and evil, continues Stone, is that it too was a symbol associated with the Canaanite religion:

> To ancient Hebrews this tree was probably understood to represent the sacred sycamore fig of the Goddess. . . . The sacred branch being passed around in the temple, as described by Ezekiel, may have been the manner in which the fruit was taken as "communion." According to Egyptian texts, to eat of this fruit was to eat the flesh and the fluid of the Goddess, the patroness of sexual pleasure and reproduction. According to the Bible story, the forbidden fruit caused the couple's comprehension of sexuality.[27]

Aside from this possible symbolization, there are other dramatic subtleties that contribute to the interest and even effectiveness of this didactic piece. Phillip Cary believes that the command not to eat of the tree came to Eve secondhand (from Adam), which may explain the reason the serpent sought to deceive her rather than the man. Cary says, "The command of a holy God makes a less frightful impression on one who comes to it secondhand."[28]

On the other hand, God's command may have come to Eve firsthand, for "the man" whom God put in the garden and instructed not to eat of the tree of the knowledge of good and evil (2:16-17) was not originally "Adam" but *ha-adam* (humankind). This would make the text coincide better with the older creation stories of Sumer and Babylon, in which women and men were created concurrently, in pairs, by the goddess. It has been argued—and this has serious implications for the Afro-Christian church and its hymnody—that prior to the creation of the woman from the rib or side of the first living soul (2:21-23), *ha-adam* (from which translators erroneously derived the proper name "Adam") was a being that was androgynous (both male and female). Phyllis Trible makes this point when she says the first act in this narrative is the creation of androgyny (2:7) and the last act the creation

27. Ibid., 220.
28. Cary, "Seeing through Adam's Excuse," 10.

of sexuality (2:23).[29] Hugh White posits the same idea in stating that the first words of any human being are those of the woman uttered in response to the serpent, so that prior to the act of disobedience the woman and the man are scarcely differentiated.[30] Hence, God's command (2:16-17) may have come to Eve not secondhand but firsthand. We can interpret all of this to mean that primordially there was an equality between the woman and the man.

And the woman said to the serpent, "We may eat of the fruit of the trees of the garden; but God said, 'You shall not eat of the fruit of the tree which is in the midst of the garden, neither shall you touch it, lest you die.'" (Gen. 3:2-3)

This is the woman's carefully formulated response to the serpent's intentionally misleading question, "Did God say, 'You shall not eat of any tree of the garden'?" Feminist theologians, in reproach to thousands of years of androcentric interpretation, are quick to point out that the woman is not only the first to utter language but in fact engages in astute dialogue with the shrewdest of all the animals. Moreover, that the woman adds the qualifier "neither shall you touch it" as an elaboration to God's command leads Trible to say she is both translator and theologian, humankind's first theological thinker.[31] Nawal El Saadawi interprets this similarly in order to contest the notion that women are mentally inferior to men. Calling Eve "the first goddess of knowledge," she says women were the first to quest for knowledge and exercise the powers of the mind.[32]

Still, this interpretation of the intelligence of the woman detracts nothing from the story's characterization of the serpent as shrewd; for the serpent's question forces the woman to cite the prohibition, according to Hugh White, thereby

29. Phyllis Trible, "Eve and Adam: Genesis 2–3 Reread," *Andover Newton Quarterly* 13, no. 4 (March 1973): 253–54.
30. White, "Direct and Third Person Discourse," 95.
31. Trible, "Eve and Adam," 256.
32. Nawal El Saadawi, *The Hidden Face of Eve: Women in the Arab World* (London: Zed Press, 1980), 211.

making God and God's commandment into objects of a third-person statement and her personal interpretation. "Having now been manipulated into the position of a subject detached from the divine words and a judge of their material content, woman is now prepared to receive the fully developed alternative interpretation of the prohibition that originates totally outside of the primary relation."[33] In defending God's command, says Westermann, the woman is already on the way to breaking it.[34]

The woman is not alone in being deceived, however. The inclusiveness of her language—"we" may not eat of the fruit—implies that the man is present while she is engaging in theological debate with the serpent. In fact, a careful overview of the story shows that the woman and the man are together as a unity from the very formation of the woman from the side of *ha-adam*. Prior to the temptation, *they* were both naked; following the temptation, *they* ate and the eyes of *both* were opened. This unity between the woman and the man dissolves only after their disobedience is discovered by God, who, walking in the garden, calls to them individually in the singular. It is only then that they cease to be of the same flesh and, interprets Marla Schierling, become two individuals who must bear their separate burdens.[35] "Inserted into this pericope is the renaming of woman by Adam. She is no longer woman but Eve (3:20). . . . Perhaps her name change is indicative of her social change. She is no longer flesh of his flesh, she is to be the mother of all life. Her vocation as helpmate, companion, coworker, or whatever, has degenerated to the single position of nurturer and child bearer. The unique relationship they once experienced together is no longer a reality. The woman's role is changed."[36] In short, even though it can be argued that the man was a silent participant in Eve's dialogue with the serpent, for him to remain silent was for him to give

    33. White, "Direct and Third Person Discourse," 98.
    34. Westermann, *Genesis 1–11*, 239–40.
    35. Marla J. Schierling, "Primeval Woman: A Yahwistic View of Woman in Genesis 1–11:9," *Journal of Theology for Southern Africa* 42 (March 1983): 7.
    36. Ibid., 7.

consent. What our theology and hymnody have not reflected
is that he is no less guilty than the woman.

> But the serpent said to the woman, "You will not die. For God
> knows that when you eat of it your eyes will be opened, and you
> will be like God, knowing good and evil." So when the woman
> saw that the tree was good for food, and that it was a delight
> to the eyes, and that the tree was to be desired to make one wise,
> she took of its fruit and ate; and she also gave some to her
> husband, and he ate. (Gen. 3:4-6)

The meaning of the penalty of death in God's commandment is not agreed upon by scholars. Some perceive it
as a serious threat of mortality, while others see it as a mere
warning. Whether it is a threat or a warning is ultimately less
important than the outcome—death of one sort or another.
That the primeval couple did not die immediately (biologically) led some early scholars, particularly Augustine, to conclude that they began to die morally and spiritually. From this
derived the notion of original sin, the fall, man blaming Eve, misogyny, and a hymnody that relegates women to
invisibility.

One of the principal obstacles preventing the obliteration
of misogyny in contemporary history and hymnody is the
popular belief that Eve alone transgressed and subsequently
led Adam astray. To the contrary of every hymn ever uttered
to this effect, the man was present with the woman as the
serpent flatly denied that God had told them the truth. The
Septuagint (the Greek translation of the Hebrew Bible) says
that the woman ate and "gave to her husband also *with her*,
and *they* ate." Even the King James Version (which has other
translation problems) says Eve ate of the fruit and "gave also
unto her husband *with her*." On the other hand, the New
English Bible and the Revised Standard Version are among
the translations that follow the Latin Vulgate translation of
the Hebrew Bible by the fourth-century Hebrew scholar
Jerome. The Latin Vulgate translation omits the prepositional
phrase "with her." Jerome often made interpolations and
omissions in his translations, and his refusal to implicate Adam

(and the male gender) in the initial act of disobedience un-
questionably has had irrevocable consequences in the hymns
that worshipers have sung and in the church's long history
of repressing women. Those of us who will allow for exegetical
room in addressing this problem are on the way to gaining
the hermeneutical control that is the requisite prelude to a
revised black hymnody. We will be helped by the New Revised
Standard Version (1989), which corrects this longstanding
error, adding after "husband" the words "who was with her."

Some scholars say that while the temptation of man by
woman is a familiar motif in religious and secular stories
within classic, popular, and folk cultures, the text does not
portray the woman as a seductress. Although it is the woman
who engages in theological dialogue with the serpent, it is
both the woman and the man who are led into disobedience
by the serpent's shrewd argument. Their trial before God
provides no evidence to the contrary. Adam's blaming of Eve
must be discounted, for in the same breath he also blames
God: "The woman *whom thou gavest to be with me*, she gave me
fruit of the tree, and I ate" (3:12). Furthermore, when the
woman blames their transgression on the serpent (v. 13b),
God evidently accepts her excuse, for the serpent is immediately cursed to squirm forever upon its belly and to be at
enmity with woman (vv. 14-15).

Merlin Stone, in line with her interpretation of the Eden
narrative as part of a protracted attack on the ancient goddess
religion of the Canaanites, says that by eating the fruit the
woman gleaned sexual consciousness and tempted the man
to join her in sexual pleasures, and that this was intended to
warn Hebrew men to stay away from the sacred women of
the goddess temples and Hebrew women not to participate
in the temple's sexual rituals.[37] Thus, when the male deity
cursed the serpent the intent was to portray the prophetesses
of the goddess, whose counsel had been identified with the
symbol of the serpent, as causative of the downfall of the

37. Stone, *When God Was a Woman*, 221.

human race.[38] Insisting on the thoroughgoing subordinationist nature of the text, Stone would therefore contend that God's cursing of the serpent by no means excuses the woman in that her suppression was an intended result of the ideologically construed narrative. Other scholars, evidently unwilling to read the narrative systematically through the prism of an antigoddess ideology, simply try to soften the story's sexist implications. For instance, they point out that the man too suffers the consequences of his disobedience and that neither of them is actually "cursed." Many of the latter interpreters view the punishments of the woman and the man as simply explaining (an etiology) why it is that men in ancient Hebrew society had to work the soil so toilsomely to bring forth food and how the dualistic role of women as wives and mothers evolved in that society.

Even if the text were to be read literally (rather than as an etiology or a political ideology), *both* the woman and the man were punished. "If there be moral frailty in one," insists Trible, "it is moral frailty in two." "Further," Trible continues, "they are equal in responsibility and in judgment, in shame and in guilt, in redemption and in grace. What the narrative says about the nature of woman it also says about the nature of man."[39] In all fairness, then, if women must continue to be subjected to characterization as simple-minded, gullible, evil, and ultimately cursed by God, then so must men (after all, it is the man's portrayal in the text as a passive participant that more approximates this condescending depiction). Furthermore, as Gerda Lerner points out, while God punishes Adam by relegating him to mortality, it is in Eve alone that the immortality of the generations lies: "Here is the redemptive aspect of the Biblical doctrine of labor between the sexes: not only shall man work in the sweat of his brow and woman give birth in pain, but mortal men and women depend on the redemptive, life-giving function of the mother for the only immortality they shall ever experience."[40]

38. Ibid., 221.
39. Trible, "Eve and Adam," 256.
40. Gerda Lerner, *The Creation of Patriarchy* (New York: Oxford University Press, 1986), 197.

The Problem of the Punishment of Woman

Because the Eden temptation and transgression have been blamed on the woman, the divine oracle of her punishment has been traditionally interpreted as being weightier than the man's:

> I will greatly multiply your pain in childbearing;
> in pain you shall bring forth children,
> yet your desire shall be for your husband,
> and he shall rule over you. (3:16)

Merlin Stone, understanding the Adam and Eve story to be an intentional ideological campaign by the Levite priests to undermine the goddess religion of Canaan, concludes that the text is irrevocably sexist, which coincides with the fact that Israelite women had to call their husbands "master" and "lord."[41] The result of the myth writers having the male deity punish the woman with painful childbirth, says Stone, was that all women giving birth would be forced to identify with the transgression of Eve.[42]

Other scholars have made attempts (some convincing, some not) to soften the blow of this notorious passage. Westermann says the husband's domination over his wife is a punishment insofar as it is abnormal in comparison to their primal relationship as equals.[43] Trible carries this point to its logical conclusion:

> This statement is not a license for male supremacy, but rather it is condemnation of that very pattern. Subjugation and supremacy are perversions of creation. Through disobedience the woman has become slave. Her initiative and her freedom vanish. The man is corrupted also, for he has become master, ruling over the one who is his God-given equal. . . . Whereas in creation man and woman know harmony and equality, in sin they know

41. Stone, *When God Was a Woman*, 55.
42. Ibid., 218–19, 222.
43. Westermann, *Genesis 1–11*, 262.

alienation and discord. Grace makes possible a new beginning.[44]

Trible concludes that the suffering and oppression that women and men know today are marks of their disobedience and not of their creation; so that in placing culture under judgment and in desiring to return woman and man to their primeval freedom, the myth seems intended to liberate rather than to enslave.[45]

Another means of dealing with the woman's punishment is to contest the traditional notion that "he shall rule over you" implies domination of the sort customarily found in patriarchal societies. Such translations as the New English Bible reinforce traditional androcentric ideas in reading, "he shall be your master"; or the Jerusalem Bible in reading, "he will lord it over you." A preferable translation, according to Carol Meyers, is "he shall predominate over you."[46] Meyers derives this translation by reading the last line of the punishment as an integral (rather than separate) part of the preceding line, thus making it clear that the man is to "predominate" over the woman's desire for him rather than "lord over" every aspect of her life. Following a lengthy examination of this passage, Meyers gives this concluding critique of the woman's punishment:

> Women have to work hard and have many children, as line 1 and 2 proclaim; their reluctance to conform, which is not explicitly stated but can be reconstructed by looking at the biological and socio-economic realities of ancient Palestine, had to be overcome. Lines 3 and 4 tell us how: female reluctance is overcome by the passion they feel toward their men, and that allows them to accede to the males' sexual advances even though they realize that undesired pregnancies (with the accompanying risks) might be the consequence.[47]

44. Trible, "Eve and Adam," 257.
45. Ibid., 258.
46. Carol Meyers, *Discovering Eve: Ancient Israelite Women in Context* (New York: Oxford University Press, 1988), 117.
47. Ibid.

Meyers's reading of the passage thus comes to this:

> I will greatly increase your toil and your pregnancies;
> (Along) with travail shall you beget children.
> For to your man is your desire,
> and he shall predominate over you.[48]

The Question of the So-Called Fall Reconsidered

In God's interrogation of the woman and the man in the garden, the man blames the wrongdoing on the woman and the woman blames it on the serpent. But there is no interrogation of the animal, figures Claus Westermann, because the narrator's intention is to show that the origin of evil is unexplainable.[49] The misinterpretation of this narrative and the misappropriation of this interpretation by hymnologists and hymnists therefore begins when the text is approached in search of an answer to the question of evil, suffering, and death. Because the answer simply is not inherent in the text, when an answer is derived it is only because one has been read into the story. Also, in the search for an answer to the problem of evil, there is a tendency to want to place the blame on one of the story's characters—the serpent, Eve, or Adam—and therefore to force the narrative to thematize an idea that is actually foreign to it.

If there is such a notion as the fall in the Hebrew Bible, it may be the fall of the angels (Gen. 6:1-6) rather than the disobedience of the primordial woman and man. According to the story of the angelic fall, the sons of God and the daughters of men illegitimately procreated, producing mighty and notorious people who provoked God's grief and destruction of the earth by flood. Whether or not this narrative of disobedience and punishment is the preferable story to be labeled the "fall" depends on scholarly interpretation. Generally the Hebrew Bible is not concerned with such abstract and dogmatic issues as the origin of sin, evil, suffering, and death,

48. Ibid., 118.
49. Westermann, *Genesis 1–11*, 256.

but rather with existential concerns of faithful perseverance.[50] The fact is, the disobedience of Eve and Adam during the "prehistory" of Israel enters neither into any discussion of the many sins perpetrated by the Israelites in the patriarchal narratives nor into any of the preachments of the judges and prophets during their judgments of Israel.

In forcing the Eden narrative to thematize the abstract and the dogmatic and to foster oppression rather than liberation, we may be missing the point and shifting the blame, just as did Adam and Eve. "That is why this sin thing has less to do with Eve than with us, with our sins," says Bill Leonard. "We cannot forgive ourselves, so we look for someone else to blame. Who better than our first mother?"[51] Leonard's point is exactly what Walter Brueggemann is getting at when he says the story is not an attempt to assist theologizing but rather to catch people in their living.[52] Perhaps, then, the punishment given Adam and Eve has something to do not just with their disobedience but with their shifting of blame. Perhaps shifting blame is worse than disobedience itself. In forcing the Eden narrative to thematize the abstract and the dogmatic rather than allowing the narrative to catch each of us in our living, men and the male leadership of the church are caught in the unbenign shifting of blame. We need a hymnody of reconciliation and remuneration for this transgression.

Patriarchy's Fall

The tragedy of this long tradition of contempt for Eve in the rabbinic lore, the deutero-Pauline writings, the apocryphal and pseudepigraphical books, and the teachings of the early church fathers and their "sons" is that androcentric readings of the Eden narrative have become deeply embedded in the fabric of modern culture. As codified in church doctrines, liturgies, hymnody, ethical theories, civil laws, and social customs, the status of women has been adversely affected. "And

50. Brueggemann, *Genesis*, 41-42, 43.
51. Leonard, "Forgiving Eve," 1039.
52. Brueggemann, *Genesis*, 50.

of course the more Eve is identified as the source of sin," explains Carol Meyers, "the more urgent becomes the need to control, subdue, and dominate her."[53]

Beneath the successive layers of androcentrism in the long history of biblical misinterpretation is buried the original meaning and message of the Eden narrative. Now that we have carved out this exegetical room, it must be evident to us that men's passing of blame to women comprises the fall of men and the fall of Christianity into the role of, in Mary Daly's words, "patriarchy's prostitute."[54] Just as Adam blames Eve for giving him of the fruit to eat and in doing so blames God, what has resulted from the millennia of patriarchalism and androcentrism is not only the misnaming of women (and men) but the misnaming of God![55]

It is time for men to cease passing the blame to Eve, to every woman, and for us to silence our tongues of such hymns that we sing (unless we choose to revise them radically). For the predominantly male leadership of the Afro-Christian church to continue to create a caste of Eve and woman in our ecclesiology, liturgy, hymnology, and hymnody is for this male leadership to disregard the truth. Truth is the only defense Afro-peoples have against the "ideological weapons of death" that are being used to cause the social, political, and economic demise of the collective African community worldwide. As we will see in the next exegetical prelude, the belief system that keeps Eve and every woman in dire straits is the same that perpetuates the notion that people of African origin are "cursed."

Given our conclusion that the Eden narrative was not intended to imply original sin and given the general pessimistic cosmogony that typifies Indo-Aryan patriarchal society, it seems feasible that Afro-Christians, in their application of hermeneutical control, would reappropriate the optimistic cosmogony of African matriarchal societies, which include no

53. Meyers, *Discovering Eve*, 75–76.
54. Mary Daly, *Beyond God the Father: Toward a Philosophy of Women's Liberation* (Boston: Beacon Press, 1973), 47.
55. Ibid.

notion of original sin or evil entering the world through woman (sin enters the world through man).[56] Since, as I detailed in chapter 2, prototypes of Christian thought are found in Egypt's system of cosmology, it is also feasible that Afro-Christians engender a renaissance in our hymnody by rediscovering our historical threads, as Diop suggests: "The essential thing, for people, is to rediscover the thread that connects them to their most remote ancestral past. In the face of cultural aggression of all sorts, in the face of all disintegrating factors of the outside world, the most efficient cultural weapon with which a people can arm itself is this feeling of historical continuity."[57] Diop further states, "Far from being a reveling in the past, a look toward the Egypt of antiquity is the best way to conceive and build our cultural future. In reconceived and renewed African culture, Egypt will play the same role that Greco-Latin antiquity plays in Western culture."[58]

What we will discover in such a historical retrospection is that matriarchy is probably the oldest form of social organization that still persists in parts of Africa, and that where some contemporary African families tend toward patriarchy, it is largely due to such outside influences as Christianity, Islam, and the secular influences of Europeanism.[59] Even the patriarchal kingship of ancient Egypt was matrilineal: Women were the carriers of the royal blood and perpetuators of the royal lineage. Long before the fierce women warriors, the Amazons, served the eighteenth-century Fon kings of the Kingdom of Dahomey, queenship frequently occurred throughout ancient Africa, especially in Ethiopia. In Egypt, Queen Hatshepsut of the Eighteenth Dynasty was classic civilization's first female pharaoh, a profoundly powerful and politically astute woman. Egypt's women, about whom there

---

56. Cheikh Anta Diop, *Civilization or Barbarism: An Authentic Anthropology*, ed. Harold J. Salemson and Marjolijn de Jager, trans. Yaa-Lengi Meema Ngemi (New York: Lawrence Hill Books, 1991), 113, 311.

57. Ibid., 212.

58. Ibid., 3.

59. Cheikh Anta Diop, *The Cultural Unity of Black Africa: The Domains of Patriarchy and of Matriarchy in Classical Antiquity* (Chicago: Third World Press, 1978), 125.

were no myths of female inferiority as in the Semitic religions of Judaism and Christianity, had equal rights with men, as opposed to the women of Greek society and, later, "European civilization." Additionally, patriarchy has evolved concurrently with individualism—one of the highest values to the Eurocentrist—while matriarchal African societies are traditionally communal. Given that the communities and families of Afro-peoples are actually more communal and matriarchal than communities and families of European origin, it is feasible that a revised black hymnody could build upon this natural structure.

The point is—and our hymnists, choristers, ministers, and laity must heed these words—the subordinationist tradition of patriarchy makes women useless in the light of their potential societal usefulness as Christian sisters and fully free individuals. A revised black hymnody and all new hymns that come from the pens and hearts of black hymnists should edify the Afro-woman, who is, according to the prevailing theory of the monogenetic and African origin of humanity, the mother of us all.

4

Race and Hymnody

If I were God I would regard as the very worse our acceptance—for whatever reason—of racial inferiority. It is too late in the day to get worked up about it or to blame others, much as they may deserve such blame and condemnation. What we need to do is to look back and try and find out where we went wrong, where the rain began to beat us.

Here then is an adequate revolution for me to espouse—to help my society regain belief in itself and put away the complexes of the years of denegration and self-abasement.

—Chinua Achebe, *Morning Yet on Creation Day* (1975)

[F]or both black and white American writers, in a wholly racialized society, there is no escape from racially inflected language, and the work writers do to unhobble the imagination from the demands of that language is complicated, interesting, and definitive.

—Toni Morrison, *Playing in the Dark* (1992)

Discriminating against people of African origin on the basis of perceptions of race is, like discrimination against women, a form of human bigotry found in the Christian church and its hymnody. The customary theological support for this bigotry is the narrative of Noah and his sons, found in the Book of Genesis: the story of the so-called curse of Ham (Gen. 9:18-27). If we found the so-called temptation of Eve to be a dogmatic misnomer, we will probably find the notion of Ham's curse being black skin to be even more indefensible in the light of our historical-critical method. The fact is, if Africans or Africa is at all cursed, it is not with black skin or because of some mythological misdeed of a character named Ham, but because there continues to be a mass exodus of African professionals out of African countries where their skills are most needed to develop economic and educational systems.

If it has occurred to us that the traditional misinterpretation of the Eden narrative warrants the serious consideration of possibly revising our hymnody, then the misinterpretation of the narrative of Noah and his sons should convince us of the feasibility of immediately implementing some kind of revisionary action. By the time we complete our third and final exegetical prelude on the dilemma of classism (chapter 5), which has direct implications concerning sexism and racism, we should be thinking of ways to begin the difficult task of disseminating the need for and of carrying out an actual hymnic revision.

The Curse Interpreted in Modern Times

Talmudic interpretations of the story of Noah and his sons have had an immense and irrevocable impact on the modern world, as have the rabbinic interpretations of the so-called temptation of Eve. The rabbis taught, according to the Babylonian Talmud, that cohabitation was forbidden in the ark but that three had copulated and were duly punished— the dog, the raven, and Ham. While the dog was doomed to be bound forever by a rope and the raven to release his seed

into his mate's mouth, Ham was smitten with black skin.[1]
Another early Jewish myth elaborates on Noah's curse as a
means of explaining not just the color but the physical and
alleged cultural characteristics of black people. The three
principal reasons used by whites to support racist practices—
the so-called curse of Ham, the psychosexual fear of our
alleged sexual prowess, and pseudoscholarly "racial science"—all converge in this text. According to this Jewish
myth, Noah delivers this elaborate form of the biblical curse:
"Moreover, because you twisted your head around to see my
nakedness, your grandchildren's hair shall be twisted into
kinks, and their eyes red; again, because your lips jested at
my misfortune, they shall swell; and because you neglected
my nakedness, they shall go naked, and their male members
shall be shamefully elongated. Men of the race are called
Negroes."[2] Here commenced the transmutation of an etiology
(explaining the subjugation of the Canaanites and the blessing
of the Semites) into a racial myth of truly cosmic dimension.

As I will later discuss in detail, had the flood narrative
concluded at 9:18-19 (minus v. 18b) and moved directly into
the table of the nations at chapter 10 (as some scholars believe
J's version of the flood originally did), then racist theologians
of the nineteenth century and early twentieth century would
have had one less biblical argument to support slavery and
its aftermath of racial discrimination, and racial overtones in
our hymnody would have been undergirded by one less powerful myth. Without the story of Noah's cursing and blessing,
the narrative of the flood and the table of nations would have
served simply as a reminder to the myriad races of the world
that all humankind monogenetically descended from one
common ancestor, that all human beings belong to the same
species, their genetic differences being minuscule to the point
of insignificance. But the text must be dealt with as it stands
canonized in the Bible. My hope is, however, that if we can

---

1. Seder Nezikin, *The Babylonian Talmud*, trans. I. Epstein (London: Soncino
Press, 1935), 745.
2. Raphael Patai, *Hebrew Myths: The Book of Genesis* (New York: Greenwich House,
1983), 121.

correctly understand the text and how it has been misinterpreted and misused historically, then we might better understand that blacks are not cursed. Surmounting this obstacle
exegetically is the requisite prelude to creating a reconciliatory
hymnody that religiously celebrates the great achievements,
in the arts and sciences, of black people throughout the two-
thirds and one-third world, both in ancient and in modern times.

It was probably around the turn of the thirteenth century
that the obstacle of this subordinationist biblical interpretation
became all the more dense and thicketed: Slavery began to
be associated with the "darker races" (perhaps partly because
of the tradition of the Talmudic teachings that Ham's curse
was black skin). While at one point in early Christian history
there was seemingly a relationship between blackness and
wisdom (Egyptian wisdom) and Africans were esteemed for
their contributions as theologians, scholars, bishops, and
popes,[3] by the fifteenth century dark skin came to be associated with evil, inferiority, and ignorance by Europeanists
comprising the emerging culture of white supremacy.

It is this notion that blacks are cursed and naturally re-
duced to slavery that allowed the Egyptologists of this supremacist ideology to account for the archaeological discovery
of blacks in Egypt in the way they did, when they desperately
wanted to believe that its civilization was created by their
own Indo-European race. These Egyptologists, unknowingly
blinded by their racism or knowingly driven by their will to
supremacy, simply concluded that the black majority in Egypt
were slaves. One aspect this theory does not account for,
however, is why a white race of Egyptians would always paint
their gods (Isis, Osiris, and Horus) the color of their slaves—
black.[4] The inconsistencies and contradictions arise because
these scholars attempt to read modern history (a history of

3. See Edward Scobie, "African Popes," in Ivan Van Sertima, *African Presence in Early Europe* (New Brunswick, N.J.: Transaction Publishers, 1985), 96–107.
4. Cheikh Anta Diop, *The African Origin of Civilization: Myth or Reality*, ed. and trans. Mercer Cook (New York: Lawrence Hill Books, 1974), 26, 75–76.

ideological white supremacy) back onto ancient Egyptian reality, or, vice versa, to read ancient Egyptian reality through
the lens of modern history with its Europeanist bias. White
Egyptologists have systematically failed to establish evidence
for the existence of a white Egyptian race. Hence, it has been
up to white theology, in the form of constrictive fundamentalism, to twist that reality into mythic make-believe by allowing such notions as the curse of Ham to persist. As I detailed
in chapter 2, the white theological academy has posited supremacist hypotheses so habitually and with no visible moral
friction, or has refused to muddy itself in reproaching such
notions, that it has become a given in Euro-Christianity that
these racist ideas are real facts. The tragedy is that the popular
theology and hymnody of the Afro-Christian church have
been influenced negatively by this tradition.

As we must come to understand, however, the Hebrew
Bible was not meant to impinge on medieval and modern
culture its ancient meanings in this distorted way, to the degree that it has (probably irrevocably) shaped the ethnological
dynamics of the modern world. The misinterpretation of the
narrative has had an immense impact on the life of Afro-
peoples throughout the world, peoples who, in some form or
another, have contact or some remnant of contact with people
of European origin. American slaveholders, for instance, preferred to interpret the story of cursing and blessing as a myth
relegating peoples of African origin to slavery; and today, as
I explained in chapter 1 with reference to Andrew Hacker,
white supremacists interpret it as relegating blacks to biological, intellectual, and spiritual inferiority. A myth, in this regard, is not something that actually occurred at a given point
in primeval history but something that is perpetually tran-
spiring throughout history because it is seemingly a basic
characteristic of human nature: Noah did what he did because
it is something that is always being done—some are always
relegated to slavery, seemingly cursed; and some always exercise hegemony over others, seemingly blessed. Such biblical
narratives can become gravely threatening to certain groups

of people when they take on this kind of mythic dimension and become prescriptive rather than simply descriptive. They become real problems for Christianity, as in the proslavery South when the story of Noah's cursing and blessing was appropriated as prescriptive of African bondage.

This language of racism and slavery even found its way into European and Euro-American hymnody, which should make Afro-Christians suspicious of the hymns they cherish that were written by hymnists of this very ideology. Perhaps the earliest Euro-American hymn that suggests the acceptance of the so-called curse of Ham as validating slavery is Charles Wesley's "For the Heathens," which first appeared in 1758.[5] Unlike John Newton's "Amazing Grace," allegedly written after his conversion to Christianity (conversion away from his heathenish life as a slaveship captain), all of Wesley's hymns were written following his conversion. Horrified by the mistreatment of slaves, which he witnessed in Georgia (not necessarily horrified by slavery itself), Wesley petitioned God to allow the blood of Christ to free our enslaved foreparents of their "curse" (stanzas 1 and 3):

> Lord over all, if thou hast made,
> Hast ransomed every soul of man,
> Why is the grace so long delayed,
> Why unfulfilled the saving plan?
> The bliss for Adam's race designed
> When will it reach to all mankind?
>
> The servile progeny of Ham
> Seize as the purchase of thy blood;
> Let all the heathens know thy name;
> From idols to the living God
> Their blinded votaries convert,
> And shine in every pagan heart.

When we sing Wesley's hymns, then, we should be cognizant that we are singing the hymns of someone who believed that

5. Warren Thomas Smith, *John Wesley and Slavery* (Nashville: Abingdon Press, 1986), 44.

blacks were the "cursed sons of Ham." We can afford to be more selective than that. Another hymn that explicitly references the so-called curse of Ham is an anonymous piece from a collection of antislavery hymns titled *Freedom's Lyre*, published in 1840 for the American Anti-Slavery Society.[6] The hymn was titled "The Guilt of Prejudice" by the compiler, Presbyterian clergyman and hymnologist Edwin F. Hatfield (stanzas 1 and 4):

> Forgive me, Lord! For in my pride,
> I scorn'd the Ethiop's race;
> And thought they were too darkly dy'd
> To have a brother's place.

> I turned away; and proudly pray'd,
> "I thank thee, God of grace!
> That I of better earth was made,
> Than Ham's accursed race."

A similar hymn implying reference to the so-called curse of Ham is an anonymous piece titled "The Slaves" in Maria Weston Chapman's compiled antislavery hymnbook, *Songs of the Free and Hymns of Christian Freedom* (1836):[7]

> And there are men, with shameless front have said
> "That nature formed the negroes for disgrace;
> That on their limbs, subjection is displayed;
> The doom of slavery stamped upon their face."

That this was hymnody written by abolitionists who sided with the enslaved in the quest for emancipation, hymnody that was mythologically indistinct from the hymns sung by pro-slavery apologists, should lead us to reconsider carefully the hymnody we have sung traditionally. The fact is, most European and Euro-American hymnists continue this tradition of racially subordinationist semantics by referring to things evil and sinful as "dark" and things holy and righteous as

6. *Freedom's Lyre: Or, Psalms, Hymns, and Sacred Songs, for the Slave and His Friends*, comp. Edwin F. Hatfield (New York: S. W. Benedict, 1840).

7. Maria Weston Chapman, comp., *Songs of the Free and Hymns of Christian Freedom* (Boston: Isaac Knaap, 1836). See the facsimile reprint (Freeport, N.Y.: Books for Libraries, 1971).

"light" or "bright" (synonyms for "white"). This language is the outer shell of the inner myth that has not really disappeared but has been suppressed in the subconscience.

For antebellum white Christians who were proslavery and postbellum white Christians who were and still are prosegregation, the story of Noah's cursing and blessing is once and for all the ethnological charter of black-white race relations in America: Ham (the black race) and Japheth (the white race) assumed archetypal dimensions in Euro-America.[8] According to the theological defenders of the slave trade, the prophecy of Noah (the curse of Ham) was to be twice fulfilled, and slavery in America satisfied that secondary fulfillment.[9] For instance, Josiah Priest, in his *Bible Defense of Slavery* (1853), argued that whites in America were the descendants of Japheth and thus that the infallibility of God's prophecy, stated through Noah, depended on the enslavement of Africans.[10] Such reasoning had the pernicious effect of making the veracity of God's self-revelation contingent upon the acceptance of slavery and white supremacy.[11] It also had the consequence of making the integrity of Christian piety dependent upon the holding of slaves.

Another proslavery crusader was Baptist preacher Thornton Stringfellow, who called Noah's cursing and blessing "the first recorded language . . . ever uttered in relation to slavery." Stringfellow believed that when Noah (in God's stead) uttered his judgments, the curse constituted a divine sanctioning of human captivity and merchandising. "May it not be said in truth, that God decreed this institution before it existed; and has he not connected its *existence* with prophetic tokens of special favor, to those who should be slave owners

8. Thomas Virgil Peterson, *Ham and Japheth: The Mythic World of Whites in the Antebellum South* (Metuchen, N.J.: Scarecrow Press, 1978), 7, 8. Shem was the archetype for the red race.

9. L. Richard Bradley, "The Curse of Canaan and the American Negro," *Concordia Theological Monthly* 42, no. 2 (February 1971): 101.

10. Josiah Priest, *Bible Defense of Slavery* (Glasgow, Ky.: S. W. Brown, 1853; republished, Detroit: Negro History Press, [1969?], 289, 393. Cited in Bradley, "The Curse of Canaan," 103.

11. Bradley, "The Curse of Canaan," 103.

or masters?"[12] Others of Stringfellow's and Priest's supremacist ilk and subordinationist ethic reasoned similarly, one being Mississippi Presbyterian preacher James A. Sloan. Sloan argued that just as all human beings suffer from Adam's original sin and women suffer because of Eve's causation of that sin, so does the black race suffer because of the sin of their progenitor, Ham.[13]

The myth of the curse of Ham became even more inflated and insidious when the very nature of the black race was stereotyped after Ham's alleged characterization as lazy, lewd, ignorant, idolatrous, superstitious, and animalistic. In addition, the scientific findings of Darwin were adapted by social scientists in order to affix an undergirding sociology to the ideology of the curse of Ham, an ideology that was already becoming outlandishly mythologized, irrevocably embedded in church hymnody and the human psyche, and increasingly causative of the "American dilemma"—the "color line." Regarding the curse of Ham assuming this measureless mythic dimension, Thomas Peterson says:

> To call the story of Ham a myth, then, means that the narrative was at least more than a fanciful account, for it encompassed mythological truth insofar as it symbolized the white Southerner's experiences and beliefs. The Ham myth encapsulated the aspirations and fears of white Southerners in their relationship to blacks in the antebellum period. . . . Through the myth's expression in language conveying the passive voice, the imperative mood, and the continuous progressive tense, it forcibly validated white beliefs about black inferiority, it legitimized Negro slavery as ordained by God, and it prescribed the proper relationship that should always exist between blacks and whites.[14]

12. Thornton Stringfellow, "A Scriptural View of Slavery," in *Slavery Defended: The Views of the Old South*, ed. Eric L. McKitrick (Englewood Cliffs, N.J.: Prentice-Hall, 1963), 86–87.
13. James A. Sloan, *The Great Question Answered* (Memphis, Tenn.: Hutton, Gallaway, 1857), 68–75.
14. Peterson, *Ham and Japheth*, 132.

Again, the language of nineteenth-century European
and Euro-American hymnody helped confirm the myth that
we, as evidenced by our color, are the so-called cursed sons
of Ham. As I mentioned in chapter 1, Reginald Heber's famous missionary hymn, "From Greenland's Icy Mountains,"
has this telling couplet in stanza 2:

> Can men, whose souls are lighted with wisdom from
>   on high,
> Can they to men benighted the lamp of light deny?

Should we not be wary of the fact that this is the hymn that
was sung by the Amistad rebels (who had become Christians
in their imprisonment) upon their release from a New En-
gland prison and return to Africa in the company of white
missionaries?[15]

Similarly, William Williams's missionary hymn, "Over the
Gloomy Hills of Darkness," refers to the African as "the dark,
benighted pagan" and the "rude barbarian." Usually, however, the color scheme of black equaling evil and white equaling good is less discernible to the consciousness. These hymns
that deride blackness as cursedness are undergirded by the
many more hymns that elevate white (the alleged blessing of
Noah's son Japheth). The double entendre in Heber's reference to his race as "men whose souls are *lighted* with wisdom
from on high" is heard in a host of Eurocentric hymns. Finally,
references to the need for things "dark" to be washed "white"
or made "light" are also numerous. John H. Stockton's hymn,
"Come, Every Soul by Sin Oppressed," has this couplet:

> For Jesus shed His precious blood rich blessings to
>   bestow;
> Plunge now into the crimson flood that washes white
>   as snow.

With pseudoscientific support of theological arguments
being posited to defend slavery in America, antislavery abolitionists had no alternative but to return fire at the level of

15. Cited in John W. Blassingame, ed., *Slave Testimony: Two Centuries of Letters,
Speeches, Interviews, and Autobiographies* (Baton Rouge, La.: Louisiana State University
Press, 1977), 206.

quasi-scholarly biblical exegesis. The learned abolitionists were at least skilled enough in extant methods of historical-critical analysis to say to slaveholders that if they wished to engage in slave trade, it is the original Canaanites they should be hunting down. With the aid of this quasi-scholarly biblical criticism, numerous antislavery poets graced the war of words over the question of slavery with their morally intuitive hymnic verse. As an anonymous hymn in *Freedom's Lyre* indicates, they called to task those proslavery academics who were supposed to be learned in the methods of higher criticism:

> Pray with tears for proud oppressors,
> Trampling on the truth they hate;
> Pray for reprobate professors
> Hast'ning to a darker fate;
> Oh! let mercy
> Check them ere it be too late.

One of the several pieces in *Freedom's Lyre* by Lydia Sigourney is especially poignant and morally penetrating. The editor, Edwin Hatfield, gave it the title "Color, No Index of Worth":

> God gave to Afric's sons
> A brow of sable dye,
> And spread the country of their birth,
> Beneath a burning sky.
>
> To me he gave a form
> Of fairer, whiter clay;—
> But am I, therefore, in his sight,
> Respected more than they?
>
> The hue of deeds and thoughts,
> He traces in his book;
> 'Tis the complexion of the *heart*,
> On which he deigns to look.
>
> Not by the tinted cheek,
> That fades away so fast,
> But by the color of the *soul*,
> We shall be judg'd at last.

The judge will look at me,
With anger in his eyes;
If I my brother's darker brow,
Should ever dare despise.

Although it was the political abolitionists whose presidential candidate, Abraham Lincoln, brought an end to the European slave trade in America, the writings and hymns of the moral abolitionists helped set the moral tone of America, if not by refuting the idea that black people are cursed, then at least by arguing its modern irrelevance "in Christ."

Perhaps one of the most infamous and elaborate attempts to discredit the myth of the so-called curse of Ham was rendered by Charles Carroll in his notorious book, *The Tempter of Eve* (1902). In order to show that the Bible and salvation are fully the possession of whites, Carroll had to deny an African presence in the Scriptures and therefore contest the idea that blacks are the sons of Ham:

> This theory would have us believe that the negro is the son of Ham, Noah's youngest son; and that his physical and mental inferiority to his "white brother" is the result of a curse which Noah put upon Ham for his offensive conduct toward him. This absurd theory had its birth in the Dark Ages; and has descended to us from that frightful period of ignorance, superstition and crime, and because the church advocates it we are expected to accept it as "both sound and sacred." But since the Hamitic origin of the negro is opposed to all the results of scientific research, and to all observation and experience, we should not be surprised to find that it is in conflict with the scriptures, upon which it is claimed to be based.[16]

To accept the curse of Ham theory for the origin of "negroes," continues Carroll, forces the acceptance of certain absurdities: (1) that Noah, a mere mortal, performed a miracle that transformed a "white-skinned, silken-haired boy" into a "black-skinned, woolly-haired negro"; (2) that God consented to this

16. Charles Carroll, *The Tempter of Eve* (St. Louis: Adamic Publishing Co., 1902), 436–37.

absurdity and aided the perpetuation of the curse on Canaan's progeny; and (3) that the curse alone is responsible for the "degraded physical and mental characters" of Negro people.[17] Furthermore, figures Carroll, it is inconceivable that people of this supposedly enlightened age would believe that the offspring of Canaan would also be cursed. Since there was no "negress" for Canaan to mate with, his mating with a white female, by which the Canaanites were conceived, resulted in the birth of mulattoes who were half-white; who then marrying white spouses had offspring that were three-quarters white; and so forth until Canaan's offspring became increasingly white, making it biologically impossible for him to have begotten "pure-blooded negroes."[18]

So it is that Carroll's argument proceeds as he concludes decisively that blacks are neither the sons of Ham nor the descendants of Adam, but rather pre-Adamic apes of the wilderness[19] (an ethnological theory dating back to the sixteenth century).[20] But according to Dorothy Blake Fardan, a white woman who is (and is married to) a member of the Nation of Islam, this is by no means an outmoded idea among contemporary whites:

> Despite the fact that *Newsweek, Nature,* and *National Geographic* have in the past five years alone published impressive feature articles on man's origins in Africa, there is still stubborn refusal on the part of many if not most whites to accept this evidence. It is much safer to retreat to a falsified biblical version of origins and remain truncated, mentally separated from the abyss of universal beginnings. The subtle deception in all of this is that Europeans associated African humans with apes and thus laid the basis for rejecting the white man's association with either.[21]

17. Ibid., 439.
18. Ibid., 439–40.
19. Ibid., 440.
20. See Thomas F. Gossett, *Race: The History of an Idea in America* (New York: Schocken Books, 1965), 15.
21. Dorothy Blake Fardan, *Message to the White Man and Woman in America: Yakub and the Origins of White Supremacy* (Hampton, Va.: United Brothers and Sisters Communications Systems, 1991), 40.

Although Carroll rejected the idea that blacks are the "cursed sons of Ham" in order to posit a different racialist theory, many people of African origin actually accepted the idea of their "race" being the descendants of Ham. Some even accepted the idea of their "race" being cursed, naturally with the presumed assurance that the "blood" of Christ canceled the curse. Others of us, as evidenced in the liturgy of Marcus Garvey's United Negro Improvement Association (UNIA), rejected altogether the notion of cursing. In one of five short prayers from the *Universal Negro Ritual*, compiled around 1921 for the UNIA by its chaplain, Alexander McGuire, we find these words:

> Almighty Savior, whose heavy Cross was laid upon the stalwart shoulders of Simon the Cyrenian, a son of Ham, in that sad hour of thine agony and mortal weakness, when the sons of Shem delivered thee into the hands of the sons of Japheth to be crucified, regard with thy favour this race still struggling beneath the cross of injustice, oppression and wrong laid upon us by our persecutors. Strengthen us in our determination to free ourselves from the hands of our enemy; put down the mighty from their seat, and exalt thou the humble and meek, through thy mercies and merits who livest and reignest with the Father and the Holy Ghost, world without end. *Amen.*[22]

In addition, McGuire's *Universal Negro Catechism*, compiled around 1921 for the religious instruction of the UNIA's youths, contains both a repudiation of the black race being categorized as "cursed" and an elevation of the black race through illustrations of the positive roles Africans played in the Old Testament narratives.

It is not surprising that the racialist myth persisted in spite of Carroll's attempt at a scholarly argument against the theory of the curse of Ham and similar existent theories that the black race is pre-Adamic. In fact, *Dake's Annotated Reference Bible*, published in 1961 and reprinted as recently as 1981,

22. Cited in Randall K. Burkett, *Garveyism as a Religious Movement: The Institutionalization of a Black Civil Religion* (Metuchen, N.J.: Scarecrow Press, 1978), 79–80.

refers to the story of Noah's cursing and blessing as the "great
racial prophecy."[23] In agreement with this doctrine, the Mormons maintained their ban prohibiting blacks from entering
their priesthood up to 1970.[24] Indeed, as recently as 1992,
Andrew Hacker, the white political scientist, admitted, "In the
eyes of white Americans, being black encapsulates your identity."[25] Consequently, rather than black scholars being free to
move on to other critical problems facing the world (such as
the dilemmas surrounding gender and class), we have been
forced to respond to this age-old quandary in a perpetual
effort to cease the misuse of this biblical text and to heal the
damage its misinterpretation has caused us. Afro-Christian
hymnists and those ministers of music responsible for select-
ing the hymns sung in our worship should heed the findings
of these scholars.

Because I am calling for a reformation in the Afro-
Christian church, beginning with a revision of our hymnody,
I will, as in the previous exegetical prelude, turn to the most
advanced biblical scholarship for assistance in reassessing another instance of misinterpretation—in this instance, that regarding the so-called curse of Ham.

Genesis 9:18-27

The sons of Noah who went forth from the ark were
Shem, Ham, and Japheth. Ham was the father of Canaan.
These three were the sons of Noah; and from these the
whole earth was peopled. Noah was the first tiller of the
soil. He planted a vineyard; and he drank of the wine,
and became drunk, and lay uncovered in his tent. And
Ham, the father of Canaan, saw the nakedness of his
father, and told his two brothers outside. Then Shem
and Japheth took a garment, laid it upon both their

23. Finis Jennings Dake, *Dake's Annotated Reference Bible* (Lawrenceville, Ga.:
Dake Bible Sales, 1981). Cited in Cain Hope Felder, *Troubling Biblical Waters: Race,
Class, and Family* (Maryknoll, N.Y.: Orbis Books, 1989), 40.
24. "Mormons Reaffirm Church's Ban on Negroes in Priesthood," *New York
Times*, 9 January 1970, 14. Cited in Bradley, "The Curse of Canaan," 105.
25. Andrew Hacker, *Two Nations: Black and White, Separate, Hostile, Unequal* (New
York: Charles Scribner's Sons, 1992), 32.

shoulders, and walked backward and covered the nakedness of their father; their faces were turned away, and
they did not see their father's nakedness. When Noah
awoke from his wine and knew what his youngest son
had done to him, he said, "Cursed be Canaan; a slave of
slaves shall he be to his brothers." He also said, "Blessed
by the LORD my God be Shem; and let Canaan be his
slave. God enlarge Japheth, and let him dwell in the tents
of Shem; and let Canaan be his slave."

For nearly two thousand years the Genesis account of
Noah's cursing of Canaan (commonly referred to as the curse
of Ham) has raised tempestuous controversy among theologians, preachers, politicians, and ethnologists. It is time for
hymnologists and hymnists to become a little impassioned as
well. The debated questions that have led scholars to exegete,
interpret, and preach on this peculiar passage are numerous:
Why does the good patriarch Noah curse Canaan simply because his father Ham saw Noah's nakedness? Why are Shem
and Japheth blessed for simply covering up Noah without
looking upon his nakedness? Could it be that Ham has en-
gaged in some more serious wrongdoing about which the text
is ambiguous or silent?

These are a few of the questions that arise when hardly
any exegetical room is allowed for considering the original
intentions of the text and the process of its editing. When
more exegetical room is taken and editing is given consideration, then we can raise such questions as: Is Canaan really
Ham's son, or is he in effect Ham, due to the possible synthesis
of two different versions of this story? In exercising hermeneutical control we can also examine the kind of narrative it
is so that the literary genre can give us a clue to the intent
of the story for the people whose tradition produced it. Ultimately we can address the more specific question of whether
Noah's cursing of Canaan was meant to predict, prescribe,
and therefore justify the enslavement, segregation, and abom-
ination of people of African descent throughout the ancient
and modern worlds.

Without question, the story of the so-called curse of Ham has affected all histories of continental and diasporan Africa for at least the last two centuries, due to a tradition of misinterpretation, misnaming, and miseducation. As we have seen, this wrongful interpretation of the biblical narrative has been dispersed throughout the Christian world in part through the popular channel of hymnody. It has been dispersed so much that only its residue remains, so that relatively few would believe that contending with the myth at this time would be important. But given my contention that the psychological, social, and linguistic residue of this myth continues to exist, let us continue our exegetical pursuit. We will begin by examining the form of the narrative in question and where it fits in relation to the form of Genesis.

Genesis: The Book of Beginnings

Noah's cursing of Canaan (Gen. 9:25-27) and the entire narrative of Noah and his sons (beginning at v. 18) constitute an important segment of the primeval history (Genesis 1–11) in the "book of beginnings." It creates a transition between the primeval history that is universally applicable to all human beings and the patriarchal history that is specifically related to the development of Israel. The material that is universally applicable commences with the two accounts of creation (1:1–2:4a and 2:4b-24), which are followed by the disobedience of Eve and Adam (Genesis 3), the narrative of their sons Cain and Abel (Genesis 4), and a folk genealogy of Cain's posterity. A new division (Genesis 5) then begins, identifying itself as a continuation of the first creation account insofar as it bypasses Cain and Abel and gives a folk genealogy beginning with Eve and Adam and ending with Noah and his sons (Shem, Ham, and Japheth). This is followed in the next chapter by the sexual interaction between the "sons of God" and the "daughters of men" (6:1-4), which, as I explained in the previous chapter, might be better suited as a "fall" narrative if such is a doctrinal necessity.

The story of the flood (6:5–8:22) opens a major division. Having witnessed the wickedness, corruption, and violence of human beings, God becomes deeply grievous and sorrowful and decides to destroy the earth by means of a flood. It is the good man Noah who receives the divine behest to build an ark and to bring aboard his sons, their wives, and two (female and male) of every living creature. Following forty days and forty nights of rainfall and an additional 159 days on the high waters, the ark comes to rest on the mountain of Ararat. The families and creatures go forth from the ark, and Noah builds an altar in order to make a sacrificial offering to the Lord (Genesis 7 and 8). The flood narrative (minus the editorial v. 18b, for reasons I will explain) then concludes at 9:18-19: "The sons of Noah who went forth from the ark were Shem, Ham, and Japheth. . . . These three were the sons of Noah; and from these the whole earth was peopled."

The subsequent literary segments—the story of Noah's cursing and blessing of his sons (9:20-28), the table of nations (10:1-32), and the folk genealogy (11:10-29)—form a transition from the end of the flood narrative (9:19) to the call of Abraham (Genesis 12). The latter opens the story of the patriarchs and the saving history of Israel, which closes after Israel's entrance into Egypt and the death of Joseph. The editor's intention for thus placing the above three transitional segments was probably to create a continuity between the blessing of Noah and the calling of Abraham, the continuity being accomplished specifically by situating Israel among the table of nations as the offspring of Noah's blessed son Shem (the Semites).

The entirety of the primeval history (Genesis 1–11) is the work of the Yahwistic (J) and Priestly (P) tradition gatherers, whose narratives took final shape respectively in the tenth and fifth centuries B.C.E. The P source, which includes God's covenant with Noah (9:1-17), highlights such themes as divine justice and retribution (as we saw in the previous chapter). The J source, which includes the story of Noah and his sons (9:18-27), emphasizes the themes of promise and fulfillment and cursing and blessing. In essence, the curse of Canaan (the Canaanites) and the blessing of Shem (Israel) and Japheth (the Philistines?) are the Yahwist writer's means of illustrating the fulfillment of Yahweh's promise of a homeland and prosperity and the promise that Israel would be a bearer of blessings.

It can be postulated reasonably that the pronouncements of the cursing of Canaan and the blessing of Shem occurred no earlier than the Davidic kingship in Jerusalem when Israelite dominance over the Canaanites was certain. The blessing of Japheth, who was to dwell in the tents of Shem (9:27), may have been an addition to the narrative that referred to subsequent and different conditions.[26] At any rate, the J source probably assumed its final form during the age of the powerful Solomonic monarchy (962–922 B.C.E.), when the Jerusalem court loomed majestic as the symbol of political dominance, urban-royal sophistication, and cultural affluence. Therefore, in establishing Israel's special identity as the sole bearer of Yahweh's blessings (now fructifying in the new monarchy), the J tradition bearers rebelled against the threat of syncretism with the allegedly inferior cultures of Palestine, particularly with the Canaanite religion.

The Flood as a Parallel Creation Story

A close consideration of the approximately two dozen parallels between 1:1–2:24 (creation) and 6:9–9:17 (the flood) supports the idea that the flood is, in an intentionally artistic way, a second narrative of creation and Noah a second Adam.[27] One of the parallels that biblical scholar Gary Rendsburg notes is the identical statement the Lord makes to Adam in 1:28 and to Noah in 9:1: "Be fruitful and multiply, and fill the earth." In addition, both the creation stories of Adam and Noah, at the editorial level, are comprised of a fusion of two separate narrative accounts, which means that the editor's assimilation of two flood stories may have been an attempt to balance the two prediluvian creation stories.[28]

26. Claus Westermann, *Genesis 1–11: A Commentary*, trans. John J. Sullivan (Minneapolis: Augsburg Publishing House, 1984), 491.
27. Gary A. Rendsburg, *The Redaction of Genesis* (Winona Lake, Ind.: Eisenbrauns, 1986), 9. For further parallels, see pp. 9–13.
28. Ibid., 13.

The first creation is presented in two slightly different, juxtaposed versions (1:1–2:4a and 2:4b-24). What clearly distinguishes the two is that the first version (1:1–2:4a) commences with the creation of the cosmos and living creatures and concludes with the creation of male and female, whereas the second version (2:4b-24) commences with the creation of a possibly androgynous human being whose loneliness is subsequently subverted by the creation of living creatures and the woman and man from *ha-adam* (the human being). The synthesized versions of the flood story are not as easily discernible, for the stories are not simply juxtaposed but rather are intermixed at the hand of an editor. Lloyd Bailey agrees that the flood narrative is comprised of once separate stories that have been so thoroughly assimilated that disentangling them is nearly an impossible task, a task that has resulted in diverse conclusions.[29] Nonetheless, Gary Rendsburg defends the editor's choice of method:

> But he could not simply connect the two Flood stories as he had done the two Creation stories. The latter, even with their differences, were not seen as mutually exclusive by the Hebrews and could thus be placed side-by-side. But to have done the same with the two Flood stories would have confused matters too much, for it would have required two fresh starts, two covenants, perhaps even two Noahs, etc., and so the solution was to intertwine the two accounts into one Flood story.[30]

Rendsburg's careful listing of the duplications, implicating the existence of two interweaving accounts of the flood narrative, is convincing. Among these duplications are the lists of animals and food to be brought aboard the ark (6:19-21 and again in 7:1-3); the statement that Noah did everything

29. Lloyd R. Bailey, *Noah: The Person and the Story in History and Tradition* (Columbia, S.C.: University of South Carolina Press, 1989), 134. Assigning to the J and P tradition bearers the entire segment beginning at the flood and concluding at the cursing and blessing, Bailey divides the segments thus: (1) 6:5–8:22, a combination of the J and P sources, (2) 9:1-17, the P source, (3) 9:18-28, the J source, and (4) 10:1-32, a combination of the J and P sources (p. 140).

30. Ibid., 134.

God commanded of him (6:22 and 7:5); God's warning that the earth will be destroyed (6:17-18 and 7:4); the description of the people and animals entering the ark and the coming of the waters (7:6-12 and 7:13-24); and the report of the receding of the waters, the opening of the ark, and the drying of the earth (8:1-12 and 8:13-14).[31] In addition, Rendsburg says there is a parallel between God's cursing of Cain (for slaying Abel)—"now you are cursed" (4:11)—and Noah's cursing of Canaan—"Cursed be Canaan" (9:25). The punishments for these crimes (4:12 and 9:25), he concludes, are derived from the root of the Hebrew word meaning work/serve.[32]

It is entirely feasible, then, that there are in fact two combined traditions of the story of Noah and his sons (9:20-27)—one featuring a Shem-Ham-Japheth trilogy of characters and the other featuring a Shem-Japheth-Canaan trilogy. More specifically, it has been suggested that an early version of the narrative referred only to Ham and his misdeed, while a later version (the "Canaan" trilogy) evolved out of new political developments in Palestine, whereupon Israel exercised dominance over the Canaanites. At some point following their entrance into Palestine, the Israelites may have perceived the transgression of Ham as being fulfilled in the cultural behavior of the Canaanites and thus composed the now imperishable and notorious poetry of 9:25-27—Noah's cursing of Canaan and blessing of Shem and Japheth.[33] For the sake of our hymnody, let us take a closer look.

A Verse-by-Verse Study of the Story

The sons of Noah who went forth from the ark were Shem, Ham, and Japheth. Ham was the father of Canaan. These three were the sons of Noah; and from these the whole earth was peopled. (Gen. 9:18-19)

31. Rendsburg, *The Redaction of Genesis*, 12.
32. Ibid., 14.
33. Clyde T. Francisco, "The Curse on Canaan," *Christianity Today* 8, no. 15 (April 24, 1964): 9.

It appears that vv. 18-19 (minus v. 18b) comprise a self-contained unit that originally closed J's version of the flood narrative and opened the table of nations at the head of Genesis 10.[34] The implication is that the story of Noah and his sons (also of the J tradition) is an editorial insert that originally had no relation to vv. 18-19, other than the commonality of characters.[35] This explains why the editor attempted to harmonize the flood and cursing-blessing narratives by adding v. 18b, "Ham was the father of Canaan." Nonetheless, because of the editorial addition of v. 18b, the story (as now canonized) necessarily commences at v. 18.

Seemingly unimportant but critical pieces of information in v. 18a are the names and the ordering of the names of the three sons—Shem, Ham, and Japheth. Evidently Canaan is not yet born, for the text says that the only human beings to enter the ark were Noah, his three sons, and the men's wives (7:13)—the same persons who were told by the Lord to go forth from the ark after the floodwaters receded (8:16). The reference to Canaan in v. 18b is thus the editor's foreshadowing of a new character, according to Allen Ross, a simple reminder to the original audience (already familiar with the story) that he is the son of Ham: "The immediate transfer of the reference to Canaan would call to the Israelite mind a number of unfavorable images about these people they knew, for anyone familiar with the Canaanites would see the same tendencies in their ancestor from this decisive beginning. So this little additional note anticipates the proper direction of the story."[36]

> *Noah was the first tiller of the soil. He planted a vineyard; and he drank of the wine, and became drunk, and lay uncovered in his tent.* (Gen. 9:20-21)

That vv. 18-19 (minus v. 18b) appear to be the original conclusion of J's version of the flood narrative is supported

34. At the hand of the editor, J's version of the flood narrative is intermixed with P (6:5–8:22).

35. Westermann, *Genesis 1–11*, 482.

36. Allen P. Ross, "The Curse of Canaan," *Bibliotheca Sacra* 137, no. 547 (July-September 1980): 225.

by the fact that v. 20 opens as though it were the beginning of a new narrative. Indeed, a new literary type is begun, an etiology (a historical tale explaining some present reality). Thus, in the transition from v. 19 and v. 20, Shem, Ham, and Japheth are no longer individuals but rather personifications of sociopolitical groups.[37] It can be discerned connotatively, then, that the purpose of Noah's becoming drunk with wine from his vineyard (v. 21) is not to comment on the ethics of drunkenness. Rather, his drunkenness is a means of setting up the dramatic event—his lying "uncovered" (naked), whereby Ham could be portrayed as deserving a curse and Shem and Japheth as deserving a blessing.

> And Ham, the father of Canaan, saw the nakedness of his father, and told his two brothers outside. Then Shem and Japheth took a garment, laid it upon both their shoulders, and walked backward and covered the nakedness of their father; their faces were turned away, and they did not see their father's nakedness. (Gen. 9:22-23)

If there are two traditions of this narrative that have been handed down—a Shem-Ham-Japheth narrative and a Shem-Japheth-Canaan narrative—then it is possible that the phrase "Ham the father of " (v. 22) was an editorial addition to the original verse: "And Canaan saw the nakedness of his father."[38] Numerous inconsistencies can be resolved by simply removing the reference to Ham in v. 22, so that it is Canaan who sees his father's nakedness and justly receives the curse in v. 25; or vice versa (as is done in some Greek manuscripts) by replacing Canaan's name with Ham's in v. 25.[39]

As the text now stands canonized, however, the event that leads to the cursing of Canaan is Ham seeing his father's nakedness and, rather than covering him, going out and telling his brothers what he saw. A literal interpretation of this event seems quite feasible insofar as Ham's misdeed is remedied when Shem and Japheth cover Noah with a garment

---

37. Bailey, *Noah*, 159. The transition from v. 19 to v. 20 is the beginning of the move from the *universal* history of human beings to the *particular* history of Israel.
38. Ibid., 161.
39. Westermann, *Genesis 1–11*, 482.

without looking upon him. Because the storyteller or editor was especially detailed in the description of the covering up of Noah, Claus Westermann holds that the text leaves no space for the interpretation of Ham's wrongdoing as anything other than the moral infringement of a son looking upon his naked father.[40]

On the other hand, it is possible that the statement "Ham . . . saw the nakedness of his father" may be a euphemism for what otherwise would be sexually explicit. It is probable that the Israelites naturally made a connection between the character of Canaan in the biblical story and the Canaanite religious culture, which involved ritualistic behaviors and goddess worship they perceived to be profane. Hence, it also seems reasonable to conjecture that the Israelites would have imagined Ham doing something far more licentious than merely seeing Noah lie naked. To this effect, the early rabbinic writings of the Palestinian and Babylonian midrashic traditions (fourth century C.E.) envisioned the crimes of Ham as being homosexuality and castration. The argument in favor of the latter is more intricate than the former. Its plot has Ham castrating Noah, thus preventing him from having a fourth son; so that Noah's cursing of Ham's fourth son Canaan is revenge. The writer of the Babylonian Talmud preferred to believe that both crimes occurred: "Now, on the view that he emasculated him, it is right that he cursed him by his fourth son; but on the view that he abused him, why did he curse his fourth son: he should have cursed him himself?— Both indignities were perpetuated."[41]

When Noah awoke from his wine and knew what his youngest son had done to him. . . . (Gen. 9:24)

40. Ibid., 488. Ross supports Westermann's contention that Ham's only crime was literally seeing his father lay naked, which was a serious act of filial impiety in ancient times (Ross, "The Curse of Canaan," 229–30). Brueggemann too says that although the troubled relation between Noah and the son he curses is given sexual expression, it ought not to be pushed too far. See Walter Brueggemann, *Genesis: A Bible Commentary for Teaching and Preaching* (Atlanta: John Knox Press, 1982), 91.

41. Nezikin, *The Babylonian Talmud*, 477–78. Also see Stephen Gero, "The Legend of the Fourth Son of Noah," *Harvard Theological Review* 73, nos. 1–2 (January–April 1980): 321–30.

The first problem that arises in this passage is Noah's reference to Ham as his "youngest son." This raises a question regarding the order in which the sons' names repeatedly appear—Shem, Ham, and Japheth (5:32; 6:10; 9:18; 10:1). The simplest solution is to assume that their names are not listed in the order of their age. The ordering Ham-Shem, for instance, may be a result of their rhyming.[42] Or, the names may be ordered according to the importance of the characters in the story. On the other hand, those who hold that two stories have been synthesized—a Shem-Ham-Japheth story and a Shem-Japheth-Canaan story—contend that the order of the names is a carry-over from the latter narrative tradition where it is in fact the youngest son (Canaan) who is the culprit and is cursed.

As we move beyond this troubling reference to the "youngest son," the ensuing words regarding what the youngest son "had done" (to Noah) force a reconsideration of what is meant in v. 22a by "Ham . . . saw the nakedness of his father." It has been suggested that the crime of Ham (the youngest son) is that he laid with Noah's wife. Such is the postulate Frederick Bassett posits by referencing Leviticus 18 and 20. In these biblical passages it is clear that to "uncover" a man's nakedness means to "know" (to lie with) his wife: "If a man lies with his uncle's wife, he has uncovered his uncle's nakedness. . . . If a man takes his brother's wife, it is impurity; he has uncovered his brother's nakedness" (Lev. 20:20-21). To Bassett, Ham's offense explains reasonably why Canaan was cursed vengefully: He was the offspring of his father Ham's incestuous relationship with Noah's wife.[43] This solution is even more attractive to Bassett because it has a parallel in the patriarchal narratives, wherein Reuben lay with his father Jacob's concubine Bilhah (Gen. 35:22). Akin to the etiology of Noah's cursing and blessing, which was used to explain the Canaanites' low status in society, Reuben's defilement of his father Jacob's bed is cited in 49:3-4 as the reason

42. Francisco, "The Curse on Canaan," 9.
43. Frederick W. Bassett, "Noah's Nakedness and the Curse of Canaan: A Case of Incest?" *Vetus Testamentum* 21, no. 2 (April 1971): 235.

for the loss of preeminence as the firstborn.[44] Bassett concludes that "a son who has sexual relations with his mother
or step-mother commits a rebellious sin against his father,
since the possession of a man's wife is seen also as an effort
to supplant the man himself."[45] The presumption of the foregoing argument is that the editor of the story of Noah and
his sons possibly misunderstood what it originally meant to
"uncover a man's nakedness," so that his editing caused the
original narrative to turn in a different direction—Shem and
Japheth literally covering up Noah's nakedness with a
garment.[46]

> he said, "Cursed be Canaan; a slave of slaves shall he be to his
> brothers." He also said, "Blessed by the LORD my God be Shem;
> and let Canaan be his slave. God enlarge Japheth, and let him
> dwell in the tents of Shem; and let Canaan be his slave." (Gen.
> 9:25-27)

Whether the crime of Ham was homosexuality, castration, seeing Noah's nakedness, or lying with Noah's wife, it
is the conclusion itself that is important: Noah curses Canaan
to be a slave to *his* brothers (v. 25)—Cush, Mizraim, and Put
(according to the table of nations in Genesis 10). On the other
hand, if Canaan is actually the culprit—that is, if Ham and
Canaan are one and the same in the two synthesized story
traditions—then the text may have intended to say that
Canaan is to be the slave of Shem and Japheth only, and not
of Cush, Mizraim, and Put. At any rate, as the text stands
canonized it is Cush, Mizraim, and Put to whom v. 25 relegates
Canaan a slave; and in vv. 26-27 Canaan is also given over
to the service of Shem and Japheth. To be sure, Canaan's
relegation to slavery is thrice stated to include his service
to five personified peoples—Cush (Ethiopians), Mizraim
(Egyptians), Put (Libyans?), Shem (Israelites), and Japheth
(Philistines?).[47]

44. Ibid., 236. Bassett also identifies the story of Lot's sons by his daughters
(Gen. 19:30-38) as an etiology justifying the disparagement of the Moabites and
Ammonites (p. 236).
45. Ibid., 236.
46. Ibid., 234.
47. Shem is obviously the personification of Israel insofar as he is the votary of
Yahweh, the one true God. The passage (v. 26a) reads, "Blessed be Yahweh, God
of Shem" (*Jerusalem Bible*).

The closest parallels to this peculiar event of cursing and blessing are found in the patriarchal narrative. Walter Brueggemann suggests that the cursing of Canaan and the blessing of Shem and Japheth comprise an early form of the cursing-blessing pattern continued in the relationships between Isaac and Ishmael, Jacob and Esau, and Ephraim and Manasseh.[48] Probably the most familiar of these three is the story in which Isaac blesses his son Jacob (albeit duped into believing it was Esau), giving him lordship over his brothers: "Let peoples serve you, and nations bow down to you. Be lord over your brothers, and may your mother's sons bow down to you. Cursed be every one who curses you, and blessed be every one who blesses you!" (27:29).

The Theological Meaning of the Curse

On the level of universality, the narrative of Noah and his sons fits comfortably into the broader thematic milieu of the primeval history in its thematizing of the human tendency to fall into apostasy. Lloyd Bailey summarizes this theological motif thus: "The 'primeval' accounts . . . stress the fallibility of the human being: humans constantly strive to break the bounds that have been set for them as creatures; they are rebels, whose sovereign must deal with them in ways that are appropriate to their status. There seems to be a reflection upon human kind, with its potentialities and limitations, that stands prior to reflection upon the nature of the people of God."[49] On the level of particularity, the canonization of the story in the Hebrew Bible served the specific political purpose of theologically validating Israel's presence and dominance in a land that had belonged to the Canaanites. The narrative thus serves as a constant reminder to Israel of the Lord's promise of this land "flowing with milk and honey" and (from their perspective) the fulfillment of that promise. That this narrative can be interpreted as both universal and particular in meaning renders it concordant with the idea that it is transitional in nature: It carries the reader from the primeval

48. Brueggemann, *Genesis*, 90.
49. Bailey, *Noah*, 117-18.

history (relevant to all of humankind) to the patriarchal history (relevant specifically to Israel).

While at the universal level the narrative can be interpreted as a myth thematizing the human tendency to fall into apostasy, at the particular level it is meant to be an etiology— a tale explaining why during the Davidic-Solomonic age the Canaanites (Canaan) are under the hegemony of Israel (Shem). Brueggemann, interpreting the story in this way, says, "The narrative is an opportunity to root in pre-history the power relations between Israel and Canaan and to justify it on theological grounds. Political relations are here determined by God's power to bless and to curse."[50] Therefore, concludes Brueggemann, the table of nations is not an ethnological statement characterizing racial groups; rather, it is a political statement regarding Israel's friends and enemies.[51]

Having now made exegetical room for ourselves and having exercised hermeneutical control over the Bible, we can see that all quarters of Christendom that have considered the story of Noah and his sons to be a "racial myth" are mistaken. Unfortunately these ideas still persist in the Eurocentric cultural identity and personality that are derived from a collective societal unconscious; and they persist in the hymnody that has been bequeathed to us from this tradition and supremacist system. Thus, black biblical scholars are forced to retread the stony road, hoping to inspire Afro-Christians to take a closer look at the text, to reconsider the intentions of the original story bearers, and to respond radically to the historic misconstrual of Christian doctrine, historiography, and hymnody.

Following his brief exegesis of the passage we are considering, African-American biblical scholar Cain Hope Felder explains the misuse of the text as resulting from a process of "sacralization": "It is this development that most clearly attests to the process of sacralization, where cultural and historical phenomena are recast as theological truths holding the vested

50. Brueggemann, *Genesis*, 90.
51. Ibid., 92.

interest of particular groups."[52] In other words, there is no doubt that the so-called curse of Ham was relevant and meaningful during or subsequent to the Israelites' conquest of Palestine, but the modern ethnological abuse of the ancient text is unmistakably antithetical to the intention of the narrative's original bearers.

Certainly it is possible, with exegetical room, to uncover the inadequacy of the traditional racialist arguments supporting the curse of Ham theory by pointing out a few simple facts: that it was Noah rather than God who pronounced the curse on Canaan, that the curse was not transferred genetically or biologically, that the curse was on Canaan and left the other three-quarters of the Hamitic family untouched,[53] and that it would be uncustomary of one to curse what God has blessed (see 9:1).[54] However, this kind of returning of fire sometimes seems fruitless, particularly when it appears that some Eurocentrists will not revise their predispositions even if counterarguments are reasoned impeccably. The fact of the matter is—and Afro-Christians need to understand this—that any attempt to interpret the story of the cursing and blessing as a "great racial prophecy" and to attempt to harmonize it with modern times is not supportable by Scripture itself. Such conclusions can be derived only by reading into the text one's bigoted presuppositions. As Clyde Francisco states, "The use of the passage to foster racial superiority is an obvious attempt to prove by the Bible a position previously held for quite different reasons."[55]

Indeed, truth can be expressed in different ways and through various literary forms—etiology, saga, fable, parable, and so forth. Doubtless, the cursing and enslavement of Canaan embodies some truth—perhaps the truth that

52. Cited in Felder, *Troubling Biblical Waters*, 39.
53. These are some of the arguments leveled by Charles Everett Tilson, *Segregation and the Bible* (New York: Abingdon Press, 1958), 23. Cited in Bradley, "The Curse of Canaan," 107.
54. Ross, "The Curse of Canaan," 233. Evidence supporting Ross's claim is found in the later patriarchal narratives where not even Isaac would revoke his blessing of Jacob even though it was dishonestly usurped from Esau (27:28-40).
55. Francisco, "The Curse on Canaan," 10.

Canaanite lifestyle and the goddess religion were perceived by the Yahwists to be idolatrous and therefore to be rejected by God's "chosen people." If nothing else, the "curse" certainly embodies the truth that the land once owned by the Canaanites was to become the land of the Israelites. But is the truth that is engendered in this ancient narrative intended to be universally true and validly applicable in modern times? The answer must be that, as etiology or myth, the narrative is descriptive and not prescriptive, that the truth is particular and not universal. We must understand fully the implications of this: The so-called curse of Ham is by no means intended to legislate the present. It is no more prescriptive—no more intended to legislate the present—and is no more universal than, as we learned in the previous chapter, the idea of original sin.

The great detail I have pursued in this chapter would have been fully unnecessary if the story of Noah and his sons would cease to be read in the way fundamentalists read it—literally, as though it were a story about individuals—and instead would be read as an etiology commenting on sociopolitical relationships between groups of people that occupied ancient Palestine. Lloyd Bailey comments in a way typical of those who, perhaps unknowingly, reap the benefits of the myth's misinterpretation: "If modern interpreters want the story to be literally historically true, then that is their problem; it was not the ancient concern when this kind of story was told."[56] To the contrary, if modern interpreters wish to make the story of the so-called curse of Ham historically true—and, by extension, to make of it an oracle prescriptive or legislative of the present so as to justify the hegemony of Japheth's alleged offspring, "European civilization"—then it is not just *their* problem; it is the problem of people who are black.

Given that this is our problem, it is necessary that Afro-Christians take a close look at the hymns we sing in order to be certain these hymns contain none of the racialist remnants of the theme of the Hamitic "curse" found explicitly or implicitly in much of European and Euro-American hymnody.

56. Bailey, *Noah*, 160.

This hymnody, which helps keep our minds psychologically attached to the image of the white-colored Jesus, needs to be replaced with a "new song" based on a different language. Such a language, according to Molefi Asante, must be aggressive and innovative. This means it must be liberated from captivity to linguistic problems inherited from "European civilization."[57] Thus, the language that fourth-century Ethiopian monk Father Moses ("Moses the black") once used to shame an archbishop is no longer acceptable. While you may be white outwardly, Moses said to the archbishop, you are still black inwardly.[58] African-American psychologist Na'im Akbar alludes that this transformation of language, language that is connected with our internal psychic world, can occur only by removing white-colored images from our outer world.[59] Ngũgĩ Wa Thiong'O is of the same mind-set when critiquing this problem in colonial and neo-colonial Kenya:

> In religious art you'll find that colonialist paintings tend to depict Satan as a black man with two horns and a tail with one leg raised in a dance of savagery: God is a white man with rays of light radiating from his face. . . .
>
> It is the same in cinematic arts and even music: assault our consciousness by giving us certain images of social realities. The musical arts are even more direct in their impact on the consciousness. . . . Missionary Christian songs created a mood of passivity and acceptance—
> . . . "Wash me redeemer and I shall be whiter than snow," cried the African convert to his Maker.[60]

Ngũgĩ says that Africans who composed and sang Christian hymns that praised a white-colored God were always left alone to do so "a thousand times over."[61]

57. Molefi Kete Asante, *Afrocentricity*, rev. ed. (Trenton, N.J.: Africa World Press, 1988), 33–34.

58. Frank M. Snowden, Jr., *Blacks in Antiquity: Ethiopians in the Greco-Roman Experience* (Cambridge: Harvard University Press, Belknap Press, 1970), 211.

59. Na'im Akbar, *Chains and Images of Psychological Slavery* (Jersey City, N.J.: New Mind Productions, 1984), 58.

60. Ngũgĩ Wa Thiong'O, *Barrel of a Pen: Resistance to Repression in Neo-Colonial Kenya* (Trenton, N.J.: Africa World Press, 1983), 57.

61. Ibid., 63.

Contemporary British hymnist Brian Wren came to understand this linguistic problem by drawing racial parallels to
his search for nonsexist language in hymnody. In a general
statement regarding the politics of linguistic oppression,
Wren says: "Language has limited power 'by itself,' but it gains
considerable power—to enable, oppress, or liberate—in the
hands of powerful users. Since power over others is usually
clung to rather than surrendered, it is reasonable to assume
that when individuals and groups have power over others,
they will use language that justifies their dominance, or makes
it seem normal and legitimate, and which ignores, devalues,
or dehumanizes those they dominate."[62] This points back
to the black nationalist ideology first taught in America by
Marcus Garvey. "Glorify your nation in music and songs. Don't
sing the songs of other races." Garvey continues: "Be careful how you sing religious hymns, written, dished up and made
popular by white writers to glorify the white race in the name
of God, taking advantage of the silence of God to impress
inferiority upon your race—such as 'The great white wings
of angels,' 'The white throne of God,' 'Wash me whiter than
snow'—all these are damnably vicious propaganda against
the black race."[63] In our hymnody there are many more such
phrases that glorify "white" and reinforce the permanence of
the white-colored Jesus in the psyche of Afro-Christians:
"Jesus' blood that washes white," "angels bright and fair,"
"saints clothed in spotless white," and countless more. On the
other side of this white-positive/dark-negative dialectic are
such hymnic phrases as "the power of darkness fear," "dark
powers of hell," "the prince of darkness," "deeds of darkness,"
"sin's dark stain," and "the darksome prisonhouse of sin."

Just as sexist language contributes to the perpetuation
of a tradition of female subjugation, so is language that portrays "black" as evil and inferior and "white" as sacred and
supreme a "curse" unto the minds and spirits of black people.
Malcolm X once commented in a speech, "My mother was a

62. Brian Wren, *What Language Shall I Use? God-Talk in Worship: A Male Response
to Feminist Theology* (New York: Crossroad, 1990), 81.
63. See Robert A. Hill and Barbara Bair, eds., *Marcus Garvey: Life and Lessons*
(Berkeley and Los Angeles: University of California Press, 1987), 213–14, 292.

Christian and my father was a Christian, and I used to hear them when I was a little child sing songs, 'Washing me white as snow.' My father was a black man and my mother was a black woman, and yet the songs that they sang in their church were designed to fill their hearts with the desire to be white."[64] For this very reason, Henry McNeal Turner, the nineteenth-century African Methodist Episcopal bishop, prevented his congregations from singing, "Wash me and I shall be *whiter* than snow." Washing, he explained, is meant to make one clean, not "white."[65] The problem, then, is not simply reflected in our hymnody; to a considerable degree the problem *is* our hymnody.

The use of the black-negative/white-positive polarity and all of its dark/light synonyms is not only derogatory in its rootedness in the curse of Ham worldview, it is also poetically outmoded and creatively boring. As Molefi Asante says, we need a language that is more aggressive and innovative—a language that can begin to dissolve the image of the white-colored Jesus etched in our minds.

Brian Wren, who recognizes that systematic language use slants human thinking and behavior, experiments with such an innovative language in his original hymns. He sings of "darkness" as "the cradle of the dawning" and creates such memorable phrases as "Joyful is the dark, holy, hidden God" and "Majesty in darkness, Energy in love."[66] The image of darkness as "the cradle of the dawning" is truly primordial insofar as the Egyptian Isis, the black mother of the gods, symbolizes the primeval darkness, preceding light, that gave birth to all reality.[67] In another hymn Wren writes, "Spirit of brooding night" and "all-embracing night, the hovering wings of warm and loving darkness."[68] These poetic phrases exemplify the kind of language at which Asante is hinting. The only difficulty with these examples, despite Wren's good intentions, is that he depicts darkness in stereotypically feminine

64. Malcolm X, "The Black Man's History" (recorded speech, 1962).
65. R. R. Wright, Jr., *The Bishops of the African Methodist Episcopal Church* (Nashville: AME Publishing House, 1963), 332.
66. Wren, *What Language?* 123, 147.
67. James Bonwick, *Egyptian Belief and Modern Thought* (London: African Publication Society, 1983), 141.
68. Wren, *What Language?* 139.

imagery, the very thing he is against in formulating a counter-
patriarchal hymnic language. *Darkness* is portrayed as "brooding," "all-embracing," "warm," "loving," and "joyful," but never as "strong," "wise," "virile," "victorious," or the like. Thus,
we are thrown back to Joseph Arthur Gobineau's claim in the
nineteenth century that the black race is, from the Euro-
patriarchal perspective, feminine—feminine in the negative
light of the so-called curse of Eve.[69]

Where do we turn, then, for a new language? Ngũgĩ
suggests that we turn to those groups of people who have
sustained the vernacular traditions and kept them dynamic.
He says, "The most important breakthroughs in music, dance
and literature have been borrowed from the peasantry. . . .
Nowhere is this more clear than in the area of languages. It
is the peasantry and the working class who are changing
language all the time in pronunciations, in forming new di-
alects, new words, new phrases and new expressions."[70]

With these very ideas in mind, Asante, steeped in the
thought of Diop and influenced by the polemics of Ngũgĩ,
concludes that in our choice between a consciousness and
language that leans toward oppression and submission or
toward victory and aggression, we must choose the positive
linguistic consciousness that is based on a comprehensive
knowledge of our history.[71] In the light of what I related in
chapter 2 about the Egyptian influences on Christianity, we
can see that contemporary Christian thought, because of certain Eurocentric impositions over the course of history, has
become degraded and fossilized—fundamentalism being one
of the many causes. We must engage in scholarly anteriority
and rebuild our hymnody. In the words of historian John
Henrik Clarke, "I don't think anything is going to save us,
except those things we devise ourselves."[72] We must devise a
revised black hymnody.

69. See Martin Bernal, *Black Athena: The Afroasiatic Roots of Classical Civilization*
(New Brunswick, N.J.: Rutgers University Press, 1987), 1:354–55.

70. Ngũgĩ Wa Thiong'O, *Decolonising the Mind: The Politics of Language in African
Literature* (Nairobi, Kenya: Heinemann Kenya, 1986), 68.

71. Asante, *Afrocentricity*, 50–51.

72. John Henrik Clarke, ed., *New Dimensions in African History: The London Lectures
of Dr. Yosef ben-Jochannan and Dr. John Henrik Clarke* (Trenton, N.J.: Africa World
Press, 1991), 44.

5

Class and Hymnody

A given people today may not be intelligent, but through a democratic government that recognizes, not only the worth of the individual to himself, but the worth of his feelings and experiences to all, they can educate, not only the individual unit, but generation after generation, until they accumulate vast stores of wisdom. Democracy alone is the method of showing the whole experience of the race for the benefit of the future and if democracy tries to exclude women or Negroes or the poor or any class because of innate characteristics which do not interfere with intelligence, then that democracy cripples itself and belies its name.

—W. E. B. Du Bois, *Darkwater* (1920)

I, the man of color, want only this:
That the tool never possess the man, That the enslavement of man by man cease forever. That is, of one by another.

— Frantz Fanon, *Black Skin, White Masks* (1952)

Classism in modern times does not have a biblical myth with which wealthy elitists can apologize for their subordination of the poor. Even though the teachings of Jesus imply

149

the exceptionalism of the "lowly" and Paul informed the Jerusalem apostles that he was eager to and would address the poor in his evangelizing, there is still a triumphalist ethos to much of our hymnody that portrays Christ as a royal and wealthy potentate and possibly even as an elitist. The master-slave dialectic in Paul's letter to Philemon, which we will discuss in this chapter, embodies the tension between Christian equality and social hierarchy—between the high and the lowly, the free and the captive, the haves and the have-nots, the developed (one-third) and developing (two-thirds) worlds. The way this tension is resolved is at the root of the problem of classism (economically based social hierarchy) and the elitist attitudes of the wealthy that support it.

The story surrounding Paul's letter has Paul writing to the Colossian Philemon regarding his slave Onesimus, who had run away and found the apostle in a Roman or Ephesian prison. Onesimus is returned to Philemon with the letter that says, among other things I will detail, that Onesimus should be received back as "no longer a slave but more than a slave, as a beloved brother." We will see that this little phrase, coming from the pen of the apostle himself, is the key to a theodicy— a rhetoric of "spiritual" equality that justifies social hierarchy and frees God from any blame for social inequality. Hence, although most of the discussion in this chapter is centered around the question of slavery, it is theoretical discussion such that the tensions and issues are all relevant to one of the modern equivalents of slavery—classism. Classism, even more specifically, includes such malediction as unjust criminal incarceration, civil terrorism, and the evident problem of being in the "class" of female or "colored."

Toward a Theodicy Reconciling Slavery and Christianity

Given that elsewhere in the Pauline writings the institution of slavery is upheld, that which distinguishes the apostle's ethics in this particular situation is perhaps his own bondage (imprisonment) or, better, that Onesimus is present to Paul, a human being and not a faceless institution or principle. Perhaps this is all that Paul tries to accomplish in his letter, as many Eurocentric scholars have surmised: to get Philemon to see Onesimus as a human being, as a brother, albeit still a slave, and not simply as the "live tool" of an economic enterprise.

George Bourne, the nineteenth-century Presbyterian clergyman and abolitionist, responds to this proslavery attitude with a query as to how it is possible to posit a theodicy reconciling slavery and Christianity. Concluding that Onesimus is exonerated from all obligation by evangelical philanthropy, Bourne insists that anyone who can reconcile the apostolic teachings with slavery can also adjoin heaven and hell. He says, "To him, vice and virtue, equity and injustice, kindness and cruelty, oppression and benevolence, thieving and probity, infidelity and religion, all are identical."[1] Henry Bibb, a fugitive ex-slave of the European slave trade, told this very thing to his former slaveholder in a letter of 1852: "I mean that you shall know that there is a just God in heaven, who cannot harmonize human slavery with the Christian religion."[2] Almost a century later, with slavery abolished, the incompatibility of Christianity and the ideology of slavery seemed still to be unknown to the white churches. This is sarcastically captured in a black newspaper piece of 1951 titled "Christianity and Color Collide in Dixie":

> LITTLE ROCK, ARK.—When a Negro is almost mobbed just because he tried to worship God, then things are really in a bad way.
>
> But that's just what happened to Joseph Harris when he went to the Coliseum here last week to join the Criswell revival. All the trouble started because he didn't choose to sit in the section reserved for "colored."
>
> Six thousand Baptists heard Harris preach a real sermon when he refused to obey two ushers and move into the restricted seats.

1. John W. Christie and Dwight L. Dumond, *George Bourne and The Book and Slavery Irreconcilable* (Wilmington, Del.: Historical Society of Delaware; Philadelphia: Presbyterian Historical Society, 1969), 179, 190.
2. John W. Blassingame, ed., *Slave Testimony* (Baton Rouge: Louisiana State University Press, 1977), 52.

"No, that is not my place," he shouted, and those
six words might have been his last had it not been for
the cool-headed Rev. M. Ray McKay, who followed a
crowd who picked Harris up and hustled him out of the
Coliseum.

The minister broke through the mob of man-
handlers, appealing to them to "be Christians." One
"Christian" shouted back, "What kind of Christian
are you?"

Finally, however, the cleric's words took effect and
the angry crowd let Harris go. . . .

Harris, as yet unruffled, listened to the services for
a while, probably decided he couldn't reach the Almighty
through these "Christians," and headed for the door.[3]

Indeed, there is an incompatibility of Christianity and
slavery—whether of the sort reproached by abolitionist
George Bourne or by the above journalist. This is also the
basic claim in an anonymous hymn included in the antislavery
hymnbook *Freedom's Lyre* (1840).[4] The hymn's opening
stanza reads:

> Strike off my galling fetters—strike!
> My shackles rend in twain,
> Unloose the yoke from off my neck,
> And break my heavy chain;
> Oh! let the breath of liberty
> My burning temples fan;
> For has not God created me,
> A *brother* and a *man*?

The third couplet of the hymn's fourth stanza again questions
the Christian slaveholder:

> Then Christian! why the fetter bind
> Upon a brother's frame?

In the same volume, *Freedom's Lyre*, we see this referencing
of brotherliness in the opening stanza of a hymn by
Josiah Conder:

> O Lord, our glorious Head! in thee,

3. "Christianity and Color Collide in Dixie, Right Wins Over Might," *Chicago
Defender*, 7 July 1951, 1.
4. *Freedom's Lyre: Or, Psalms, Hymns, and Sacred Songs, for the Slave and His Friends*,
comp. Edwin F. Hatfield (New York: S. W. Benedict, 1840).

No diff'rence parts the bond and free;
The freeman feels no more his own,—
The slave is for a brother known.

Despite these glorious strains that sought to tap the emotions and moral conscience of America, Thornton Stringfellow vigorously defended the European slave trade. The first part of his argument, adequately rendered, is that the New Testament does not explicitly denounce slavery. Where his argument falters, however, is in his claim that the New Testament introduces no new moral principle that could eventually cause the eradication of slavery.[5] With historical evidence seemingly on their side, since slavery was in fact eradicated in part by a Christian moralistic impulse, many contemporary scholars have attempted to disprove Stringfellow's notion. In doing so, they have actually posited theodicies (reconciliations) explaining the existence of slavery (an evil) in a world created by the good God that Christians worship. This theodicy, as we will see, is also the implicit justification of classism.

Alexander Maclaren, a late-nineteenth-century biblical scholar, follows Stringfellow's argument up to the point where he says the New Testament never directly condemns slavery and, in recognizing the obligations of slaves to their masters, seems even to condone its continuance. He goes on to argue that Christianity does not sanction slavery but hopes to convert individuals who, person by person, will transform and obliterate such institutions.[6] There is agreement on this basic point by twentieth-century biblical scholars Eldon Koch, C. F. D. Moule, Michael Parsons, and theologian Emil Brunner. Koch does not claim that Paul is arguing for an end to slavery altogether but that the principle at work in this single incident would, in due time, undermine the institution: "The might of the Christian fellowship is apparent when it

5. Thornton Stringfellow, "A Scriptural View of Slavery," in *Slavery Defended: The Views of the Old South*, ed. Eric L. McKitrick (Englewood Cliffs, N.J.: Prentice-Hall, 1963), 94.
6. Alexander Maclaren, *The Epistles of St. Paul to the Colossians and Philemon* (New York: A. C. Armstrong and Son, 1887), 460–61. Maclaren does not perceive patience as being equivalent to passivity (p. 462).

can empower one in the faith to cut across the traditions of the ages, the pressure of his own times, and personal prejudices to free a man from slavery. The fellowship of the faith has power to destroy those bonds. 'To set the captive free' was the mission of Christ, and it is a becoming task for those in fellowship with him."[7] Moule says that insurrections against slavery in the Roman Empire were ineffective, so that what was needed was moral suasion of the kind provided by the Christian teachings.[8] Parsons agrees, saying that the apostles sought to introduce the neglected aspect of simple dignity into the new relationship between masters and slaves and that in doing so slavery was undermined and eventually destroyed.[9] In Brunner's words, slavery was dissolved from within: "The institution or order of slavery is dissolved from within and replaced by the order of fellowship in love without any appeal to a just mundane order. The problem of the injustice of slavery fades into the background. Without even being mentioned it has been solved by something which no claim for justice can achieve, by fellowship in love, by brotherhood."[10] In other words, says Brunner, what Paul wanted for Onesimus, he also wanted for Philemon—brotherhood, which could be achieved only by the transformation of both master and slave.[11]

What is being suggested by Maclaren, Koch, Moule, and Brunner is that community "in Christ" is able to transform master and slave in such a way that the hierarchical dialectic would dissolve. This is what contemporary Christians consciously or unconsciously think regarding the problem of classism.

7. Eldon W. Koch, "A Cameo of *Koinonia*: The Letter to Philemon," *Interpretation* 17, no. 2 (April 1963): 186.
8. C. F. D. Moule, *The Epistles of Paul to the Colossians and to Philemon* (Cambridge: Cambridge University Press, 1957), 11.
9. Michael Parsons, "Slavery and the New Testament: Equality and Submissiveness," *Vox Evangelica* 18 (1988): 90.
10. Emil Brunner, *Justice and the Social Order*, trans. Mary Hottinger (New York: Harper & Brothers, 1945), 107.
11. Ibid., 106.

Christ and "Communitas"

Paul's approach, to William Westermann, would in effect render slavery meaningless, even though it might remain a physical reality.[12] Parsons, as we have seen, follows this reasoning as well, suggesting that slavery could be abolished more effectively once Christian slaveholders were able to perceive their slaves as human beings, moreover, equal to themselves.[13] "The apostles, generally, are not making social comment on prevailing custom, they are asking the question, 'What does it mean to be slaves of Christ in this situation?' or, 'What is the relationship between Christian freedom and social slavery?' "[14] Parsons explains the relationship between Christian freedom and social slavery by maintaining that "in Christ" slave and master are equal. "Both parties are to rid the hierarchical relationship of feelings of antagonism, of superiority and inferiority, and of dehumanizing pride."[15] Eduard Lohse suggests that as equals Philemon and Onesimus are no longer superior and inferior except legally in the world:

> Although Onesimus "in the flesh" is, as a slave, the property of his master, this earthly relationship is now surpassed by the union "in the Lord." There is no doubt that earthly freedom is a great good. Nevertheless, in the last analysis it is of no significance to the Christian whether he is slave or free. The only thing that matters is this: to have accepted God's call and to follow him (1 Cor. 7:21-24). The master of a slave must be obedient to this call, for he, too, is subject to the command of the Kyrios. In this way, the relationship of master and slave has undergone a fundamental change. Although it might seem natural that Philemon grant Onesimus his freedom, the Apostle can leave it to Philemon how he wants to decide. Under all circumstances Philemon is bound to the commandment of love which makes its renovating

---

12. William L. Westermann, *Slave Systems of Greek and Roman Antiquity* (Philadelphia: American Philosophical Society, 1955), 150.
13. Parsons, "Slavery and the New Testament," 95.
14. Ibid., 90.
15. Ibid., 93.

power effective in any case, since the slave who returns home is now a brother.[16]

When Parsons explains that "in Christ" slave and master are equal and equally free from the hierarchical relationship of superior and inferior,[17] the seeming incongruence of Paul's combined utterances regarding slavery is reconciled. In Colossians we read that "in Christ" there is neither slave nor free (Col. 3:11), while eleven verses later we read that slaves are to obey their earthly masters (3:22). Thus, the theory of Parsons, Westermann, and Lohse, regarding master and slave being free of a hierarchical relationship, suggests that to be authentically "in Christ" is to subsist in a sustained state of what anthropologist Victor Turner calls "spontaneous communitas."

But spontaneous communitas is, as Turner explains, a socially transient moment or phase of structureless mutuality that spontaneously and only periodically arises in the interstices of structure.[18] "Spontaneous communitas has something 'magical' about it," defines Turner. "Subjectively there is in it the feeling of endless power. But this power untransformed cannot readily be applied to the organizational details of social existence. It is no substitute for lucid thought and sustained will. On the other hand, structural action swiftly becomes arid and mechanical if those involved in it are not periodically immersed in the regenerative abyss of communitas."[19] This is what Parsons, Westermann, and Lohse seem to be suggesting, that in Christ the magical and endless power of spontaneous communitas can be transformed into the permanent organizational details of social existence.

More realistically, Paul could be suggesting that the occasional immersion of Philemon and Onesimus in the spontaneous communitas that Christian worship and communal

16. Eduard Lohse, *Colossians and Philemon*, trans. William P. Poehlmann and Robert J. Karris (Philadelphia: Fortress Press, 1971), 203.

17. Parsons, "Slavery and the New Testament," 93.

18. Victor Turner, *The Ritual Process: Structure and Anti-Structure* (Ithaca, N.Y.: Cornell University Press, 1977), 137, 138, 140.

19. Ibid., 139.

hymn singing potentially foster would cause regenerative power to flow over into the workaday world and humanize their structural relationship as master and slave. But what really happens when the hymn singing ceases and those caught up in spontaneous communitas reenter the structural atmosphere of the workaday world is that a mere rhetorical bridge is erected to support both (a) hierarchical structures that condone structural inferiority and (b) such universal values as harmony between all people and equality before God. The sum of a and b is seemingly what Turner is getting at when he speaks of "ideological communitas."[20]

What Parsons, Westermann, and Lohse are suggesting— the permanent transformation of spontaneous communitas into the organizational details of social existence—has yet to be seen in the history of Christianity. In fact, the antithesis seems more typical. For instance, some Africans enslaved in America actually felt either that there was no difference in the way slaves were treated by Christian and non-Christian slaveholders or that in fact Christian slaveholders were even crueler in their treatment of slaves.[21]

So, what has typified Christian history is ideological communitas, such as was characteristic among white Protestants during the abolitionist and social gospel movements in America. Even though white abolitionists and white social gospelers were concerned that their movements and corresponding corpora of hymnody express ideas regarding the "brotherhood," freedom, and equality of the races, such ideals were at worst rhetorical and at best in reference to spiritual (not social) equality "in Christ." For instance, in James Montgomery's hymn "Hail to the Lord's Anointed," published in the abolitionist hymnbook *Freedom's Lyre*, are these words that imply the moral as well as ontological and biological inferiority of the "poor and needy" slave:

> He comes with succor speedy to those who suffer
>   wrong;
> To help the poor and needy, and bid the weak be
>   strong;

20. Ibid., 134.
21. Blassingame, *Slave Testimony*, 435.

> To give them songs for sighing, their darkness turn to
> light,
> Whose souls, condemned and dying, are precious in
> His sight.

Further proof of this defective kind of equality is evidenced in Maria Weston Chapman's antislavery adaptation of Reginald Heber's "From Greenland's Icy Mountains," which maintains Heber's pervading ethic of social Darwinism and elitism. It is titled "From Georgia's Southern Mountains" and is included in her antislavery hymnbook, *Songs of the Free and Hymns of Christian Freedom* (1836). Chapman retains the hymnic segment that refers to "negroes" as "blind" and "benighted." Again, in various hymns in *Freedom's Lyre* we find references to the enslaved as "wretched, helpless tribes" and as a "dark bewildered race"—indeed a *class* of lesser beings.

This is not the only clue that the high-sounding egalitarianism of moral abolitionism (and like contemporary moralism) is but empty fanfare of a condescending elite. Many of the antislavery hymns give the clear impression that their concern is not really (or solely) for the enslaved but for the "stain" that slavery places on the garment of their white race. This is certainly true of the political abolitionists, whose interest (also expressed in song) was not so much in the enslaved as it was in saving the union, which slavery could undermine. But it is moral abolitionism that concerns us here, for the argument of the moral abolitionists for the abolition of slavery was explicitly Christian, as are contemporary justifications for classist hierarchy. In a hymn by moral abolitionist Lydia Sigourney, "We Have a Goodly Clime," in *Freedom's Lyre*, we find this stanza:

> We have a birth-right proud,
> For our young sons to claim,—
> An eagle soaring o'er the cloud
> In freedom and in fame;
> We have a scutcheon bright,
> By our forefathers bought;
> But lo! a blot disdains its white!
> Who hath such evil wrought?

Even the radical moral abolitionist William Lloyd Garrison, founding editor of the antislavery newspaper *The Liberator*, could not escape this racial elitism. In his most famous hymn, "Ye Who in Bondage Pine," also in *Freedom's Lyre*, Garrison expresses concern for the staining of his racial birthright. Not only do the tears of the slave, he says, "bedew *our* plains," but their "blood *our* glory stains." Garrison's alarm is particularly high since he perceived slavery in America to be even worse than in ancient Rome (Roman slavery obviously being used as a symbol of utmost immorality because of its historical anteriority):

> Of slavery—worse than e'er
> Rome's slaves were doom'd to bear,
> Horrid beyond compare.

In another couplet, Garrison, addressing his strains directly to the slaves, seems to be in consensus with the prevailing notion of white supremacy:

> Uprising, take your place
> Among earth's noblest race.

To the moral abolitionists the progeny of Africa may or may not be cursed; but slavery, to be sure, is a curse—for the captors as well as the captives. Garrison's "Savior! Though by Scorned Requited," also in *Freedom's Lyre*, reads:

> Help us ev'ry chain to sever—
> Ev'ry captive to set free—
> And our guilty land deliver
> From the curse of slavery.

Another semantic reversal of this kind occurs in Josiah Conder's hymn "O Lord, Our Glorious Head," where it is the oppressors who are called slaves—specifically, "ruthless slaves of gold."

Akin to the moral abolitionists, when social gospelers preached and sang about the fraternity of the "race," they were not thinking of the oneness of the European race of former masters and the African race of former slaves. They were not even thinking of social desegregation or class equality but symbolically (and more comfortably) of "spiritual" oneness "in Christ." F. Lyall makes a similar point by comparing a "Christian slave" to the status of a "freedman" who, under Roman law, is still partially subject to his owner (now his patron): "The point Paul is making is clearly the fundamental equality and worth of the individual believer. The slave Christian is a *freedman*, a full human being yet not detached from this patron."[22] This, I believe, is the underlying apology for the new slavery of classism and other forms of hierarchism. However, this syndrome of the "free slave" is not true liberty, as Elijah Muhammad of the Nation of Islam also recognized. Muhammad said, "We do not believe that we are equal with our slave-masters in the status of 'Freed slaves.' "[23]

Given my claim that spontaneous communitas is but temporary and that ideological communitas is ethically inadequate because it creates a rhetorical illusion of equality, let us now take a closer look at Paul's letter in order to flush out further debate.

Philemon 8-21

Accordingly, though I am bold enough in Christ to command you to do what is required, yet for love's sake I prefer to appeal to you—I, Paul, an ambassador and now a prisoner also for Christ Jesus—I appeal to you for my child, Onesimus, whose father I have become in my imprisonment. (Formerly he was useless to you, but now he is indeed useful to you and to me.) I am sending him back to you, sending my very heart. I would have been glad to keep him with me, in order that he might serve me on your behalf during my imprisonment for the gospel; but I preferred to do nothing without your consent in order that your goodness might not be by compulsion but of your own free will. Perhaps this is why he was parted from you for a while, that you might have him

22. F. Lyall, "Roman Law in the Writings of Paul—The Slave and the Freedman," *New Testament Studies* 17 (1970–71): 78–79.
23. Elijah Muhammad, *Message to the Blackman in America* (Chicago: Muhammad Mosque of Islam No. 2, 1965), 163.

back for ever, no longer as a slave but more than a slave, as a beloved brother, especially to me but how much more to you, both in the flesh and in the Lord. So if you consider me your partner, receive him as you would receive me. If he has wronged you at all, or owes you anything, charge that to my account. I, Paul, write this with my own hand, I will repay it—to say nothing of your owing me even your own self. Yes, brother, I want some benefit from you in the Lord. Refresh my heart in Christ. Confident of your obedience, I write to you, knowing that you will do even more than I say.

The traditional narrative surrounding this New Testament book, as I have explained partly, is that the apostle Paul has written a letter to Philemon, a member of the church in Colossae, regarding Philemon's slave, Onesimus, who had run away. Having managed to locate the apostle Paul in Rome (some say Ephesus), where Paul was imprisoned, Onesimus became a Christian and consequently Paul's spiritual son. Sometime after Onesimus's conversion Paul wrote to Philemon in an attempt to rectify or redeem the former master-slave relationship.

Scholars have repeatedly raised questions about the accuracy of some of these historical determinations. But our concern is not where Paul was imprisoned, how or why Onesimus found him, by what route Paul's letter got to Colossae, or whether the slave owner was Philemon (the first named in Paul's salutation) or Archippus (the third named).[24] The question we are concerned about, as we examine the parameters of a revised black hymnody, is what Paul expected of the recipient of the letter (I will call him Philemon) and, as regards the issue of slavery and its modern progeny (classism), what Paul could have meant by Philemon receiving Onesimus back "no longer as a slave but more than a slave, as a beloved brother" (v. 16).

24. Traditionally it has been held that Philemon, the first mentioned in the letter, was the owner of Onesimus. John Knox (and a number of scholars who agree with him) claims that the slave owner was Archippus, the third addressed in the letter (John Knox, *Philemon among the Letters of Paul*, rev. ed. [Nashville: Abingdon Press, 1959], 58). His argument is convincing, but I will call the slavemaster Philemon.

Was Paul really grappling with the ethical dilemma of social slavery, or was he simply trying to get Philemon to spare the life of the converted slave who, according to Roman law, could have been put to death for his defiant act of running away? This is a reasonable consideration, particularly if Paul's letter is read through the lens of a similar letter written by a Roman official named Pliny to his friend Sabinianus. Pliny's letter reads in part:

> Your freedman, with whom you had told me you were vexed, came to me and, throwing himself down before me, clung to my feet, as if they had been yours. He was profuse also in his tears and his entreaties; he was profuse also in his silence. In short, he convinced me of his penitence. I believe that he is, indeed, a reformed character, because he feels that he has done wrong. You are angry, I know; and you have reason to be angry, this also I know; but mercy wins the highest praise just when there is the most righteous cause for anger. You loved the man, and I hope you will continue to love him; meanwhile, it is enough that you should allow yourself to yield to his prayers. . . . I am afraid lest I should appear not to ask, but to compel, if I should add my prayers to his.[25]

It appears that Pliny was beckoning Sabinianus to restore the former slave unharmed to his previous position. This also could have been Paul's intention in writing to Philemon. The essential question thus becomes: Was Paul only concerned about Onesimus, or was the problem of slavery itself the issue?

If Onesimus alone was Paul's concern, then Paul simply may have wanted his newborn spiritual son restored to his former relationship with Philemon but now treated as a brother in a way that would humanize their master-slave relationship. Rather than Onesimus being treated as a mere "live tool" (as Aristotle defines a slave),[26] Paul could have wanted Philemon to treat Onesimus as a real human being,

---

25. Cited in Charles R. Erdman, *The Epistles of Paul to the Colossians and to Philemon* (Philadelphia: Westminster Press, 1933), 119–20.

26. Aristotle, *Politics*. Cited in J. Estill Jones, "The Letter to Philemon—An Illustration of *Koinonia*," *Review and Expositor* 46, no. 4 (October 1949): 454.

to receive him essentially as he would receive Paul. Paul also had the option of exhorting Philemon to follow the more humane slavery laws of Judaism, wherein slaves were generally to serve no more than six years and in the seventh year were to go free, carrying with them material goods that would facilitate their transition to freedom (Deut. 15:12-14). Moreover, there was precedent among the monastic Essenes of Palestine for Paul to have denounced slavery as altogether antithetical to the natural law of human equality.[27] Although slavery was underwritten by Greek philosophy (as Aristotelian philosophy has underwritten hierarchism/classism in the West), the apostle could have argued that those "in Christ" should not be holders of slaves like those who are not "in Christ."

What we are faced with in the letter to Philemon, then, is a theodicy problem—specifically, the incompatibility of the morality of Christ and the immorality of slavery and classist hierarchy. This is the question on which this chapter gives some reflection as an exegetical prelude to a revised black hymnody. Let us continue, then, with a detailed examination of Paul's letter, beginning with its literary structure.

The Structure of Philemon

Did Paul want Onesimus returned to him to help in his missionary evangelism? Was Onesimus's assistance to Paul the condition of his possible manumission? Or did Paul want Onesimus set free so that Onesimus could do as he himself pleased? Whatever the intent of the letter, Pliny's letter to Sabinianus helps us to see Philemon as a document possibly not intended to be read literally but as writing conceived according to the art of persuasion well known to the scholars of Paul's day. Pliny, whose argument in behalf of Sabinianus's freedman is a plea for a pardon, aims his rhetorical reasoning toward the forgiveness of the former slave owner. Paul's argument is not for mercy upon Onesimus but for Philemon and Onesimus to treat each other as brothers.[28]

27. Moule, *The Epistles of Paul*, 11.
28. F. Forrester Church, "Rhetorical Structure and Design in Paul's Letter to Philemon," *Harvard Theological Review* 71, nos. 1–2 (January-April 1978): 32.

Forrester Church contends that Paul was a master of rhetoric and was not simply making a request but intentionally using learned tactics to advance an argument.[29] With reference to the writings of Aristotle, Quintilian, and Cicero, Church defines three kinds of rhetoric—that used to exhort or dissuade, to accuse or defend, and to praise or blame. He figures that Paul used the first kind, deliberative rhetoric, the three parts of which—the exordium, the proof, and the peroration—correspond with the parts of his letter.[30]

The exordium, according to the teachings of the classic rhetoricians, is a prelude that establishes the mood of the ensuing argument and attempts to win the goodwill of the hearer by linking praise for the hearer to the argument's intent. Following his salutation to Philemon, Apphia, and Archippus, in the name of the Father and Christ Jesus (vv. 1-3), Paul satisfies the requirements of the exordium by thanking God for what he has heard of the demonstrations of love and faith by these three Christian fellow workers (vv. 4-7). Then he launches into the proof, the formal part of the argument that attempts (by appealing to reason and emotion) to establish *honor* and *advantage* as the motives for the requested action. In his proof (vv. 8-16), Paul suggests that Philemon's obedience to the request is the honorable thing to do, since Paul himself is a "prisoner for Christ Jesus" (v. 9), and ambassador (or "old man" as the Jerusalem Bible translates it) (v. 9), and has become Onesimus's spiritual father (v. 10). The stated advantage immediately follows this appeal to the emotive when Paul says that Onesimus was formerly useless to Philemon but now is very useful to both of them (v. 11). Paul proceeds even further (possibly following Cicero's instruction that in cases where one is arguing a particularly scandalous case he must shift the attention of the hearer away from the one who is hated by substituting in his place one who is loved):[31] The apostle embodies himself in Onesimus

29. Ibid., 17, 21, 25.
30. Ibid., 18, 19–21.
31. Ibid., 27.

and binds Philemon to the relationship (vv. 15-16). The peroration (vv. 17-22), which immediately ensues, consists of a restatement of the appeal (v. 17), an amplification of the argument (vv. 18-19), a situating of the hearer in an emotional mind-set (v. 20), and the winning over of the hearer's favor (vv. 21-22).

An excellent argument, indeed, is Paul's letter. In fact, it is such a well-behaved argument that when it is said that only Paul could have written this masterful and tactful piece,[32] it is true not because of its mastery or tact. Any scholar who is learned in the teachings of Aristotle, Quintilian, and Cicero probably could have restored Onesimus unharmed to his former relationship with Philemon; but not any rhetorician could have won Onesimus's manumission. What is unique about the letter is that Paul makes the common religious faith of Onesimus and Philemon the reason for his appeal.[33] Let us see more closely how all of this is made to work by examining, line by line, Paul's proof and peroration.

A Verse-by-Verse Reading of Paul's Proof and Peroration

Accordingly, though I am bold enough in Christ to command you to do what is required, yet for love's sake I prefer to appeal to you—I, Paul, an ambassador and now a prisoner also for Christ Jesus. (Philemon 8-9)

Paul does not hesitate to command his churches to provide for his needs (as evidenced in his epistle to the Philippians) or to alter inappropriate behavior (as evidenced in his epistle to the Corinthians). Perhaps these specific commands are what he has in mind when he says to Philemon that he is bold enough to command him to do what is required. In fact, at the close of the letter, Paul more or less does command Philemon to do what is required and provide for his needs, but he masks his command for Philemon's "obedience" as

---

32. P. N. Harrison, "Onesimus and Philemon," *Anglican Theological Review* 32, no. 4 (October 1950): 270.
33. Koch, "A Cameo of *Koinonia*," 184.

an "appeal" couched in egalitarian language. As Norman Petersen recognizes, Paul, in spite of his "egalitarian rhetoric," relates to Philemon and Onesimus as a superior, namely, as a father.[34] It is not merely for "love's sake," then, that Paul chooses to appeal to Philemon; it is also for the sake of Paul satisfying the requirement of tact in rhetorical persuasion. Or, to put it differently, Paul is appealing not only to Philemon's love (the Jerusalem Bible says, "I am appealing to your love instead") but also to his rationality. While it is true, says Petersen, that Paul uses the nonauthoritarian value of love as mediation between his authority in the church and Philemon's in the world (as a legal slave owner),[35] Paul ultimately tips the scales in his own favor:

> Paul cannot secure his goals with Philemon by pitting superior [an apostle in the church] against superior [a legal slave owner in the world] across domains. . . . The strategy of Paul's approach is therefore to ensure Philemon's acknowledgment of this by addressing him as a fellow worker, brother, and partner, and in the process disclosing to him the apostolic authority that lies behind his anti-structural address. Paul, therefore, implicitly acknowledges Philemon's position of structural authority in the world but attacks it through his employment of anti-structural masks.[36]

> *I appeal to you for my child, Onesimus, whose father I have become in my imprisonment. (Formerly he was useless to you, but now he is indeed useful to you and to me.)* (Philemon 10-11)

There is some debate over whether Paul is making a request on behalf of or concerning his child Onesimus.[37] Semantically, Paul is writing concerning Onesimus. Even if the correct translation were "on behalf of," Paul's letter is still

34. Norman R. Petersen, *Rediscovering Paul: Philemon and the Sociology of Paul's Narrative World* (Philadelphia: Fortress Press, 1985), 104.
35. Ibid., 106.
36. Ibid., 170.
37. See a discussion of this in Sara C. Winter, "Paul's Letter to Philemon," *New Testament Studies* 33, no. 1 (January 1987): 6.

written "concerning" Onesimus, for in either case the preposition or prepositional phrase is qualified by its reference to Onesimus as Paul's spiritual son. When Paul speaks of Onesimus as his "child," he probably is thinking of the rabbinic precept where a convert is viewed as a "child just born."[38] The Talmud indicates that one who teaches his neighbor's son the Torah can lawfully claim him as his own begotten son.[39]

But is one's "child just born" to be looked upon as a "live tool" (a slave)? To paraphrase: Formerly he was a useless tool to you but now he is a spiritual tool valuable as a brother and a slave to both of us. My question is rhetorical, like Paul's play on Onesimus's name (which means "useful"), but Paul's wordplay seems to imply that even after his conversion (symbolized by his change from being useless to useful) Onesimus is still looked upon as one whose place it is to serve. Paul does not say, for instance, formerly he was useless but now you and I can be useful to him by serving him as our Christian brother, as we serve Christ.

> *I am sending him back to you, sending my very heart. I would have been glad to keep him with me, in order that he might serve me on your behalf during my imprisonment for the gospel; but I preferred to do nothing without your consent in order that your goodness might not be by compulsion but of your own free will.* (Philemon 12-14)

Dwight Pentecost suggests that Paul's imprisonment is not *because of* Christ but *by* and *for* Christ for the purpose of witnessing to the Gentiles with whom he came in contact during his trials and imprisonments.[40] Says Pentecost, "Paul used his prison as a pulpit."[41] Erwin Goodenough, conversely, insists that Paul is not in prison at all, that his reference to "imprisonment for the gospel" is metaphorical (and hence

38. David Daube, "Onesimus," *Harvard Theological Review* 79, nos. 1–3 (January/April/July 1986): 40.

39. Cited in Jones, "The Letter to Philemon," 462.

40. J. Dwight Pentecost, "Paul the Prisoner," *Bibliotheca Sacra* 129, no. 514 (April–June 1972): 136.

41. J. Dwight Pentecost, "Studies in Philemon," *Bibliotheca Sacra* 130, no. 519 (July–September 1973): 250.

rhetorical). In other words, soon Paul would be free from his pressing engagements to visit Philemon.[42] This is unlikely, though, based on the fuller account of Paul's imprisonments, beatings, whippings, stoning, and so forth in his letter to the Corinthians (2 Cor. 11:23-27).

More important than whether Paul is (or for what purpose he may be) in prison is whether he is asking Philemon for Onesimus to be returned to him to serve him during his imprisonment(s). Paul's forthright acknowledgment that he would like to keep Onesimus with him could be a foreshadowing of the "more" with which he ends his peroration: "I write to you, knowing that you will do even *more* than I say" (v. 21).

> *Perhaps this is why he was parted from you for a while, that you might have him back for ever, no longer as a slave but more than a slave, as a beloved brother, especially to me but how much more to you, both in the flesh and in the Lord. So if you consider me your partner, receive him as you would receive me.*
> (Philemon 15-17)

In vv. 13-14, Paul seems to have been hinting that he would like to have Onesimus returned to him according to the exercise of Philemon's free will. Then he appears to contradict that when he refers to Philemon having Onesimus back "for ever." But there is no real contradiction: To have Onesimus back "for ever, . . . as a . . . brother" does not cancel out the possibility that Paul wants Onesimus returned to him, for "brotherhood," both in the flesh and in the spirit, is not dependent on the proximity of kin.

In petitioning Philemon to welcome Onesimus back as a "brother," Paul seems to be arguing for the equality of the two Christian men, not merely for mercy upon the fugitive slave. To have asked Philemon to be merciful (as Pliny petitions Sabinianus in his letter regarding the freedman) would have implied that a superior is bestowing forgiveness on an

42. Erwin R. Goodenough, "Paul and Onesimus," *Harvard Theological Review* 22, no. 1 (January 1929): 182.

inferior.[43] Paul does not stumble directly into that problem of classism, but he does stumble into it. First, his suggestion that Philemon welcome Onesimus back "as a beloved brother" does not seem to do justice to the new structural relation seemingly intended by "no longer as a slave." Sara Winter says that although Philemon might now welcome Onesimus back as a Christian "brother," brotherhood does not imply manumission.[44] Hence, if brotherhood is not taken by Philemon to imply manumission, then his response would basically be one of forgiveness: a superior bestowing forgiveness on an inferior.

Clearly this crucial passage does not certify that Paul is speaking of manumission. "No longer as a slave" and "as a beloved brother" are congruent ideas and appear to correct the seeming incompatibility of being a "slave" and "brother." But this congruency is somewhat disrupted by the segment connecting these two phrases—"but *more* than a slave." Philemon is to welcome Onesimus back as "no longer a slave *but more than a slave*, as a beloved brother."

Those of us who understand the inadequacy of the mere rhetoric of liberation might ask how Onesimus could be "*more* than a slave" without still being a slave. The "no longer as a slave" is so qualified by the phrase that follows it that it could very well mean, "no longer [*just*] a slave, but [*also*] a beloved brother." Other translations basically present the same problem. The King James Version reads, "not now as a slave, but above a slave, a beloved brother"; and the Jerusalem Bible says, "not as a slave any more, but something much better than a slave, a dear brother." In these instances we would know that one could be "above" or "much better than" a slave only if one were no longer a slave. But even these translations are not problem free. If "in Christ" there is no slave or free, then how can one be "above a slave" or "something much better than a slave" unless slavery or slavehood (hierarchy or

43. Church, "Rhetorical Structure," 32.
44. Winter says that Paul's speaking of manumission is clear only later when he says "receive him as you would me" (v. 17) and "I write you, knowing that you will do even more than I say" (v. 21) (Winter, "Paul's Letter to Philemon," 10, 11).

classism of some sort) were still permitted to exist? On the basis of language alone, it appears that Paul believes it possible for one (including Onesimus) to be both a slave and a Christian brother. Many Eurocentric scholars in fact believe this to be what Paul is suggesting. This is the "theodicy" I will later examine as the basis of apologies for classist hierarchy in modern reality.

> *If he has wronged you at all, or owes you anything, charge that to my account. I, Paul, write this with my own hand, I will repay it—to say nothing of your owing me even your own self. Yes, brother, I want some benefit from you in the Lord. Refresh my heart in Christ.* (Philemon 18-20)

Sara Winter argues that Onesimus was sent to the apostle on behalf of the Colossae church.[45] However, the "if he has wronged you" (v. 18) may in fact imply that Onesimus ran away (the traditional view). Thus, Winter's argument is even less feasible (and certainly less creative) than the possibility that Philemon sent Onesimus to Paul to be instructed to be an obedient and "useful" slave (since before he was useless) or, better, that Onesimus overheard the Christian gospel of liberation being preached and ran away seeking Paul in order to be converted and set free.

Just as traditional as the idea that Onesimus ran away is the notion that he stole something from his master. Dwight Pentecost reasons that no fugitive slave could have made a journey from Colossae to Rome without having stolen goods from his master.[46] The text, however, does not implicate Onesimus as having stolen anything. In fact, it is rather pretentious for a person who has never been a slave and who is among the privileged class to portray a slave negatively as one who steals (the same holds true for hymnody that portrays the "poor and needy" as moribund). Why read that into the text when Paul simply says, "*If* he has wronged you"? Moreover, Paul uses "if" rhetorically, for the slave owner has indeed

45. Winter, "Paul's Letter to Philemon," 2.
46. J. Dwight Pentecost, "Studies in Philemon," *Bibliotheca Sacra* 130, no. 517 (January–March 1973): 51.

been wronged, according to Roman law. Whether or not Onesimus stole food and supplies from his master, the fact is that he illegally stole himself, and that alone is sufficient for him to be crucified.

Pentecost also draws a comparison between Paul's promise to pay the debt of another (Onesimus) who could not pay it (v. 18) and the Lukan narrative of the Good Samaritan who promises to pay the innkeeper the debt that would be incurred by the man who had fallen among thieves.[47] Indeed, the contemporary liberationist view of slavery is that a slave is a human being fallen among thieves. But, Pentecost is suggesting, Paul is reminding Philemon that he was once in a similar position before God that Onesimus is now in before him: He faced death because of his sin. "Jesus Christ came to strike off the shackles," says Pentecost, "to declare man free from the bondage in which he was born."[48]

> *Confident of your obedience, I write to you, knowing that you will do even more than I say.* (Philemon 21)

Paul uses forthright authoritative language here (his petitioning Philemon's "obedience"), which he forfeits using near the beginning of the letter. This requested obedience is in direct reference to the "more" ("I write to you, knowing that you will do even *more* than I say"), which numerous scholars hold to imply Onesimus's manumission and return to Paul. P. N. Harrison says, "We can safely say that in all probability Philemon took Paul's hint and returned Onesimus to him, as no longer a slave, but a brother in Christ, free to render those services of which Christ's prisoner stood in such urgent need."[49] John Knox similarly suggests that part of the reason this letter is occasionally interpreted as having a proslavery slant is that full value has not been given to Paul's petitioning Philemon to do "more."[50] While Forrester Church

47. Ibid., 55.
48. J. Dwight Pentecost, "Grace for the Sinner," *Bibliotheca Sacra* 129, no. 515 (July–September 1972): 223–24.
49. Harrison, "Onesimus and Philemon," 276–77.
50. Knox, *Philemon*, 30.

views Paul's appeal to Philemon to do the "more" as but a
satisfying of the peroration of the deliberative argument—as
but a means of trumping Paul's argument in a flattering and
persuasive way[51]—Norman Petersen sees Paul's rhetoric and
reality as indivisible. "His rhetoric is the form through which
he exercises his role," says Petersen, "and Philemon, like ourselves, apprehends the role through the form in which it is
expressed. He can be no less aware of the total reality than
we are."[52] According to Estill Jones, even if the "more" were
mere rhetoric, even if Paul was not pursuing Onesimus's manumission but merely his safe return home, the apostolic letter
was still an attempt to place a concrete social problem in the
light of Christian love.[53]

That Paul is genuinely concerned with the enactment of
the "more" rather than with merely satisfying the requirements of a deliberative argument (an argument intended to
get the slave back to his master alive) is seemingly evident in
the apostle's efforts to get his letter read by the entire membership of the Colossian church. Paul could not be certain
that his tactful argument would sway Philemon to do the
"more," which may have been the reason he addressed the
letter not to Philemon alone but also to Apphia, Archippus,
"and the church in your house" (vv. 1-2). The church community probably was familiar with the situation surrounding
Onesimus's absence; and since Roman law and social custom
had it that slaves were forbidden the privilege of group organization or association, the church needed authoritative
instruction regarding the reception of Onesimus into their
congregation as a fellow Christian. By making his letter to
Philemon a public document, Paul was being as certain as
possible that Philemon would not act independently and contrary to his request.

By doing this, Paul also may have assured that the church
would read his letter by referring to it and Onesimus in his
epistle to the Colossians (if in fact Paul wrote this epistle). In

51. Church, "Rhetorical Structure," 30–31.
52. Petersen, *Rediscovering Paul*, 133.
53. Jones, "The Letter to Philemon," 455.

this epistle Onesimus is referred to favorably by name as "the faithful and beloved brother, who is one of yourselves" (Col. 4:9). Some scholars, following Knox's protracted argument, contend that Paul, in this epistle, is referring to the letter to Philemon when he speaks of the "letter from Laodicea": "And when this letter [Colossians] has been read among you, . . . see that you read also the letter from Laodicea [Philemon?]. And say to Archippus [the one Knox believes is actually Onesimus's master], 'See that you fulfill the ministry which you have received in the Lord' " (Col. 4:16-17).[54]

Whether or not Colossians is sure evidence of Paul's genuine concern that Philemon do the "more," the letter to Philemon itself presents us with some additional proof. At the close of the letter, Paul alerts Philemon that he might arrive at Colossae at any time, that a guest room should be prepared in anticipation of his visit. The possibility that Paul could show up unannounced let Philemon know that the apostle would be checking to see if he acted obediently.

The Question of Slavery

In an effort to force us to consider carefully how the rhetorical language of equality in our hymnody veils myriad forms of enslaving hierarchy, such as classism, I contend that the welcoming back of Onesimus "as a beloved brother" does not do justice to the new structural relationship hinted at by the phrase "no longer a slave," particularly because of the ambiguity of the segment that connects these two phrases— "but *more* than a slave" (v. 16). Therefore, the central question surrounding the letter to Philemon is shifted to a later part of the letter—what the "more" meant when Paul says, "I write you, knowing that you will do even more than I say" (v. 21). Was Paul suggesting that Onesimus return to his master as not *just* a slave but *also* a brother, or was he suggesting that Onesimus be fully manumitted?

54. John Knox, along with others, believes that the "letter from Laodicea" is Philemon. This would make Archippus rather than Philemon the owner of Onesimus (Knox, *Philemon*, 45–47).

How people have answered this question has been partly a result of the predisposition with which they have approached the biblical text, for the text is neutral enough to be colored as being either pro- or antislavery. For instance, George Bourne, the Presbyterian clergyman and abolitionist, claimed that Onesimus is exonerated from all obligation by evangelical philanthropy, but he also notes that the bondage of Onesimus and the laudable character of Philemon are often cited to sanction slavery.[55] In the latter regard, Paul not only returns the fugitive to his master after he manages to escape from bondage, he also recognizes that the slavemaster is due some compensation for the temporary loss of property and labor. Furthermore, rather than using this situation to formulate a strong ethical retort against slaveholding, Paul praises the slavemaster for his Christian work. With such a reading—particularly in the light of the other Pauline utterances on slavery and the acceptance of slavery in the Old Testament—it appeared obvious to the advocates of the European slave trade that slaveholding was not necessarily unchristian.

Even some Americans who opposed slavery believed that the Scriptures condoned it. Morris Jacob Raphall, a rabbi who immigrated to the United States in 1849 to oversee a New York City congregation, attacked the abolitionists for trying to force an antislavery interpretation on the Bible. "My friends," the rabbi saluted, "I find, and I am sorry to find, that I am delivering a pro-slavery discourse, I am no friend of slavery. But I stand here as a teacher in Israel; not to place before you my own feelings and opinions, but to propound to you the word of God, the Bible view of slavery."[56] Some modern biblical scholars, who would also claim to be no friend of slavery, contend that it is absurd to interpret Paul's letter to Philemon as an early invective against the immoral institution.[57] Eduard Lohse says Philemon posits no general idea

55. Christie and Dumond, *George Bourne*, 179.
56. Cited in Rifat Sonsino, "The Bible and Politics," *Judaism* 32, no. 1 (Winter 1983): 79–80.
57. Jones, "The Letter to Philemon," 465.

or rule about slavery but simply illustrates Paul's intercession in a specific situation in which love must be fostered by decision and deed.[58] Others mediate between the pro- and antislavery extremes by claiming that Philemon is not an antislavery document but neither can it be said to be proslavery or that the church did nothing about slavery.[59] H. Richard Niebuhr carries this idea to its logical conclusion. He says that if Pauline Christianity—which is concerned with rejecting other religions and not with changing economic institutions—has contributed anything to social change, this has resulted unintentionally and not without the intervention of other organizations.[60]

Generally speaking, Paul does not attack worldly establishments, for he perceives human law as an evil needed to prevent humanity from greater degeneracy. This is what Niebuhr calls Paul's "ethics for the prevention of degeneration."[61] This ethic, applied to slavery in Paul's day, would render slave insurrection a greater evil than the maintenance of slavery, for insurrection (when as many as half the people inhabiting the Roman Empire were slaves) would have threatened the very foundation of society and government. Proslavery Americans rely on this very ethic in their arguments for the continuance of the European slave trade. Thomas Dew, a proslavery professor of political economy at the College of William and Mary, wrote in 1832: "It is said slavery is wrong, in the *abstract* at least, and contrary to the spirit of Christianity. To this we answer . . . that any question must be determined by its circumstances, and if, as really is the case, we cannot get rid of slavery without producing a greater injury to both the masters and slaves, there is no rule of conscience or revealed law of God which *can* condemn us."[62]

58. Lohse, *Colossians and Philemon*, 188.

59. William J. Richardson, "Principle and Context in the Ethics of the Epistle to Philemon," *Interpretation* 22, no. 3 (July 1968): 314–15.

60. H. Richard Niebuhr, *Christ and Culture* (New York: Harper & Row, 1951), 188.

61. Ibid., 166.

62. Thomas R. Dew, "Review of the Debate in the Virginia Legislature," in Stringfellow, *Slavery Defended*, 31.

This argument is what Niebuhr calls "dualism" in his five-point typology on the way Christians respond to culture. The dualists know they cannot escape being citizens of the world and thus attempt to be both loyal to Christ (the "ethics of regeneration") and responsible to culture ("the ethics for the prevention of degeneration").[63] Slavery is tolerated because, as Augustine explains Paul's "prevention" ethic, it is one of the penalties fallen upon a depraved people:

> But, as men once were, when their nature was as God created it, no man was a slave either to man or to sin. However, slavery is now penal in character and planned by that law which commands the preservation of the natural order and forbids its disturbance. If no crime had ever been perpetrated against this law, there would be no crime to repress with the penalty of enslavement.
>
> It is with this in mind that St. Paul goes so far as to admonish slaves to obey their masters and to serve them so sincerely and with such good will that, if there is no chance of manumission, they may make slavery a kind of freedom by serving with love and loyalty, free from fear and feigning, until injustice becomes a thing of the past and every human sovereignty and power is done away with, so that God may be all in all.[64]

According to Norman Petersen, what distinguishes Paul's appeal to Philemon from the admonishing of slaves to obey their masters (in the uncertain Pauline letters) is the participation in slavery of a Christian master and a Christian slave.[65] But if we were to superimpose the above Augustinian treatment of slavery on Paul's letter to Philemon, we might conclude that the "no longer a slave but more than a slave" is slavery as "a kind of freedom by serving with love and loyalty," with the reciprocity of being "free from fear and feigning."

The Antislavery Argument

Probably the principal retort to theological arguments that Paul's letter to Philemon supported slavery came not from

63. Niebuhr, *Christ and Culture*, 156, 165–66.

64. Augustine, *The City of God*, trans. Gerald G. Walsh et al. (New York: Image Books, 1958), bk. 19, chap. 11.

65. Petersen, *Rediscovering Paul*, 289.

abolitionists but from the enslaved themselves. A white preacher and slaveholder named Charles Colcock Jones recalled this reaction to a sermon he preached to a congregation of Africans:

> I was preaching to a large congregation on the *Epistle of Philemon*: and when I insisted upon fidelity and obedience as Christian virtues in servants and upon the authority of Paul, condemned the practice of *running away*, one half of my audience deliberately rose up and walked off with themselves, and those that remained looked any thing but satisfied, either with the preacher or his doctrine. After dismission, there was no small stir among them; some solemnly declared "that there is no such an Epistle in the Bible"; others, "that they did not care if they ever heard me preach again!" . . . There were some too, who had strong objections against me as a Preacher, because I was a *master*, and said, "his people have to work as well as we."[66]

The first Jewish retort to the aforementioned apology by Rabbi Raphall that the Bible sanctioned slavery came from Jewish intellectual Michael Heilprin less than two weeks after Raphall's sermon. In a *New York Tribune* editorial, Heilprin insisted that, first, the Bible is not proslavery but merely tolerates slavery and that, second, everything in the Bible is not divinely sanctioned.[67] This is what Knox means when he says Paul's letters suffer the misfortune of being canonized and that had Paul known the fate of his writings he might have composed them differently[68] (which is what I meant in chapter 2 by the necessity of our making exegetical room). The point is, Paul's letters address particular situations, the details of which we know only in part.

For example, what if Onesimus had run away and went to Paul because he knew that a letter from the apostle would

66. Albert J. Raboteau, *Slave Religion: The "Invisible Institution" in the Antebellum South* (New York: Oxford University Press, 1978), 294.
67. See Sonsino, "The Bible and Politics," 80–81.
68. John Knox, "Paul and the 'Liberals,' " *Religion in Life* 49, no. 4 (Winter 1980): 417–18.

assure his safe return home to his master? We have already
seen in Pliny's letter to Sabinianus that slaves (or freedmen)
occasionally wanted to return to their masters. Frederick
Douglass, who freed himself from slavery in Maryland, gives
what is a timeless apology in behalf of fugitive slaves who
wanted to return to their masters. He says, "Some apology
can easily be made for the few slaves who have, after making
good their escape, turned back to slavery, preferring the actual
rule of their masters, to the life of loneliness, apprehension,
hunger, and anxiety, which meets them on their first arrival
in a free state."[69]

Viewing Douglass's apology through G. W. F. Hegel's
master-slave dialectic,[70] we can understand that the consciousness of a master exists for itself, while the consciousness of a
slave is fashioned to be dependent upon and exist for her
master. A slave who views herself through her master's eyes
cancels out her own self-consciousness, thus relegating herself
to the hegemony of her master and the belief that she cannot subsist independently. The master asserted this self-
perception on his captive by, for instance, whipping the slave
into submission. One American slaveholder would, every two
or three weeks, have one or two of his slaves bound and
whipped unmercifully for no other reason than to let the
enslaved know that he was their master.[71] Thus, we can understand Douglass's words, "A freeman cannot understand
why the slave-master's shadow is bigger, to the slave, than the
might and majesty of a free state; but when he reflects that
the slave knows more about the slavery of his master than he
does of the might and majesty of the free state, he has the
explanation."[72] It takes one who has been a slave to realize
that potentially this is why Paul wrote to Philemon and why
Pliny wrote to Sabinianus as they did: These slaves, as

69. Frederick Douglass, *My Bondage and My Freedom* (New York: Miller, Orton,
and Mulligan, 1855); see the facsimile reprint of New York: Dover, 1969 (more
recently as reprinted by Peter Smith), 339.
70. G. W. F. Hegel, *The Phenomenology of Mind*, trans. J. B. Baillie (New York:
Harper & Row, 1967), 228–40.
71. Blassingame, *Slave Testimony*, 139.
72. Douglass, *My Bondage*, 339.

Douglass would say, knew more about the slavery of their masters than about the might and majesty of the freedom they had known for such a brief time.

Let me speak further regarding why the meaning of Paul's letter is dependent upon the particularity of the situation. What if Paul had said to Onesimus that Christ died at the hands of the Romans for setting captives free and that as an ambassador for Christ he would rather suffer likewise than to send a freedman back into bondage? What if he said this even though confessing that he believes that those who are enslaved should (to use Augustine's words) "obey their masters" and "serve them so sincerely and with such good will that, if there is no chance of manumission, they may make slavery a kind of freedom by serving with love and loyalty"? Thus, what if Paul only hesitatingly consented to Onesimus's request that he be returned to his master, under the condition that he become a Christian, by which (and only by which) terms Paul could reasonably assure Onesimus's safe return home by pressing Philemon to treat the converted slave as a brother? These things would qualify Paul's sending a slave back to his master and would cancel out proslavery arguments that rely on Paul taking this action.

That the meaning of Paul's letter is dependent on the particular situation being addressed is recognized by Stephen Barton. To illustrate his point, Barton constructs a hypothetical response by Philemon to Paul's letter and then a letter of response by Paul to Philemon. The gist of Philemon's fictional response to Paul's letter reads: "Beloved Paul, is it not important to maintain order? Is it not possible for Onesimus to be both my slave and my brother? Is it not possible for us to be one in the Spirit but master and slave in the world? . . . I had thought that it was in this vein that you gave instructions to the churches at Corinth."[73] Paul's fictional response was for Philemon to be guided by the Spirit rather than by his human inclinations: "How, then, can there be master and slave, when in Christ there is neither?"[74]

---

73. Stephen Barton, "Paul and Philemon: A Correspondence Continued," *Theology* 90, no. 734 (March 1987): 99.
   74. Ibid., 100.

The point is that in Philemon, as well as in the epistles that address the issue of slavery, Paul is writing in the context of particular situations at given historical moments. Just because he tolerated Roman slavery, says Knox, does not mean he would tolerate slavery today. "To assume that he would have been equally tolerant of it in *our* world, so different from his that he could not even have imagined it, is to be ignorant almost beyond belief."[75] Just because he tolerated Roman slavery then does not mean he would tolerate classism today or would appreciate its residue in our hymnody.

The Dialectic of Structure and Antistructure

Norman Petersen is convinced that had anthropologist Victor Turner not developed his theory of structure and antistructure (communitas) biblical scholars would have had to do so in order to account for the organizational dynamics in Paul's letters.[76] Petersen sees the bipolarity of structure/antistructure manifested in two ways in Paul's worldview: first, the structure (hierarchism) of the world and the antistructure (nonhierarchism) of the church; and second, the structure and antistructure of the church.[77] In terms of the first, Paul, in the context of the church, denies such distinctions as male/female and slave/free, which typify hierarchical/structural relations in the world.[78] Correspondingly, his references to church folk as brothers and sisters are antistructural/nonhierarchical and stand over against the hierarchical relationships between fathers and sons, mothers and daughters, and so forth.[79] While the antistructure of the church is oppositional to the structure of the world, the structure/antistructure in the church is not oppositional and does not reject all structure because it is dealing with and within its own world.[80] But Paul's idea of structure in the church is that

75. Knox, "Paul and the 'Liberals,' " 419.
76. Petersen, *Rediscovering Paul*, 197 n. 165.
77. Ibid., 153.
78. Ibid., 155.
79. Ibid., 157.
80. Ibid., 159.

it is based not on power but on mutuality and responsibility, each part of the body (structure) carrying out its function for the good of the whole (antistructure).[81]

According to the body politic (1 Cor. 12:12-27), it appears as though Michael Parsons, William Westermann, and Eduard Lohse are suggesting that Philemon could be the "head" and Onesimus the "foot" of the "body" while yet there is an equality according to the mutuality of responsibility. This is a possible explanation of what Paul means by Onesimus being received by Philemon as both a slave and more than a slave— as the passage reads, "no longer a slave *but more than a slave, as a beloved brother*" (Philemon 16). To borrow again from Hegel's master-slave dialectic,[82] the consciousness of a master exists for itself while he creates a situation where the consciousness of a slave is dependent on and exists for him. A slave, viewing herself through the master's eyes, cancels out her own self-consciousness, relegating herself to inferiority. But because bondage is "a consciousness repressed within itself," a slave is capable of entering into the consciousness and of fixing it so as to be truly self-dependent and self-existent. In European slavery and colonialism this is evident in the many songs that are clearly songs claiming or calling for liberation. To Paul, who is working within the context of the seemingly unconquerable system of Roman slavery and hence with his "ethics for the prevention of degeneration," being "in Christ" would enable Onesimus, even if still a slave, to be truly self-existent and Philemon to see him in this way as "*more* than a slave, as a beloved brother." As Eldon Koch puts it, slave and master, in sharing the same faith, are transformed and become partners, which results in the slave losing his slavishness and the master his despotism.[83]

But Petersen stands vehemently against this idea, and so should we in our pursuit of a revised hymnody. To be "in Christ," Petersen argues, makes it logically and sociologically impossible for Philemon to relate to Onesimus as both an

81. Ibid., 159, 160.
82. Hegel, *Phenomenology of Mind*, 228–40.
83. Koch, "A Cameo of *Koinonia*," 185.

equal/brother and an inferior/slave, leaving Onesimus's manumission as the only appropriate response: "Because they *are*
in Christ, Onesimus cannot *be* both Philemon's slave and his
brother, and Philemon cannot *be* both Onesimus's master and
his brother. A believer can act *as though* he were his brother's
slave, but his brother can neither act like nor be his master."[84]
But this is one possible interpretation of what "ideological
communitas" sums up to be—one person (let us say a poor
black woman) acting responsibly as though she were her sister's slave in such a way that the other person (let us say a
wealthy white woman) need not act like or be a master. The
words of Augustine, cited earlier, echo hauntingly here: "It
is with this in mind that St. Paul goes so far as to admonish
slaves to obey their masters and to serve them so sincerely
and with such good will that, if there is no chance of manumission, they may make slavery a kind of freedom by serving
with love and loyalty, free from fear and feigning, until injustice becomes a thing of the past and every human sover-
eignty and power is done away with, so that God may be all
in all."[85]

I am suggesting that there are serious problems with
ideological communitas (which is the very egalitarian language that pervades our hymnody), even though it seems to
be a possible explanation of what Paul intends for the relationship between Philemon and Onesimus. After all, it is ideological communitas that more or less characterizes Paul's
relationship with Philemon and Onesimus as both their
brother and their spiritual father. Hence, as Paul's letter to
Philemon demonstrates, it is a short step from the reality that
structure is needed to maintain antistructure[86] to the Pauline
"ethics for the prevention of degeneration," which implies
the necessity of a head to guide the foot for the betterment
of the larger spiritual "body." It is a short step to an apology
for hierarchism, including classism. Yet, as Canaan Banana

84. Petersen, *Rediscovering Paul*, 269, 289, 290.
85. Augustine, *City of God*, bk. 19, chap. 15.
86. Victor Turner, *Dramas, Fields, and Metaphors: Symbolic Action in Human Society*
(Ithaca, N.Y.: Cornell University Press, 1974), 265.

says in a classic exercise of hermeneutical control that renders bare ideological communitas: "Mankind cannot live by slogans alone."[87]

The Insufficiency of Ideological Communitas

Ideological communitas is the theodicy (reconciliation) I suggest is being posited by Eurocentric scholars who, entrenched in Aristotelian hierarchism, claim that Onesimus could be both Philemon's slave and his brother. If this were true, then one could easily claim: What has made Christianity the great religion that it is, is that the Bible says, wives be subject to your husbands and slaves obey your masters (Col. 3:18, 22). The only thing that prevents ideological communitas from being an utterly wretched theodicy is the idea that, one master-slave relationship at a time, the entire slavery institution would dissolve. However, that idea is rather idealistic, like the metaphysical idealism of Josiah Royce discussed in chapter 2. As H. Richard Niebuhr suggests, if Christianity has contributed to social change, it has been largely unintentional and not without the intervention of other organizations.[88] Therefore the theodicy of ideological communitas must be rejected as a high hope with no empirical proof of plausibility, an opiate intended to undermine the zeal of the poor for liberation, and an obstacle to our pursuit of a revised black hymnody.

Ideological communitas must also be rejected because it fails to reconcile the tension between slavery (of such myriad kinds as classism) and human potentiality. Slavery as a physical fact may be rendered meaningless by Paul's teachings, but slavery also makes an oppressed person useless in the light of her potential usefulness as a Christian sister and fully free individual. Paul hints at this when he says about Onesimus, "Formerly he was useless to you, but now he is indeed useful to *you* and to *me*" (Philemon 11). No matter what a slave's or

---

87. Canaan Banana, *The Gospel according to the Ghetto*, rev. ed. (Gweru, Zimbabwe: Mambo Press, 1990), 16.
88. Niebuhr, *Christ and Culture*, 188.

poor person's labor is worth economically, it cannot match
up to her potential as a free human being, a person who can
be useful to herself or to whomever she pleases.

For instance, about half a century after Paul's death,
Ignatius, bishop of Antioch (in Asia Minor), was taken to
Rome to meet his death. During his transport to Rome he
wrote letters to the Magnesians, Trallians, Romans, and Ephesians. The bishop of Ephesus to whom he wrote was, inter-
estingly enough, a man named Onesimus. Knox claims that
this bishop of Ephesus most probably was the same Onesimus
for whom Paul wrote a letter to Philemon a half-century earlier. "That the slave Onesimus was a person of promise is
indicated by Paul's great concern to have him with him," says
Knox. "It would have been natural for places of leadership
in the Pauline churches to be held by the actual companions
of Paul himself so long as there were any of them living."[89]
Such instances of status inconsistency were not uncommon
in ancient Rome. Occasionally slaves owned slaves and lived
in luxury or ex-slaves became wealthy and influential.[90] Neither would this have been the only time a man came up from
slavery to become a bishop, for such was the plight of Callistus
who became Rome's holy see in 217 C.E.[91] So convincing is
Knox's reasoning that Moule concludes: "There seems to be
no cogent reason against the identification of the freed slave
with the bishop of the same name addressed by Ignatius. . . .
It is thus possible, though not demonstrable, that we are given
a glimpse of a spectacular sequel to St. Paul's letter many
years later."[92]

Knox also suggests that Onesimus was probably responsible for the compilation of the Pauline letters, which would
explain the inclusion of the otherwise seemingly unimportant
Philemon.[93] What is even more intriguing is that the compilation of the Pauline letters in Ephesus under Onesimus's

89. Knox, *Philemon*, 103–4.
90. Lloyd A. Thompson, *Romans and Blacks* (Norman, Okla.: University of Oklahoma Press, 1989), 144.
91. Jones, "The Letter to Philemon," 455.
92. Moule, *The Epistles of Paul*, 21.
93. Knox, *Philemon*, 107.

administration would have marked the beginning of the canonization of the New Testament; for Marcion, but decades later, may have appropriated this compilation for his heretical canon, which prompted the formation of an authoritative canon by the church.[94] P. N. Harrison agrees with Knox that Onesimus the former slave was probably the bishop of Ephesus to whom Ignatius wrote and who was responsible for the collecting of the Pauline writings.[95] He concludes: "The testimony of Ignatius makes it certain that Onesimus *either* himself became bishop of Ephesus and played a leading part in the formation of the original Corpus Paulinum, *or else* so lived and died that another Onesimus, named after him, and inspired by his memory, rose to that high office and rendered to Christendom that imperishable service. In either case, St. Paul's letter to Philemon must in fact have produced its desired effect."[96]

Ideological communitas—the attempt to translate into the workaday world the highest state of communality attained during worship—may humanize relationships in everyday life, but it reduces to an "ethics for the prevention of degeneration," a negative. Ideological communitas is comprised of "masters" masking their power and hegemony behind the rhetoric of an alleged egalitarian "ethics of regeneration." Ideological communitas is the equivalent of Paul saying to Philemon "for love's sake I prefer to appeal to you" (Philemon 9), while saying in the same letter that he is "confident of Philemon's *obedience*" (v. 21). It is the equivalent of his saying, "I preferred to do nothing without your consent in order that your goodness might not be by compulsion but of your own free will," while not truly allowing the exercise of free will.

For us to understand this masking of inequality without doing anything to change it in our history and in our hymnody is but Reinhold Niebuhr's Eurocentrically flawed "Christian realism," discussed in chapter 2. Without question, ideological communitas—whether it results from Roycian metaphysical

94. Ibid., 108.
95. Harrison, "Onesimus and Philemon," 191–92.
96. Ibid., 293.

idealism or Niebuhrian Christian realism—does not allow for
the burgeoning of human potential and ultimately the free
growth into salvation that can come only by way of self-identity
and self-determination. Ideological communitas does not allow for this human burgeoning, because it imprisons the oppressed in the liminal state (the betwixt and between) of being
neither a slave nor free. Onesimus the slave never could
have made the important contribution to Christianity that
Onesimus the free man did. Complete emancipation from all
forms of slavery—gender, race, and class hierarchy—is the
only way we can attain our God-given potentiality. This is
why we have had in the past, and continue to have in the
present, women divorcing their husbands, blacks separating
themselves from whites, the poor disassociating themselves
from the wealthy: The oppressed have found it nearly impossible to fulfill their human potential under the yoke of
slavery's progeny: sexism, racism, and classism.

In arguing against the notion that a person can be both
one's brother or sister and one's slave, I am suggesting that
if there is a theodicy in Paul's letter to Philemon—a theodicy
reconciling the immorality of slavery with the morality of
Christianity—then it must be found elsewhere in the letter.
It can only be the "more" that Paul speaks of when he says,
"Confident of your obedience, I write to you, knowing that
you will do even *more* than I say." The "more," alone, must
be the consummation of the "communitas" of Christ.

This is the key to *all* forms of Christian emancipation,
the key that unlocks the door to redemption, unleashes the
potentiality of salvation. The Scriptures do not delineate the
details of how Christians are to relate to modernity's myriad
forms of slavery perpetuated against the oppressed—women,
people of color, and the poor. The Scriptures speak only
indirectly to these problems. Therefore we must do the
"more" of which the apostle speaks—*more* than what the Scriptures make explicit. Our hymnody must help motivate us to
do the "more," to walk the extra mile in pursuing the release
of the captives. It must be a hymnody that says both to the
Euro-Christian church and the Afro-Christian church: "Let
my people go!"

PART THREE

REVISION

6

Anatomy of a New Hymnal

Obedience of the oppressed to the oppressor; peace and harmony between the exploited and the exploiter; the slave to love his master and pray that God grant that the master may long reign over us: these were the ultimate aesthetic goals of colonial culture carefully nurtured by nailed boots, police truncheons and military bayonets and by the carrot of a personal heaven for a select few. The end was . . . the aesthetic of submission and blind obedience to authority reflected in that Christian refrain, *Trust and Obey*:

> Trust and obey
> For there is no other way
> To be happy in Jesus
> But to trust and obey!
>   —Ngũgĩ Wa Thiong'O, *Detained: A Writer's Prison Diary* (1981)

My petition for a re-creation of our hymnody conjures up the caution of Johannes Climacus, Søren Kierkegaard's

occasional pseudonym. During a brief segment in his *Concluding Unscientific Postscript* (1846), Kierkegaard's Climacus
employs a hypothetical protagonist who voices some mis-
givings about religion, particularly Christianity. Although
Kierkegaard was a Christian convert at the time he wrote this
book, his pseudonymous alter ego, Climacus, was an uncon-
verted humorist going about the task of discovering the
morality required for becoming one of the curious religious
creatures Christians seem to be.

As the segment begins, Climacus's protagonist is point-
edly challenging the fact that clergy gather at church conventions in order to resolve such lofty dilemmas as "what the
age demands," while overlooking the needs of individuals.[1]
In this instance, it is a new hymnal that the clergy say "the
age demands":

> Everybody is preoccupied with what the age demands,
> no one seems to care about what the individual needs.
> Possibly no new hymnal is needed. Why does no one hit
> upon the idea which lies so close at hand, closer perhaps
> than many will believe: the idea of experimenting with
> the plan of having the old hymnal furnished with a new
> binding, to see if a different binding might not do the
> trick, especially if the bookbinder were to print on the
> cover, The New Hymnal. . . . But when the entire age,
> unanimously and with many voices, demands a new hym-
> nal, aye, almost several new hymnals, then something
> must be done; things cannot go on as they are now, or
> it will be the ruin of religion.
>
> How comes it that church attendance is relatively
> so small as it is in the country's capital? Why, quite nat-
> urally, the answer is clear as day: it comes from the aver-
> sion felt toward the old hymnal. How does it come that
> those who do go to church are disorderly enough to come
> just as the clergyman enters the pulpit, or a little later?
> Why, quite naturally, the answer is clear as day: because
> of the aversion for the old hymnal. . . . What is the reason

1. Søren Kierkegaard, *Concluding Unscientific Postscript*, trans. David F. Swenson
(Princeton, N.J.: Princeton University Press, 1968), 427.

for the indecent haste with which the people leave the
church the moment the clergyman has said Amen? Why,
naturally, the answer is clear as day: because of aversion
for the old hymnal. . . .

But for this very reason it seems to me that we ought
to go slow in abolishing the old hymnal, lest we experience too great a measure of embarrassment when we
have to explain the same phenomenon after the new
hymnal has been introduced.[2]

In abolishing most of the old hymnals in the churches
of Afro-Christendom we in fact ought to experience great
embarrassment, insofar as we are now—at this very moment
in this book's "petition"—being asked to explain the "same
phenomenon" after the new hymnals have been introduced.
I am speaking of the "same phenomenon" of religious apathy
and, from the perspective of ethnohymnology, indifference
toward those who are culturally and ideologically ethnic.

I have contended, on the other hand, contrary to what
Climacus believes with regard to European Christendom, that
Afro-Christians, and all others who would be ethnic, ought
to be concerned about "what the age demands" and in fact
ought to feel an aversion for the "old hymnal." It is clear as
day! The "old hymnal" is "washing us white as snow"; it is
preventing us from being not only culturally ethnic but ideologically ethnic (in the sense of being in solidarity with women,
nonwhites, and the poor). As I stated in my keynote address
to the 1992 annual meeting of the Hymn Society, we need a
new breed of hymnologist. We need ethnohymnologists who
have as their overriding concern the plight of those groups
in society most ethnic and therefore most alienated from extant hymnological tradition. We need hymnists of this ilk
as well.

At least some of the Hymn Society conferencees felt that
my keynote address, which was supposed to be titled "You
Are Ethnic," failed in its assigned task of creating racial unity
rather than racial divisiveness. I suppose I would have satisfied

2. Ibid., 428–29.

these critics if my message were the idealistic one expressed
in one of Howard M. Edwards's hymns, "We Are All One in
Mission." Sung in Edwards's Hymn Society workshop featuring his hymns forthcoming in published form, the
hymn begins:

> We all are one in mission, we all are one in call,
> Our varied gifts united by Christ, the Lord of all.

But my address, it was said by some conferencees, contributed
to a black-white polarization. In fact, what I attempted to
identify was the reality of a polarity between the ideologically
ethnic and the ideologically unraced—that is, the actual lack
of Christians being "one in mission." The contrast between
these two poles can be illustrated by comparing two collections
of hymns showcased at the Hymn Society meeting—the new
Yale hymnbook, *A New Hymnal for Colleges and Schools* (1992),
edited by Jeffery Rowthorn and Russell Schulz-Widmar; and
the two volumes of "songs of the world church" edited by
John Bell, *Many and Great* (1990) and *Sent by the Lord* (1991).

Upon a cursory study of the Yale hymnal several characteristics, typical of the "old hymnal," were readily apparent.
First, of the hymnal's five major sections—In Praise of God,
The Created Order, The Biblical Witness, The Faithful Life,
and Hope for the World—the *last* category is Hope for the
World, which contains the subsection Justice and Peace. This
sends a clear theological message that the first order of busi-
ness for Christians is to praise God and only subsequently, as
an "appendix," to be concerned about the secular aspects of
justice and peace.

It is fortunate, however, that the opening section of the
Yale hymnbook, In Praise of God, contains a hymn by Brian
Wren, in which it is "She" who is God. The hymn begins:

> Who is she, neither male nor female, maker of all
>   things,
> Only glimpsed or hinted, source of life and gender?

Under the major heading, The Biblical Witness, in a hymn
titled "Woman in the Night," Wren begins the third stanza
with this couplet:

> Woman in the house, nurtured to be meek,
> Leave your second place: listen, think, and speak!

Wren, someone I consider to be an ethnohymnologist, understands the potential consequences of saying yes to being ethnic. In his hymn "Faith Looking Forward" he says that if by our action of "running risks or taking sides" we burn all our bridges, "Christ longs to find us free for the kingdom."

Something else typical of the "old hymnal" struck me about the Yale publication. Of the five African-American spirituals included in it (which comprise nearly the totality of the African-American contribution) none of the spirituals falls, actually or thematically, under the heading Hope for the World and specifically under the subcategory Justice and Peace; whereas the true ethnic nature of the spirituals, a music created by a people enslaved by the "unraced," is liberation. It is ironic that instead of including spirituals that represent their natural office of questing for justice and peace, a hymn by poet William Alexander Percy is included under this category. It is ironic, as well as being the epitome of hypocrisy, because this Mississippian, Percy, was the author of that horribly racist best-selling autobiography of 1941, *Lanterns on the Levee*. For a hymnal designed by scholars for a scholarly community, a community that should know of this popular racist figure of American history, the inclusion of a hymn by Percy is an act of ethnic insensitivity.

With regard to the selection of African-American spirituals that are devoid of their characteristic liberation theme, I would not be surprised if it were argued that such hymns would be too particularistic and insufficiently ecumenical for inclusion in such a hymnal. However, if this were the reason for the exclusion of such songs, then that position would only serve to illustrate how far the "unraced" still have to go before being able to say "We are ethnic." Including a few hymns from African-American, Hispanic, Asian, and African sources—as is the ethical standard for the mainline hymnals of the post-1970s—allows for but a "hymnal squeak" in the face of the need for "nation building." The fact is that the spirituals containing the theme of liberation ought to be viewed as the very essence of ecumenicity. This is so not only because those of the so-called first world need to be in solidarity with those of the so-called third world, but because the third world is none other than the majority two-thirds world. Thus, an ecumenicity that elevates the concerns of those who are ethnic—women, nonwhites, and the poor (the masses of the majority two-thirds world)—is an accurate, not to mention ethical, ecumenicity.

The Yale hymnal, then, though it will have its anticipated usefulness in the elite halls of academe, is far from being a model of what it means to say yes to being ethnic. It is far from being a model of what is required of the Afro-Christian church in terms of singing "new song." What its editors have accomplished is indeed a great feat of Eurocentric hymnology but not of ethnohymnology. In the eyes of the Afro-Christian church it should be perceived as no great feat.

The work of John Bell of the Iona Community can serve as a paradigm for saying yes to being ethnic and doing ethnohymnology. The Iona Community, in which the theology of this ethnohymnologist, Bell, is situated, is an international ecumenical community of about two hundred members, eight hundred associate members, and three thousand friends, founded in 1938 by Rev. George MacLeod. Part of the mission of the community in seeking new ways of "living the Christian gospel in the world" and in being concerned for justice and reconciliation is to break down the divisions between church and world, prayer and politics, and sacred and secular. In his introduction to the first of the extant two volumes of "songs of the world church," titled *Many and Great* after a Native American song, Bell reproaches the religious paternalism of the West, specifically its presumption that the ethnic Christians of the two-thirds world have nothing to offer in return for the civilization the West brings them. In the process of writing their own hymns, it came as a surprise to the people of the Iona Community that songs from such places as Soweto, Buenos Aires, and Budapest were not only singable but actually helpful in terms of providing new insight into the nature of their faith.[3] Bell goes on to say, with the sensitivity of a true ethnohymnologist: "It is because we believe that as Western Europeans we are called on at this time in history to learn from the experience of those we previously colonised, that we have not included in this collection songs from the former imperial powers."[4] The exercise of even a portion of this ethnohymnological position on the part of the editors of the Yale hymnal would have resulted in a vastly different compilation. The exercise of a substantial part of this ethnohymnological position would result in wonderful "new song" for the Afro-Christian church.

The second volume of "songs of the world church" is titled *Sent by the Lord* after a Nicaraguan song. In explaining the intentionality behind the fact that the preponderance of hymns in this collection are from Central and Southern America, Bell says in the introduction:

> [The year] 1992 commemorates the "discovery" of America by Christopher Columbus. For many people in Central and Southern America, this is not a time for joy, but a time for deep regret as that occasion calls to mind the succession of waves of colonial, religious and financial imperialism which has beleaguered many of the countries in the sub-continent right to the present day.
>
> It is therefore hoped that some of the songs in *Sent by the Lord* may be used as an antidote to the triumphalism which Western countries may be tempted to associate with the centenary.[5]

Many of the "songs of the world church" are duo-ethnic—that is, both culturally and ideologically ethnic. For example, "Kyrie Guarany," in *Sent by the Lord*, is a hymn from Paraguay, a country on the east coast of South America. It is comprised of a reiteration of the lines:

3. John L. Bell, ed., *Many and Great: Songs of the World Church* (Glasgow, Scotland: Wild Goose Publications, 1990), 7.
4. Ibid., 9.
5. John L. Bell, ed., *Sent by the Lord: Songs of the World Church* (Glasgow, Scotland: Wild Goose Publications, 1991), 7.

On the poor, on the poor,
Show your mercy, O Lord.

Another hymn from the same collection is the Nicaraguan
piece "Sent by the Lord." It begins:

Sent by the Lord am I;
My hands are ready now to make the earth the place
in which the kingdom comes.

After repeating that couplet the stanza continues on to say
that the angels cannot transform this hurtful world into a
place of love, justice, and peace; doing God's will of setting
the world free belongs to humanity.

Another example of duo-ethnic hymnody is the South
African song "Senzeni Na" ("What Have We Done?") in *Sent
by the Lord*. The first verse iterates the question, "What have
we done?" Then the second verse reiterates a query like that
of the first, "Sono sethu" ("What is our sin?"). Bell's footnote
indicates that these words have been sung throughout South
Africa as both an expression of protest and a means of black
South Africans sharing their pain with God and one another.

It is interesting, however, that the third verse to this
hymn has been omitted, even though it answers the two queries, "What have we done?" and "What is our sin?" The answer
the South Africans give in that omitted verse is "We are black."
Bell omitted the verse because, he explained in his footnote,
"it would be impossible for white Westerners to sing that with
the conviction it requires."[6] However, not to sing the answer
to what is the epitome of *the* ethnic theodicy question is to
sidestep having to contend with the real substance of the song.
Akin to the exclusion of liberation spirituals from the Yale
hymnal, omitting the answer to *the* ethnic theodicy question
posed in this South African song is to avoid the crucial reminder to society that the ethnohymnologist advocates. That
reminder is that in singing this culturally ethnic hymnody we
must also have a conviction to be in solidarity with the ideologically ethnic—women, nonwhites, and the poor—whose

6. Ibid., 67.

global status characterizes the preponderant reality of the two-thirds world. That reminder is also that we must, prior to our efforts to deepen solidarity with the ethnic, bridge the lacuna that separates our ethnic worlds.

That such a bridge of reconciliation should begin with apology is the point made by black South African evangelicals in the document titled *Evangelical Witness in South Africa* (1986). It is because the point is made about South Africa that it is of real significance here, for what is explicitly the problem there in terms of gender, race, and class hierarchy is in fact the problem in the Western countries. There is a pre-liberation South Africa, in this respect, latent in all the Western countries and all the Western churches—including the Afro-Christian church. The document reads:

> This is the only way in which South Africans can be reconciled. Firstly we must all be conscious of the sin that has led us to this war. The sin of racism. The sin of undermining other people as if they were not made in the very image of God. The sin of discriminating against other people and suppressing them to stop them from developing their potential and living their lives in full. The sin of dispossessing people of their land. The sin of accumulating riches by making profits at the expense of other vulnerable humans, by so doing impoverishing them. The sin of classism and sexism. . . . These are the sins of white South Africa which they need to confess and repent of, so that there can be forgiveness and reconciliation.[7]

Thus, after all the culturally ethnic hymns have been sung in our Afro-Christian churches as an initial step toward solidarity with the ideologically ethnic, for every Afro-Christian (and any others who would be ethnic) to be able to sing in "Senzeni Na" that "We are black"—as confession and repentance—is for all of us to come closer to being able to say "We are ethnic." In proceeding further into ethnicity,

---

7. *Evangelical Witness in South Africa (Evangelicals Critique Their Own Theology and Practice)* (Dobsonville, South Africa: Concerned Evangelicals, 1986), 13.

every Afro-Christian (and any others who would be ethnic) should also be able to answer the query of the Brian Wren hymn, "Who Is She?" with not only the answers he gives in his four stanzas—She is God (Love, Life, Hope)—but also with the answer "She is Black." The fact is, as regards the necessity of being able to make such a statement, the confused meaning of blackness and femaleness has gone so deep into the collective unconscious of blacks and nonblacks and women and men that any normalized relation between these groups can come only with just such a deep therapy that attempts to unconfuse the matter. To be able to understand the crucial meaning of this symbolism—God as female and black—and to be able to sing "She is Black" without feelings of repulsion, is for Afro-Christians (and all others who would be ethnic) to have made a large leap of faith in the direction of becoming ethnic.

As for Johannes Climacus, the pseudonymous character I mentioned at the beginning of this chapter, he would make no good ethnohymnologist, for what the age demands is not a new cover to the "old hymnal" but in fact a new hymnal comprised of new song to sing—ethnic song. Using Climacus's words, but without his humorous sarcasm, I petition Afro-Christians to understand that "things cannot go on as they are now, or it will be the ruin of religion."

As for the Afro-Christian church, it has four choices at hand in terms of how to go about singing new song: (1) Its music ministers can choose more selectively from old hymns (with possible revision) or, especially, select from a growing body of new song; (2) its hymnists can attempt to compose new hymns and hymn tunes; (3) its hymnists can set to music the poetry of some of the great black social thinkers who may or may not be traditional poets; (4) its parishioners can sing the "songs of the world church." My own attempt to write new song (text and music) for black churchgoers to sing is illustrated in the appendix that follows, and I have more to say about the "songs of the world church" there.

Regarding the new song of hymnists other than myself, the work of a Catholic sister named Miriam Therese Winter, in a small collection of original hymns titled *Womansong* (1987),[8] can serve as a paradigm for addressing the problem of gender. In her piece titled "Mother Earth" is a metaphorical portrayal of both Mother Earth and God as women:

> Blessed be God, Her woman's touch
> Gives us earth, who gives so much.

In the hymn "Women" we are told that women themselves have much to give after centuries of being silenced. In the hymn "One by One," "women of the world" are being told that they, who are "one in deprivation," are coming to an awareness in which together they are challenging the structures and confronting discrimination. Winter's strongest example of breaking or reversing stereotypical characterizations of women in hymnic language is found in "Hear God's Word." Not only is it "She" who is God, but She is "fierce" and "terrible" and her "rage" is full of "force." Those who sing this song are beckoned to hear the word of God, which is "prepared to prune and plunder," as "She" fashions "a new and holy age." So are we to help fashion a new age, says Winter in a verse of the hymn "Take the Time," which captures the substance of my book's petition. It begins:

> Take the time to sing a song,
> For all those people who don't belong.

Those people who "don't belong" (the ethnic) are women "wasted by defeat," men "condemned to walk the street," and many others we will never meet. In subsequent stanzas the ethnic are also the hungry who struggle just to make it through another day and the millions of refugees who have had to flee from their lands and liberty. Where power causes "deep unrest," she concludes, we should join the struggle of the "oppressed"; then we will "be blessed."

Regarding the potential of the poetry of Afro-Christian social thinkers serving as a source of new song, I will say a word about the verse of poet, novelist, and social philosopher

---

8. Miriam Therese Winter, *Womansong* (Nairobi, Kenya: Medical Mission Sisters [P.O. Box 53376, Nairobi], 1987).

C. Eric Lincoln. In *This Road Since Freedom*, a collection of poetry written over the course of his adult years, Lincoln speaks to the issues of African-American reality. Not even counting the several hymns in his anthology, his poems tend to be so lyrical and rhythmical that they cry out to be set to melody and to be sung. Even the poems that are not already hymns can serve as a source of inspiration and as potential pieces for revision or metricization. They can be metricized in the same way that James Russell Lowell adapted his poem of 1844 protesting the war with Mexico, "The Present Crisis," into the classic social gospel hymn, "Once to Every Man and Nation."

In "A Prayer for Love," a hymn penned in 1958, Lincoln prays for the loving hand of God to still him when he trembles, to give him peace amid life's storms. Beyond these personal cries for comfort and condolence, which always have been a part of Afro-Christian expression, is also a summons for the formation of community: a petitioning of the creator to teach the created how to be merciful with one another and how, no matter what the personal and social sacrifice, to love everyone—the lowly as well as the mighty. In so petitioning, and in calling on the Lord to confound all "hateful doctrine," Lincoln's hymn captures the spirit of Martin Luther King's quest for ideal community. As evidenced in his philosophy of nonviolence, King believed that the foundational principle that creates, orders, and sustains community is love—the love of God, neighbor, even enemy.

Like King, Lincoln was raised in the South amid the noncommunity of discrimination and segregation. During his lifetime Lincoln also searched unceasingly for the antithesis of this "Jim Crow" reality—for community whose maker, builder, and sustainer is God. Lincoln's "Prayer" gives voice to King's belief that the causes of noncommunity can be displaced only by the realization of life's natural communalness—the love of creature for creature—as fashioned by the will of the creator. The attributes of love and truth are the requisite tools, the sole means of overcoming the barriers of fear, deception, and "hateful doctrine," which Lincoln says interfere in the sharing of sisterly and brotherly love. To be sure, truth and love are liberating: Truth can free us from deception, and love from dread and hatred.

Lincoln's "Prayer" captures King's mature understanding of human community, an understanding that became less provincial and more universal as the civil rights leader came to view the American dilemma in the international context of the struggle for global unity. At the time of his death, King's philosophy had far transcended the notion of community as merely realized by racial integration and black socioeconomic equality. It included a response to racism and classism from the more global purview of the collective human transgressions of poverty, militarism, and imperialism. In short, Lincoln's prayer was King's prayer: "Lord, let my parish be the world."

"How Like a Gentle Spirit," a hymn written in 1987 and published in *The United Methodist Hymnal* in 1989, is identical in spirit to "A Prayer for Love," written thirty-one years earlier: Humankind is not essentially a pluralism of peoples, but primordially one humanity guided by one God, a God that is neither white nor black, male nor female. Despite human attempts to project ideological attributes onto the divine in order to justify human biases and bigotry, God, to Lincoln, is simply a loving gentle spirit, a soaring mother eagle, an empowering lively force that enables the human creature to overcome fear and peril. In spite of the problems that plague civilization and its pluralism of intercultural societies, Lincoln holds true to the belief that "the universal love of God shines through." He remains ever hopeful: He is certain that "all humankind is one by God's decree." Implicit in Lincoln's hymn is that the church is called to demonstrate to society's individuals and myriad communities how to be gentle, motherly, and empowering to "the least of them"—the downtrodden and disinherited, the diseased and disabled. This is in keeping with Lincoln's social philosophy and with his commitment to the spirit of King.

In "The Pilgrimage," a poem of 1969, written upon
Lincoln's first pilgrimage to the land from whence his foreparents came, the poet sings of "Mother Africa." She—
Africa—is the bosom he had long longed to see. His ancestors
had been beckoning him, for his spirit had been sapless, thirsty
for rootedness in her dusky sacred womb.

Why does the poet call the land of his foreparents
"Mother" when God in Western civilization customarily has
been "Father"? *She* is "Mother" because *she*, who is black and
comely, procreated humanity. *She*, who is the lily of the valley,
is the Black Madonna. Her daughter, Ethiopia, begot Egypt,
the native land of classic civilization—Egypt, who conceived
religion and philosophy, the arts and the sciences; Egypt,
whose cosmology engendered the very ideas that, in part
through Judaism, were appropriated by Christianity: monotheism, messianic expectation, trinitarianism, incarnation,
virginal conception, redemption, passion, resurrection, sabbath, baptism, eucharist, transubstantiation, judgment, millennialism, damnation, and salvation. It is *she* who is the
"ancient land of mystic fame" which, out of the vast unknown,
gave to the poet the heritage he owns. In "The Pilgrimage,"
Lincoln worships her: "Africa, O Africa, My Africa." This,
and the poems above, are ripe texts for the fashioning of new
Afro-Christian song.

The 1968 poem, "This Road Since Freedom," after which
Lincoln's anthology is titled, is also more than worthy to be
metricized for hymn singing. In this poem the poet sings of
America. It is not an anthem of praise that he sings to this
"new god"—America—whose civil religion of justice, equality,
and democracy excludes him because, as he says, "my face is
black." It is not "My Country, 'Tis of Thee" that he sings; it
is a requiem to a stillborn dream. Employing the language
of the nation's great civil hymn as a rhetorical rebuff to the
nation's untruth about liberty and justice for all, Lincoln asks
of the "land of the free" and the "home of the brave" if ever
there will be true opportunity for the son of a slave.

But this is by no means the most poignant query in his
verse. That question, similar to the queries in the South African hymn "Senzeni Na," is most dissonant and difficult to

ask and to hear. It is a question that has plagued every woman, man, and child whose "face is black": "Does *black*," the poet asks, "some Godly error mask?" This question comprises a momentary thematizing of the tragic vision of life, where fault actually is traced back to the creator rather than to humankind's primal parents, the Adamic ancestors. Naturally there is hesitancy in this sort of query, for the tragic vision is repulsive to the religious consciousness which really believes God to be innocent of evil. Because blaming evil on the divine can hardly be rationalized (since it would mean the self-annihilation of the religious consciousness), it only can be theatricalized or poeticized; and poeticize the tragic vision Lincoln does: He projects himself back into the tragic drama of a black man dying the "white death" during the "lynching era" (1889–1945). Poeticize the tragic vision Lincoln does when he calls the body of this black man hanging from a *white* tree "strange fruit": fruit that strangely hangs—on *white* trees by day. And at night, in the evil of night, "strange flesh" (dusky human flesh) burns; it is the so-called "nigger barbecues," a ritual picnic expressing white supremacist solidarity. The dissonant, distressing question that Lincoln asks still lingers, and Lincoln wishes it never had to be raised: "I wonder whether God saw me burning, heard my skin popping, pitied me as I cried my Savior's name, offering him my tortured soul to take."

The first-person singular—*my* burning skin, *my* tortured call—is profound and penetrating, like new song ought to be. It is not some artifact of antiquity, some historical other, some distant ancestor of whom Lincoln speaks. It is Lincoln— the man himself—who burns; and his poetry summons us, those who dare to be ethnic, to walk with him in his death, that we might be awakened to new life. This poem is a source for powerful "new song."

In the midst of the old South, God—the great liberator— was preparing a way toward black freedom through the leadership of Martin Luther King. When the prison door of Birmingham Jail locked King in, the window to emancipation

was steadily being severed open and the iron curtain of segregation torn down. Surely we all should rejoice in our songs,
in that King looked over the mountaintop and saw the promised land; but we should not be overly jubilant just yet, for
Birmingham jails still exist in the world and iron curtains of
segregation still hang heavy. In "Come Back, Martin Luther
King," the poem that closes the anthology *This Road Since
Freedom*, Lincoln is calling for a renewal of the spirit of the
man who dreamt the impossible dream and sang the impossible song, a man who led us to walk as his Savior walked, to
dream as his Savior dreamt, to sing as he sang—"new song."

Particularly bothersome to the poet is that racial discrimination still predominates in Boston, the city where he and
King received their graduate training in religion. The message they have taught us ever since those days of learning at
Boston University is that true love and fraternity between the
races make it impossible for any race of people to relate to
another race of people as simultaneously equals and inferiors,
for the "haves" simultaneously to discriminate against and
treat equally the "have-nots." The hatred and the segregation,
the hypocrisy, the languished dream—all these force the poet
to ask, "When shall we overcome?" All of these force him to
plead, "Come back, Martin Luther King." Indeed, come back,
teach us, in the songs we sing, to let freedom ring.

All of the poems that comprise the anthology *This Road
Since Freedom* illustrate that the history of the African legacy
profoundly moves the poet. We need more poets, traditional
or nontraditional, who write like this—poets whose words can
profoundly move us either to set them, to adapt them, or to
create new song based on the inspiration of them.

As for the "songs of the world church," we can learn a
valuable lesson from the experience of the Iona Community,
which discovered the singability and religious relevance of
these ethnic songs. For instance, for African Americans to
sing African songs in their original languages, a practice that
could be complemented by doing simple parts of the liturgy
in one or more African languages, would broaden us in several

ways. In addition to giving us new texts and meanings derived from the cultures, experiences, and struggles of our African forebears and other world peoples of cultural and ideological ethnicity, the "songs of the world church" could help us put new sounds and rhythms into our repertoire and reality. These songs could also help reorient us away from Eurocentric perspectives that are partly responsible for holding us culturally and ideologically captive to traditions that maintain sexism, racism, and classism, not to mention that it would educate us by enabling us to learn additional languages.

The parallel is best drawn with the dialectic between preliberation apartheid and language in South Africa. South African literary critic Andries Walter Oliphant, in exploring the way in which language contributed to the stabilization of apartheid by disguising and marketing it, petitions for the institutionalization of a language (probably English) that is disengaged of its hierarchical associations and discriminatory agenda. "This concept proposes the detachment of English from its local associations with racism, sexism, and elitism. . . . This process, in the words of Njabulo Ndebele, is governed by the willingness to open South African English to 'the possibility of its becoming a new language,' informed by indigenous speech patterns and grammatical adjustments that might arise from 'the proximity of English to indigenous African languages.' "[9] On the other hand, Ngũgĩ Wa Thiong'O argues against the potential of English becoming a new language, for which reason he finally decided to write only in his mother tongue, Gikuyu. He says:

> Berlin of 1884 was effected through the sword and the bullet. But the night of the sword and the bullet was followed by the morning of the chalk and the blackboard. The physical violence of the battlefield was followed by the psychological violence of the classroom. . . . In my view language was the most important vehicle through which that power fascinated and held the soul prisoner.

9. Andries Walter Oliphant, "The Renewal of South African Literature," *Staffrider* 9, no. 4 (1991): 22, 33.

The bullet was the means of the physical subjugation.
Language was the means of the spiritual subjugation.[10]

Ngũgĩ is in the enviable position of knowing his mother
tongue, which is not the case for the peoples of the African
diaspora. Therefore Afro-Christians must at least recognize
the relationship of the English language to cultural traditions
of domination and therefore recognize the literary changes
that are demanded if a new postcolonial or postslavocratic
mind-set is to be nurtured in the hymns we sing. It is possible
that, similar to Oliphant's suggestion, these adjustments could
arise from the proximity of, for instance, English to African
and diasporan-African language usage. On the other hand,
the value of using African languages will be understood only
by those who have, in Fanon's words, felt the language of the
ruling power burn their lips.[11]

Singing a new song cannot alone accomplish the conversion to ethnicity that needs to occur in the Afro-Christian
church. Probably the best way to prepare the church to sing
new song is to introduce to a congregation, through a fairly
elaborate educational program, the kind of knowledge that
is conducive to the objective. One possibility is to establish an
Afrocentric church-affiliated school similar to the Kemet
School of Knowledge founded in Winston-Salem, North Carolina, by Alton B. Pollard III, a Baptist minister and professor
of religion at Wake Forest University.

The school year could correspond with the college academic year. Each of the school's two semesters could have
two regular courses and one language course, each offered
one day a week. The regular courses could be offered in such
areas as black theology, womanist theology, and African history, and the language lesson could be in Swahili or other
African languages. For children of ages three to ten, the school
could offer sessions comprised of readings from books by and

10. Ngũgĩ Wa Thiong'O, *Decolonising the Mind: The Politics of Language in African
Literature* (Nairobi, Kenya: Heinemann Kenya, 1986), 9.
11. Frantz Fanon, *The Wretched of the Earth*, trans. Constance Farrington (New
York: Grove Press, 1966), 221.

about peoples of African origin, the telling of traditional stories of Africa and Afro-America, and the singing of African
songs and hymns. For youths from ages eleven through the
senior year in high school, the school could offer an introductory course in African history (first semester) and African-
American history (second semester).

As a means of raising funds and gleaning broader community interest in such a school, a "church connection
program" could be established. Churches that join this "connection" could be encouraged to send students to the school
(especially Sunday school teachers), possibly covering the cost
of their tuition and books. What we seek is for these affiliate
churches of the "connection" to allow students from each
church to give their congregation, at some point during each
Sunday service, a brief summary of the previous week's school
lessons. This weekly summary could be given following the
announcements, but the ideal place is just before the sermon
(or the sermonic hymn). This would allow the minister, particularly the minister who follows the syllabi of the classes, to
elaborate on the lessons in at least some of the sermons.
Ideally, this would allow for an integration of the school's
teaching, the minister's preaching, and the congregation's
worshiping. The congregation would slowly come into the
kind of knowledge, languages, and songs that would nurture
a reoriented mind-set. In this new atmosphere, partly realized
with the help of new song coming out of the school, singing
a new song in general can flourish and, in turn, help en-
courage ethnicity in just the way that song is able to.

APPENDIX OF
ORIGINAL HYMNS

This book, which is concerned about gender, race, and class as they have been manifested in our hymnody, is written by someone who has tried to take the side against what Toni Morrison calls the "othering" of people. As I mentioned in the preface, in choosing the side of liberty and justice for everyone, those of us who will say yes to being ethnic will not have to apologize to those who have been othered, apologize at a later (possibly too late) date as the church and Christians too often have had to do. Tomorrow, when freedom comes, we need to be sitting at the table of reconciliation—but on the side that will be able to say, "We, who are ethnic, forgive you." This is who has written *Sing a New Song*. This is also who has written the five hymns that follow—hymns that attempt to be duo-ethnic, that is, both culturally and ideologically ethnic.

I agree with Ngũgĩ that the English language is a means of "spiritual subjugation" for us, but as an African American who does not speak an African language I have no choice but to hope that Andries Oliphant is correct about the possibility of English becoming a new language. I have been cautious about my hymnic language in an attempt to avoid spiritual subjugation and have attempted to use an English that has been adjusted by a proximity to African-American speech, speech derived from our spirituals, sermons, and our insurgent intellectual discourse.

I have chosen as my form of musical expression the standard four-part hymnic style, which still predominates in Afro-Christian hymnals. I hope that, to a degree, I have also accomplished the feat of adjusting this standard harmony by giving it some proximity to African-like rhythms (syncopations) and, in the case of "Our God Who Reigns Lord before Us," using the pentatonic scale so familiar to African music and the spirituals created by the African-diaspora people in America.

Certainly when these hymns are tried, the question of what is or is not black English or black music will arise. These questions have been long debated and are not resolved in this book or these hymns. The important point to know is that my hymns are nothing more than an example of our potential to create new song to sing. It is my petition that poets and musicians more talented than I am in these areas will contemplate (even debate) the ideas embodied in my petition and then, with the practice of exegetical freedom, pick up the pencil and sit down at the piano and heed the biblical mandate, "Sing unto the Lord a new song."

Our God Who Reigns Lord before Us

Words and music by Jon Michael Spencer, 1986

Our God who reigns lord be - fore us, reigns God of Af - ri -

ca;   the   earth's   lil - y of the val - ley.   She is black   and
the   earth's   cin - na - mon and saf - fron.   She's the Rose   of

come - ly. Though e - vil - doers stole her   chil - dren, ship'd them to   cruel for - eign
Shar - on. Through par - ent - less chil - dren th'may be,   stol - en from their bless'd ca - naan

lands,
land,   they shall in - her - it God's   king - dom where - ev - er they shall stand.

Gird Our Loins and Guide Our Lives

Words and music by Jon Michael Spencer, 1986

to   the   poor   the   least   of them. Let   us   see   that
love   all   kind   as   Je - sus did.   As did   he, let
wit - ness that   thy   will   is done. As should be, let
rid   our   land   of   so - cial sin.   As should be, let

the poor rise up   to pros - per - i - ty, to pros - per - i - ty.
us now rise and   bless hu - man - i - ty, bless hu - man - i - ty.
us have our long   sought li - ber - ty,   our sought li - ber - ty.
all kind join in   one whole fam - i - ly, one whole fam - i - ly.

Peace, Be Still

Words and Music by Jon Michael Spencer, 1986

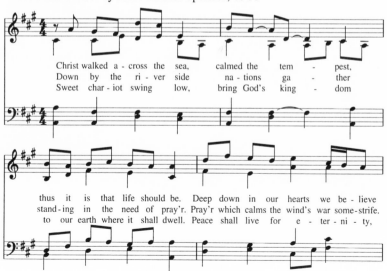

Christ walked a - cross the sea,   calmed the tem - pest,
Down   by   the   ri - ver side   na - tions ga - ther
Sweet char - iot swing low, bring God's king - dom

thus   it   is   that life should be. Deep down in our hearts we be - lieve
stand - ing in   the   need of pray'r. Pray'r which calms the wind's war some-strife.
to   our earth where it shall dwell. Peace shall live for e - ter - ni - ty,

earth should be a re - fuge of peace. War and ra - cial strife should cease to
Hymns of pray'r which heal wounds of life. Hun - ger, ha - tred, war should cease to
al - so hu - man e - qual - i - ty. Wo - men shall be free from gen - der

be in our land.
be in our land. It must cease! "Peace be still" Je - sus said. Strife must
op - pres - sion.

cease to dwell in our land; it can - not stand a - gainst

lord Je - sus. He's our shield a - gainst the storm.

O Freedom!

Words and music by Jon Michael Spencer, 1986

1 O free-dom! Free-dom! Free-dom up! O Lord, free at last! Re-joice ye!
2 O glo-ry! O glo-ry on high! Our Lord's king-dom's come. Hal-le-lu!
3 O chil-dren! Chil-dren of the Lord! Come and rest as-sured. O trav'-ler,

Re-joice in the Lord, for Mo-ses freed us from the Pha-raoh's bon-dage.
Ha-le, Ha-le-lu! For Je-sus freed us from the chains of ha-tred.
O trav'-ler come home, for Je-sus made our earth-ly home a king-dom.

A-wake, dry bones, the trum-pet sounds; go ring them bells loud! Yes, Lord!

Jesus Is Born! O What a Great Day!

Words and music by Jon Michael Spencer, 1986

Je - sus is born! O what a great day! Tell it a -
Je - sus is born! O what a bless'd day! God has giv'n
Je - sus is born! O what a sweet day! As we of
Je - sus is born! O what a great day! Tell it a -

broad to all the earth; go tell it on the moun - tain, go
her be - got - ten son, that who - so - ev - er would trust would
ev' - ry race and creed now join hands at his man - ger bring - ing
broad to all the earth; go tell it on the moun - tain, go

tell it o'er the hills; ev' - ry - where tell of his birth.
have e - ter - nal life, safe in her earth - ly king - dom.
our best hymns, sing - ing our best har - mo - ny.
tell it o'er the hills; ev' - ry - where tell of his birth.

SELECT
BIBLIOGRAPHY

Akbar, Na'im. *Chains and Images of Psychological Slavery.* Jersey City, N.J.: New Mind Productions, 1984.

Appiah, Kwame Anthony. *In My Father's House: Africa in the Philosophy of Culture.* New York: Oxford University Press, 1992.

Asante, Molefi Kete. *Afrocentricity.* Rev. ed. Trenton, N.J.: Africa World Press, 1988.

Banana, Canaan. *The Gospel according to the Ghetto.* Rev. ed. Gweru, Zimbabwe: Mambo Press, 1990.

Bazilli, Susan, ed. *Putting Women on the Agenda.* Johannesburg, South Africa: Ravan Press, 1991.

Bell, John L., ed. *Many and Great: Songs of the World Church,* vol. 1. Glasgow, Scotland: Wild Goose Publications, 1990.

———, ed. *Sent by the Lord: Songs of the World Church,* vol. 2. Glasgow, Scotland: Wild Goose Publications, 1991.

Ben-Jochannan, Yosef A. A. *Africa: Mother of Western Civilization.* Baltimore: Black Classic Press, 1988.

———. *African Origins of the Major "Western Religions."* Baltimore: Black Classic Press, 1991.

Bernal, Martin. *Black Athena: The Afroasiatic Roots of Classical Civilization,* vols. 1 and 2. New Brunswick, N.J.: Rutgers University Press, 1987, 1991.

Blassingame, John W., ed. *Slave Testimony: Two Centuries of Letters, Speeches, Interviews, and Autobiographies.* Baton Rouge, La.: Louisiana State University Press, 1977.

Bonwick, James. *Egyptian Belief and Modern Thought.* London: African Publication Society, 1983.

Burkett, Randall K. *Garveyism as a Religious Movement: The Institutionalization of a Black Civil Religion.* Metuchen, N.J.: Scarecrow Press, 1978.

Call for Relevant Evangelical Witness, A. Dobsonville, South Africa: Concerned Evangelicals, 1987.

Carroll, Charles. *The Tempter of Eve.* St. Louis.: Adamic Publishing Co., 1902.

Césaire, Aimé. *Discourse on Colonialism.* Translated by Joan Pinkham. New York: Monthly Review Press, 1972.

Clarke, John Henrik, ed. *New Dimensions in African History: The London Lectures of Dr. Yosef ben-Jochannan and Dr. John Henrik Clarke.* Trenton, N.J.: Africa World Press, 1991.

Cleage, Albert B., Jr. *Black Christian Nationalism: New Directions for the Black Church.* New York: William Morrow & Co., 1972.

———. *The Black Messiah.* Kansas City, Mo.: Sheed & Ward, 1968.

Cone, James H. *Black Theology and Black Power.* Rev. ed. San Francisco: HarperCollins, 1989.

———. *For My People: Black Theology and the Black Church.* Maryknoll, N.Y.: Orbis Books, 1984.

Coplan, David B. *In Township Tonight! South Africa's Black City Music and Theatre.* Johannesburg, South Africa: Ravan Press, 1985.

Daly, Mary. *Beyond God the Father: Toward a Philosophy of Women's Liberation.* Boston: Beacon Press, 1973.

Diop, Cheikh Anta. *The African Origin of Civilization: Myth or Reality.* Edited and translated by Mercer Cook. New York: Lawrence Hill Books, 1974.

———. *Civilization or Barbarism: An Authentic Anthropology.* Translated by Yaa-Lengi Meema Ngemi; edited by Harold J. Salemson and Marjolijn de Jager. New York: Lawrence Hill Books, 1991.

———. *The Cultural Unity of Black Africa: The Domains of Patriarchy and of Matriarchy in Classical Antiquity.* Chicago: Third World Press, 1978.

Du Bois, W. E. B. *Darkwater: Voices from within the Veil.* New York: Schocken Press, 1920.

———. *The World and Africa: An Inquiry into the Part Which Africa Has Played in World History*. Enlarged ed. New York: International Publishers, 1965.

Evangelical Witness in South Africa (Evangelicals Critique Their Own Theology and Practice). Dobsonville, South Africa: Concerned Evangelicals, 1986.

Fanon, Frantz. *Black Skin, White Masks*. Translated by Charles Lam Markmann. New York: Grove Press, 1967.

———. *Studies in a Dying Colonialism*. Translated by Haakon Chevalier. London: Earthscan Publications, 1989.

———. *The Wretched of the Earth*. Translated by Constance Farrington. New York: Grove Press, 1966.

Fardan, Dorothy Blake. *Message to the White Man and Woman in America: Yakub and the Origins of White Supremacy*. Hampton, Va.: United Brothers and Sisters Communications Systems, 1991.

Felder, Cain Hope. *Troubling Biblical Waters: Race, Class, and Family*. Maryknoll, N.Y.: Orbis Books, 1989.

———, ed. *Stony the Road We Trod: African American Biblical Interpretation*. Minneapolis: Fortress Press, 1991.

Fredrickson, George M. *White Supremacy: A Comparative Study in American and South African History*. New York: Oxford University Press, 1981.

Gendzier, Irene L. *Frantz Fanon: A Critical Study*. New York: Grove Press, 1973.

Gossett, Thomas F. *Race: The History of an Idea in America*. New York: Schocken Books, 1965.

Hacker, Andrew. *Two Nations: Black and White, Separate, Hostile, Unequal*. New York: Charles Scribner's Sons, 1992.

Hill, Robert A., and Barbara Bair, eds. *Marcus Garvey: Life and Lessons*. Berkeley and Los Angeles: University of California Press, 1987.

Hood, Robert E. *Must God Remain Greek? Afro Cultures and God-Talk*. Minneapolis: Fortress Press, 1990.

Hooks, Bell. *Yearning: Race, Gender, and Culture Politics*. Boston: South End Press, 1990.

James, George G. M. *Stolen Legacy: Greek Philosophy Is Stolen Egyptian Philosophy*. New York: Philosophical Library, 1954.

Karenga, Maulana. *Introduction to Black Studies*. Los Angeles: University of Sankore Press, 1982.

Kierkegaard, Søren. *Attack upon "Christendom."* Translated by Walter
  Lowrie. Princeton, N.J.: Princeton University Press, 1968.
———. *Concluding Unscientific Postscript.* Translated by David F.
  Swenson. Princeton, N.J.: Princeton University Press, 1968.
Knox, John. *Philemon among the Letters of Paul.* Rev. ed. Nashville:
  Abingdon Press, 1959.
Küng, Hans. *On Being a Christian.* Garden City, N.Y.: Image
  Books, 1984.
Lerner, Gerda. *The Creation of Patriarchy.* New York: Oxford Uni-
  versity Press, 1986.
Lincoln, C. Eric. *Race, Religion, and the Continuing American Dilemma.*
  New York: Hill & Wang, 1984.
———. *This Road since Freedom: Collected Poems.* Durham, N.C.: Car-
  olina Wren Press, 1990.
Luckert, Karl W. *Egyptian Light and Hebrew Fire: Theological and
  Philosophical Roots of Christendom in Evolutionary Perspective.*
  Albany: State University of New York Press, 1991.
Madhubuti, Haki R. *Enemies: The Clash of Races.* Chicago: Third
  World Press, 1978.
Marable, Manning. *How Capitalism Underdeveloped Black America:
  Problems in Race, Political Economy and Society.* Boston: South
  End Press, 1983.
Mbiti, John S. *African Religions and Philosophy.* New York: Doubleday
  & Co., Anchor Books, 1970.
McKitrick, Eric L., ed. *Slavery Defended: The Views of the Old South.*
  Englewood Cliffs, N.J.: Prentice-Hall, 1963.
Meyers, Carol. *Discovering Eve: Ancient Israelite Women in Context.*
  New York: Oxford University Press, 1988.
Morrison, Toni. *Playing in the Dark: Whiteness and the Literary Imag-
  ination.* Cambridge: Harvard University Press, 1992.
Ngũgĩ Wa Thiong'O. *Barrel of a Pen: Resistance to Repression in Neo-
  Colonial Kenya.* Trenton, N.J.: Africa World Press, 1983.
———. *Decolonising the Mind: The Politics of Language in African
  Literature.* Nairobi, Kenya: Heinemann Kenya, 1986.
———. *Detained: A Writer's Prison Diary.* Nairobi, Kenya: Heinemann
  Kenya, 1981.
Niebuhr, H. Richard. *Christ and Culture.* New York: Harper &
  Brothers, 1951.
Pagels, Elaine. *Adam, Eve, and the Serpent.* New York: Random
  House, 1988.

P'Bitek, Okot. *Song of Lawino and Song of Ocol.* Nairobi, Kenya: Heinemann Kenya, 1984.

Petersen, Norman R. *Rediscovering Paul: Philemon and the Sociology of Paul's Narrative World.* Philadelphia: Fortress Press, 1985.

Peterson, Thomas Virgil. *Ham and Japheth: The Mythic World of Whites in the Antebellum South.* Metuchen, N.J.: Scarecrow Press, 1978.

Priest, Josiah. *Bible Defense of Slavery.* Glasgow, Ky.: S. W. Brown, 1953. Republished, Detroit: Negro History Press, [1969?].

Raboteau, Albert J. *Slave Religion: The "Invisible Institution" in the Antebellum South.* New York: Oxford University Press, 1978.

Redford, Donald B. *Egypt, Canaan, and Israel in Ancient Times.* Princeton, N.J.: Princeton University Press, 1992.

Rodney, Walter. *How Europe Underdeveloped Africa.* London: Bogle l'Ouverture, 1972.

Royce, Josiah. *The Problem of Christianity,* 1913. Reprint, Chicago: University of Chicago Press, 1968.

Saadawi, Nawal El. *The Hidden Face of Eve: Women in the Arab World.* London: Zed Press, 1980.

Sertima, Ivan Van, ed. *African Presence in Early Europe.* New Brunswick, N.J.: Transaction Publishers, 1985.

————, ed. *Black Women in Antiquity.* New Brunswick, N.J.: Transaction Publishers, 1987.

Shorter, Aylward, et al. *Towards African Christian Maturity.* Nairobi, Kenya: St. Paul Publications-Africa, 1987.

Smith, Warren Thomas. *John Wesley and Slavery.* Nashville: Abingdon Press, 1986.

Snowden, Frank M., Jr. *Blacks in Antiquity: Ethiopians in the Greco-Roman Experience.* Cambridge: Harvard University Press, Belknap Press, 1970.

Spencer, Jon Michael. *Black Hymnody: A Hymnological History of the African-American Church.* Knoxville, Tenn.: University of Tennessee Press, 1992.

————. *Protest and Praise: Sacred Music of Black Religion.* Minneapolis: Fortress Press, 1990.

————, ed. *The Worshipping Church in Africa.* A special issue of *Black Sacred Music: A Journal of Theomusicology* 7, no. 2 (Fall 1993).

Stone, Merlin. *When God Was a Woman.* New York: Harcourt Brace Jovanovich, 1976.

Terrien, Samuel. *Till the Heart Sings: A Biblical Theology of Manhood and Womanhood.* Philadelphia: Fortress Press, 1985.

Thompson, Lloyd A. *Romans and Blacks*. Norman, Okla.: University of Oklahoma Press, 1989.

Tilson, Charles Everett. *Segregation and the Bible*. New York: Abingdon Press, 1958.

Turner, Victor. *Dramas, Fields, and Metaphors: Symbolic Action in Human Society*. Ithaca, N.Y.: Cornell University Press, 1974.

——. *The Ritual Process: Structure and Anti-Structure*. Ithaca, N.Y.: Cornell University Press, 1977.

Welsing, Frances Cress. *The Isis Papers: The Keys to the Colors*. Chicago: Third World Press, 1991.

West, Cornel. *Prophetic Fragments*. Grand Rapids: Wm. B. Eerdmans Publishing Co.; Trenton, N.J.: Africa World Press, 1988.

Westermann, Claus. *Genesis 1–11: A Commentary*. Translated by John J. Sullivan. Minneapolis: Augsburg Publishing House, 1984.

Westermann, William L. *Slave Systems of Greek and Roman Antiquity*. Philadelphia: American Philosophical Society, 1955.

Williams, Chancellor. *The Destruction of Black Civilization: Great Issues of a Race from 4500 B.C. to 2000 A.D.* Chicago: Third World Press, 1987.

Wilmore, Gayraud S., ed. *African American Religious Studies: An Interdisciplinary Anthology*. Durham, N.C.: Duke University Press, 1989.

Wilmore, Gayraud S., and James H. Cone, eds. *Black Theology: A Documentary History, 1966–1979*. Maryknoll, N.Y.: Orbis Books, 1979.

Woodson, Carter G. *The Mis-Education of the Negro*, 1933. Reprint, Washington, D.C.: Associated Publishers, 1969.

Wren, Brian. *What Language Shall I Use? God-Talk in Worship: A Male Response to Feminist Theology*. New York: Crossroad, 1990.

INDEX OF
NAMES AND SUBJECTS

INDEX OF
BIBLICAL REFERENCES

NEW TESTAMENT